TRISTEN WILLIS

The Genesi Cure

This book is dedicated to my husband and children.

Contents

Foreword

Please be advised that although this story is intended for a young adult audience it does contain content which may be triggering to some readers.

Please see below list of potential triggers:

- *Violence*
- *Blood / Gore / Death*
- *Strangulation / Suffocation*
- *Mental Health / Anxiety / Panic Attacks*

Acknowledgments

I would like to take a moment to express my gratitude towards those who have been with me since the beginning of this journey.

The Genesi Code was my first published novel in 2017, and although I took many detours along the way, I have finally completed this duology.

To those who have read The Genesi Code and persistently asked when the sequel would be released, thank you. Without your persistence, The Genesi Cure would not have come to fruition.

Prologue

Sam

Year: 2248

Our past experiences mold us into the individuals we are today. To erase that past would be to erase a piece of our identity. However, the past has a way of resurfacing when we least expect it...

Panic etched its way into my consciousness before my eyes even fluttered open. A cold, hard surface pressed against the length of my back—metal, unyielding and chilling to the touch. My limbs were heavy, lethargic as if wading through a swamp. Confusion clawed at the edges of my mind, blurring the lines between reality and the void that was my memory.

"Where am I?" The question slipped through my lips in a barely audible whisper. As my eyes adapted to the surroundings, the once blurry scene sharpened into view, presenting a stark, sterile laboratory illuminated by a harsh, unyielding white light.

I tried to sit up but met resistance. Straps held my wrists and ankles, fastening me to the table. Panic surged in my chest, almost too much to bear, as I pulled at the restraints in vain—a primal urge to escape racing through me.

"Ah, you're awake."

The voice cut through the silence, authoritative and chillingly recognizable. Chancellor Cain stood before me, his aura as commanding as the forcefield enclosing our divided city. His intense gaze locked onto me, holding my attention more powerfully than the restraints ever could.

"Father," I managed to say, the word tasting like ash on my tongue.

"Chancellor Cain," he corrected, his voice that of a ruler rather than a parent. "But you will learn to answer to much more when all is said and done."

"Has it worked, Chancellor?" another voice interjected. General Thorn emerged from the shadows. He stood a step behind Chancellor Cain, close-cropped black hair a dark halo around his tanned face. Despite his deferential position, his posture radiated an air of quiet control—one that belied his title as lackey.

"Thorn," I acknowledged with a nod, the effort sending a wave of nausea crashing over me. A forced show of respect for the man who orchestrated my capture. Every fiber of my being wanted to recoil from them both, but I remained composed, my own survival instincts as sharp as the scalpel I imagined slicing into my skin not long ago. "Your predicament, as you so aptly call it, son, was necessary," Cain began, his words meticulously chosen, each one carefully placed. "A means to an end."

"An end that justifies this?" I challenged, straining against the straps once more, muscles protesting under the strain.

"Yes," he replied without hesitation, his conviction as unwavering as the walls around us. The laboratory, with

2

its gleaming instruments and the scent of antiseptic, became a theater in which I was both the audience and the unwilling star. And there, beneath those scrutinizing eyes, I realized the true depth of my entrapment.

"Recruitment was only your beginning, Sam," Cain said, looming over me. "You were chosen for something greater—a transformation into what our society needs."

"Transformation?" The word hung between us, its meaning I couldn't yet grasp. "Delta Force was merely a prelude," he continued, eyes gleaming with pride—or was it possession? "You are eighteen, at the precipice of potential, and that potential has been… unlocked. You are my son, Samyaza, and now, a Genesi soldier."

A Genesi. The elite soldiers, the altered—the ones spoken of in hushed tones on the streets, their abilities shrouded in awe and terror. How many nights had I lain awake as a child, listening to tales of how the Genesi almost erased the human race before they went into hiding?

"Genesi," I echoed, the title foreign on my tongue.

"Indeed," my father affirmed with an imperious nod. "You see, our efforts have not been without merit. We captured one, a true Genesi." His voice took on the cadence of a man who'd rehearsed his triumph many times over. "From them, we extracted the essence, the very coding that makes them superior. And with it, we've begun crafting an army."

"An army?" I could feel the weight of his ambition pressing down upon me.

"An army under my command," Chancellor Cain declared, his words slicing through the sterile air. "And you, Sam, you are the inaugural soldier of this new era. Our enemies will cower, and our power will be unrivaled. You are the firstborn of a legacy that will reshape our world."

I scrutinized his features, searching for traces of the man who had once been my father rather than the ruthless Chancellor. All I found was an unwavering determination in his eyes and a fierce ambition driving him forward. My heart raced within my chest as Cain drew nearer, his gaze cutting through any facade of choice I might have clung to.

"Sam," he started, his voice a low rumble resonating in the chilly atmosphere, "this goes beyond mere soldier creation. It's about achieving perfection—about control. The new Genesi genetic code we've developed surpasses the original design, transcending their primal instincts and violent tendencies."

Struggling against the unforgiving restraints, the cold metal dug into my wrists, mirroring the overwhelming sense of powerlessness creeping over me.

"Control?" I managed to croak out, fear seeping into the single word.

"It's absolute," he confirmed with a chilling composure. "Your mind, your will - they're mine to command now. You'll obey without question, without hesitation. I won't repeat the mistakes that triggered The Genesi War."

The room spun around me, and I shut my eyes briefly, grappling with the gravity of his words. No longer just his son; I was now his creation, a mere piece in his calculated game where he held all the power.

"And what if I refuse?" My voice was a whisper, almost lost amidst the beeping of machines.

"Refusal is not within the parameters of your new existence," he said, turning away from me to face General Thorn, who stood silent, an impassive sentinel. "Show him."

Thorn approached, a small device in hand, and pressed it

against my temple. A shockwave of pain ripped through my consciousness, and for a brief moment, I was submerged in darkness, my sense of self slipping away like sand through fingers.

"Understand, Sam," Cain continued, as if discussing the weather instead of commandeering my very being, "to become a Genesi, you must first be stripped of life. Your death was a necessary sacrifice for rebirth."

His words settled over me like a shroud, heavy with truth. *I had died.*

The realization clawed at my insides, a scream building behind the walls of my chest. But I couldn't afford to show weakness, not now. With effort, I schooled my features into stoicism, though inside, a tempest raged.

"Rebirth or enslavement?" I asked, the defiance in my tone belying the dread that twisted in my gut.

"Semantics," Cain replied curtly, his back still turned. "You are the vanguard of a new order, my son. In time, you will see the grandeur of our purpose."

His dismissal was a clear signal that the conversation was over. I lay there, motionless, listening to the retreating footsteps of the two men who held my fate. The lab's silence was oppressive, filled with the echo of a heartbeat that I wasn't even sure was my own anymore. In the solitude of my thoughts, I grappled with the duality of my existence—the boy who once was and the soldier I had become. Death had claimed me, but something deep within stirred—a flicker of rebellion, a spark of the person I used to be. It was this ember I clung to, a silent vow to myself that while I may have died in the process, Samyaza Cain was far from gone.

"Father," I began, my voice steady despite the storm inside.

"Your vision is... extraordinary." The words tasted like acid on my tongue, but I needed him to believe I was compliant, broken—a pawn in his grand scheme. Cain paused mid-stride, and General Thorn's retreating footsteps ceased. Both turned to regard me with an air of expectation.

"Indeed. We have achieved what many thought impossible, especially after Dr. Christopher Foster's untimely death. You are vital to our success," Cain replied, his eyes glinting with dangerous pride.

"Then let me prove my worth," I said, trying to push myself up into a sitting position before remembering that I was still held down by my restraints. My muscles coiled, ready to snap, but I held back. Any act of aggression would only tighten their control over me. No, subtlety was my ally now. "Show me my role in this new order you speak of."

Thorn exchanged a glance with Cain, a silent conversation passing between them. After a moment's deliberation, he approached and released the straps binding me to the table. I masked the surge of relief with a grateful nod, careful not to reveal my true intentions. "Your training begins immediately," Thorn declared, his voice gruff as he handed me a set of dull-gray fatigues. "Remember, you're no longer just Sam Cain—you are a Genesi soldier now."

"Understood," I replied, slipping into the uniform that symbolized my supposed rebirth. It felt foreign against my skin, a constant reminder of the line I had crossed from human to something other.

"Serve us well, and you will ascend to heights unknown," Cain said, a trace of affection weaving through the command in his tone. It was a masterful performance, one that might have swayed me if I hadn't known better.

"Of course, Father," I responded, injecting a loyalty into my voice that I did not feel. "I will serve your cause with all that I am." As I spoke, my mind raced, dissecting every word, every gesture for any clue that could lead to my escape. I had to be patient, observant. The Genesi might be bound to his will, but Sam was still very much alive within me—and he would not yield so easily.

"Good," Cain said, a smile tugging at the corners of his mouth. "Welcome to the future, my son."

As they led me out of the lab and down the corridor lined with armed guards, I kept my head high, my steps sure. My father believed he had created the ultimate weapon in me, unaware that he had forged the key to his own undoing. I would play the part he envisioned until the moment to strike presented itself. Until then, I would be the dutiful soldier, the obedient son.

But when the time came, I would reclaim my life and shatter the chains he thought unbreakable. For now, I was Samyaza Cain, the first of a secret Genesi army—awaiting the chance to rise anew.

Chapter 1

Luka

Year: 2258

I slammed my palms onto the cold, stone surface of the makeshift table, causing the flickering holographic map to disappear. The cavernous space echoed with our raised voices, tension thick in the air.

Sam stood opposite me, his broad shoulders rigid beneath a worn leather jacket that marked his command of the genesi. His piercing blue eyes held mine with an intensity bordering on desperation.

"Harsher methods, Luka!" Sam growled, his voice resonating off the walls hewn from the heart of the mountain. "We cannot afford to be merciful - not when Chancellor Cain is breathing down our necks!"

"Mercy has nothing to do with it," I shot back, my own voice betraying the turmoil inside me. For six weeks since arriving at this Genesi rebel stronghold, I had been locking horns with Sam over the same issue - six endless weeks of trying to convince him that there were lines we shouldn't cross.

"Those 'harsher methods' will make us no better than him - no better than your father."

Sam bristled at the mention of Chancellor Cain and for a moment, I saw a shadow of the boy he once was - a boy turned into a weapon by the very man we were fighting against. A part of me regretted ever agreeing to become Sam's weapon in this war, helping him lead a rebellion. Doubt was a constant companion, whispering that I lacked the ability to carry such a burden.

"Sometimes, Luka, you have to fight fire with fire. My father won't hesitate to use everything in his arsenal against us." Sam's fists clenched and his knuckles whitened as his gaze bore into me. I could see the strain of command etched in his face, the weight of his legacy as commander of the genesi and as Cain's son - a weight I now shared.

"Using bioweapons... genocide..." I murmured, the words tasting like ash on my tongue. "That's not winning, Sam. That's just surviving through annihilation."

"Survival is the first step to victory," he countered, his voice hard as the rock surrounding us.

I looked around the throne room at the mountain-carved throne itself - a symbol of strength and resilience. It stood as a stark reminder of the choices before us - holding onto our humanity or succumbing to the darkness of warfare.

"Survival without principles is just another form of death," I said quietly.

Sam began to speak, most likely with another snide remark already formed on his tongue.

"Enough, Sam!" My voice echoed off the stone walls of

the throne room, matching the coldness of the mountain that entombed us. The argument had spiraled and I stood defiantly before him, unwilling to yield to his increasingly drastic measures.

I noticed the flicker in Sam's piercing blue eyes, a storm brewing underneath his calm exterior. "We don't have time for hesitation, Luka," he growled.

"Using bio weapons crosses a line we can't come back from," I argued, my ash blonde hair falling into a messy curtain as I shook my head in frustration. Sam clenched his jaw, and I knew my words had struck a nerve. But whether they would sway him or not was uncertain. The silence that followed was heavy, filled with unspoken fears and the looming weight of decisions yet to be made.

In the end, I couldn't stay there, under the overpowering gaze of the stone throne and the pressure of Sam's expectations. Without waiting for his dismissal, I turned on my heel, my boots echoing against the rock as I left the throne room. I needed air, space... I needed to find Liz and the others, to ground myself with their human touch that felt so distant in these moments of strife.

As I made my way through the cavernous hallways, my mind raced with thoughts of our conversation and the realization that every choice we made now held countless lives in the balance. And deep down, a small part of me feared what it would mean if we couldn't navigate this without becoming the very monsters we were fighting against.

The sharp clacking of footsteps mirrored my own, too rhythmic to be a coincidence. I spun around, my heart racing. "Go back to shadowing, Troian," I called out sharply without turning.

She stopped mid-step, her figure standing rigid in the dimly lit corridor. I could envision her long, dark hair framing her tanned face as she hid in the shadows. "Just making sure you don't do anything rash, Luka."

"Return to your role as Sam's shadow," I snapped back, bitterness coating my words from our earlier confrontation. "You don't need to monitor my every move."

Without waiting to see if she complied, I walked away. Troian was Sam's second-in-command, and it seemed like there wasn't an hour in the day where I didn't feel her watchful gaze. It was as if she had a constant need to remind me of my outsider status, the variable in their otherwise calculated rebellion.

The further I got from the throne room, the clearer my mind became with each step. Troian had never warmed up to me, and I couldn't blame her - I had been thrown into their world, disrupting the delicate balance they had maintained. She must have felt threatened by my sudden presence and the trust that Sam placed in my abilities - abilities that I wasn't even sure I possessed.

Nate, on the other hand, was different. He was Sam's third-in-command and the only one who treated me with any kind of friendliness. His sense of humor was a rare commodity in these dreary halls, and it was reassuring to know that not everyone was plotting against me. But even Nate's jokes couldn't ease the weight of responsibility that weighed heavy on my shoulders.

As I walked, my thoughts began to clear with each step. I had memorized the twists and turns of the seemingly endless hallways that led to the outside.

As I walked, I could hear snippets of quiet conversations

swirling around me like leaves in a storm. "I don't know if humans can be trusted…" "…there's a spy among us…" "Chancellor Cain won't stop until he's crushed the rebellion." Their words were stinging reminders of the fragile thread holding our alliance together. Doubt and fear were just as deadly as any weapon, and they had found their way into the hearts of those living within these mountains.

Could I blame them? The future was uncertain, and I was asking them to follow me blindly. Seeking a moment of refuge, I slipped past the murmurs of unrest and found myself in a shadowed alcove. The noise of the encampment faded into a distant hum, granting me a brief respite from the weight of leadership on my shoulders.

In this moment of quiet, my facade crumbled. Sinking to the ground, my ash blonde hair curtained my face as my trembling hands reached for the cool earth. Grief washed over me like an unyielding tide, threatening to erode the shores of my composure.

"How am I going to do this?" I whispered into the uncaring darkness. "How am I supposed to stop Cain and win a war?" Time pressed close, suffocating like the dense fog that crept over the valley at dawn.

There were truths I kept locked behind a stoic gaze, knowing that they could unravel the fragile seams of our alliance. Every decision felt like a gamble in a game where the rules changed with each breath and the stakes were lives - lives that I had sworn to protect.

"Stand up," I commanded myself in a barely audible voice. "You are Luka Foster. You do not yield." Taking deep breaths to try and quell my anxiety, I forced myself to move from my hiding spot and make my way towards the exit of the mountain.

My mind raced with potential plans and backup strategies as I walked, the cool air of the underground tunnels doing little to calm the frustration burning within me. I had come here to fight alongside them, not become a pawn in a game of power and control. And Sam... he was pushing for something I couldn't give him. Harsher methods, he said. As if becoming more like the monsters we were fighting against was the answer to our problems. But no matter how much I argued, it felt like I was talking to stone walls instead of open minds.

Would they ever understand? Could I make them see there has to be another way?

I hoped Liz would have insight. She always cut through chaos with clarity that I desperately needed now. If anyone could help me navigate this mess, it was her.

Training. I needed to see something real, something grounded. The human side of this struggle - my friends honing their skills, preparing for what was ahead. They hadn't been altered or turned into weapons like me. Their humanity was intact, and in that, I found hope. Above all, I longed for Liz's sage advice. She had been my captain once, her words a guiding light in the haze of difficult choices and ethical dilemmas.

As I neared the end of the tunnel, daylight filtered in, casting elongated shadows on the rough-hewn walls. The sound of metal against metal grew louder, and I braced myself for the sight of my companions locked in combat. The training area was situated in the valley just beyond the entrance of the largest mountain.

Stepping out from the gaping mouth of the mountain, I blinked against the sudden onslaught of sunlight. The training grounds spread out before me, a stark contrast to the suffocating caverns inside. My friends' laughter filled the crisp air as they finished their sparring session. There they were - Lewis, Skai, Ian, Ren, Harvey, and Liz - engaged in a symphony of movement, their bodies an extension of their will to survive and fight back.

I stayed at a distance, watching them spar with discipline born from desperation. They moved gracefully despite the violence of their actions, each strike a testament to their determination. Liz's form was flawless, her presence commanding even amidst the chaos of training. She noticed me first and paused mid-motion to acknowledge my arrival with a nod. Her deep blonde hair was pulled back tightly into a ponytail.

I waited patiently as they finished their exercises one by one - their muscles glistening with sweat, chests heaving with exertion. They were warriors in their own right, unaltered yet powerful. My gaze lingered on Liz, the wisdom in her eyes promising the advice I sought. Soon, we would talk, and perhaps within her words, I would find the strength to sway Sam from his destructive path.

"I'll see you guys later. I'm headed back to the computer lab to meet with Lars," Lewis called out to the group, wiping sweat from his brow with the back of his hand. His casual remark didn't escape me, nor did the fact that Harvey and Ren lingered, exchanging hushed words. They glanced at me expectantly, searching for any sign of how my morning meeting with Sam had gone.

"Give me a second, guys," I murmured to them, spotting Liz gathering her gear near the edge of the clearing. I needed her - her experience, her advice

"Liz," I called out, and she looked up at me. Her eyes immediately registered the urgency in my stance.

"Can you walk with me?" I asked, gesturing for her to join me. Together, we moved away from the others, seeking privacy amidst the tall pines that surrounded us.

I confided once we were out of earshot, "Sam believes Cain's army will be here within the month. He wants to consider using a bio weapon to delay their advance."

Liz's gaze hardened, lines etching onto her face as she became consumed by concern. "That's a dangerous path, Luka," she cautioned.

"I know," I admitted, feeling the weight of the world settle on my shoulders. "I don't want to resort to extreme measures, but he's pushing for it."

"Then we'll find another way," Liz said firmly, determination lacing her voice. "We always do."

Silence enveloped us as we continued our walk, circling back towards where our friends waited. With Liz by my side, maybe there was still hope that we could navigate this war without sacrificing ourselves in the process.

"Leadership isn't about making easy decisions," Liz began, her wisdom cutting through the chaos of my thoughts. "It's about making the right ones. Have you considered sabotage? Or spreading misinformation?"

"I've thought of every possibility," I confessed, frustration gnawing at me. "But sabotage is too risky and spreading misinformation could backfire horribly. We're not just fighting against an enemy army; we're also fighting against other genesi soldiers who are under Cain's mind control. And they are stronger than the rebel genesi fighters we've managed to gather..."

"Then let's bring more minds into this," Liz suggested, scanning the area before turning back to me. "Ren and Harvey have different perspectives. Maybe together, we can find a solution you haven't thought of yet."

"Maybe," I murmured, holding onto a sliver of hope.

"Ren! Harvey!" Liz called out, her voice carrying across the training grounds.

The two approached, their expressions curious. Ren's eyes were sharp and analytical while Harvey exuded quiet strength.

"Let's hear your meeting recap," Liz said, turning her attention back to me. "We need to brainstorm - Cain's army is on the move and we have to be ready to push back without losing ourselves to darkness."

Chapter 2

Sam

I slumped onto the stone throne, my body sinking into the cold embrace of the mountain. A storm had raged inside our cave-like chamber moments before, Luka's words still echoing off the walls, stinging like hail.

"You just don't get it, Sam!" she had shouted, her ash blonde hair a wild halo around her face, olive green eyes aflame with that stubborn spark I both admired and cursed.

"Of course, I don't," I muttered to the empty room, sarcasm seeping from each syllable. "Understanding is overrated anyway." The throne, carved from the very heart of this forsaken mountain, was no cushion for comfort, nor did it offer any solace for the frustration coiling in my gut like barbed wire.

As if the argument wasn't enough of a headache, Troian, ever the loyal watchdog, had slipped out after Luka without a sound; her silent footsteps were a testament to her earned place by my side.

Second in command didn't come with instructions but if

it did, 'Follow Luka' would be scrawled on the first page in Troian's meticulous hand no doubt. With a sigh, I stood from the throne and began pacing the length of the chamber.

My mind raced with potential outcomes and consequences as I tried to map out my next move. "Can't say I trust Luka either," I admitted to the shadows; the words were a confession meant only for these ancient stones. "But I bet you're not just tailing her; are you?" I pictured Troian's journey beyond the chamber likely crossing paths with Skai. They'd become two threads tightly woven together since humans arrived at our encampment. Skai's unruly nature and Troian's unyielding loyalty made for a volatile combination— one that often left me with a mess to clean up.

Troian had clawed her way up to stand beside me, her hands as scarred as the rest of us, every mark a story of survival. We looked into the abyss together, she and I, and when it stared back, it was her steady gaze that held it at bay. Trust her with my life? That was the easy part; it was trusting her with our future that kept me awake at nights. I stopped my pacing and sank back into my throne.

"Speaking of futures," I whispered, the weight of leadership pressing down once more as I ran a hand along the armrest, the stone cool beneath my skin, "we've got a storm coming, and it's bringing hell with it."

And with Luka out there, somewhere between rage and revelation, time felt like sand slipping through my fingers. I needed her to see what lay within her, the power that could tip the scales. But that was a battle for another day, another argument I was bound to have—and lose—if something didn't give.

"Stubborn as the earth we're standing on," I grumbled, rising from the throne to pace the room once more. My boots crunched over the scattered debris, my restless energy trailing behind me.

"There has got to be a way to delay Cain's forces," I mused aloud, my pacing bringing me back to stand before my throne. My gaze fell on the scattered plans and maps sprawled across the stone surface, as if they might hold the answers I sought.

I slumped back on the throne, every inch of its hard, unforgiving surface reminding me that the world was equally so. Luka's refusal to embrace her Genesi gifts was like trying to teach a rock to swim – pointless and frustrating.

"You're not just strong, you're Genesi-strong," I'd told her earlier, my voice echoing off the stone walls, only to be met with her characteristic scowl.

"Genesi… What a cursed blessing," I muttered under my breath, my mind wrestling with the irony. To have such power at our fingertips, yet denied by the very hands that should wield it with pride. She didn't understand, couldn't see that this wasn't about control—it was survival. Luka's stubbornness could damn us all if she didn't learn to let go and let the Genesi within her take hold.

"Damn it, Luka," I sighed, knowing deep down that my frustration was born of fear – fear for her, for all of us. If she only realized that accepting the gift wasn't surrendering—it was arming herself for the inevitable battles ahead.

"Talking to the ghosts or just practicing your royal decrees?" The familiar voice snapped me out of my reverie, and I looked up to find Nate leaning against the stone doorway, a wry grin plastered across his tawny face.

"Meeting went as well as expected," I replied, the corner of my mouth twitching upward despite myself. "Throne room's still standing, so I'd say I kept my temper fairly in check."

"Fairly? That's a new record." Nate strolled over, the lightness in his step a stark contrast to the leaden atmosphere that had settled around me since Luka stormed out.

"Should we mark the day? Sam Cain keeps his cool. News at sunrise," he chuckled, patting my shoulder with a brotherly affection that somehow made the weight I carried feel a touch lighter.

"Only because sunrise is a myth in these parts," I shot back, allowing a momentary pause from the gravity of our situation. But even as we bantered, the unease remained—a constant companion whispering warnings in my ear.

Nate's question sliced through the banter like a knife. "Heard anything from our spy on Cain's movements?"

I shook my head, the weight of failure settling on my shoulders. "Nothing. It's been too quiet. I fear the worst—that Winston has been killed." My voice was a low rumble, each word laced with regret. Winston was determined to prove he had never been a spy for Cain. We both understood the risks when we sent him in, but it didn't make the potential loss any easier to stomach.

"Damn," Nate muttered under his breath. His expression tightened, the playful spark in his eyes momentarily snuffed out by the gravity of our situation. "Before he went dark, he gave us something though, right? That Cain's forces are mobilizing."

"Yeah," I confirmed, my gaze fixed on the rough-hewn walls of our mountain sanctuary. "They know where we are... or at least, where we might be." I offered a small smile, a silent acknowledgment of the unspoken fears that lingered between us.

"Lars has been trying to recover any video footage from Winston's biometric eye camera feed," I explained. Before we sent him back to Delta Force as our spy, we made sure that Lars had adjusted his biometric eye so that only we could access the footage it captured. The camera would send the footage to us through an encrypted network.

"You look like hell, man." Nate's concern broke through my contemplation. He studied me with those keen eyes of his, ones that missed nothing. "You're burning the candle at both ends."

"Sleep is a luxury we don't have," I said tersely. "We're running out of time, Nate. If Luka doesn't come to terms with who she is—"

"Her Genesi abilities?" he finished for me.

"Exactly." I stood and paced once more, restless energy coursing through me. "Without her embracing her power, we can't delay Cain's forces, let alone dream of bringing him down."

"Maybe give her some space, Sam. These things can't be rushed."

"Space is what Cain will invade if we don't act fast!" Frustration flared within me, hot and demanding. I stopped pacing, turning to face him squarely. "Luka is our linchpin, Nate. I just need to figure out how to get her to see that."

"Look, I get it, man. Luka's got you wrapped around her little finger," Nate said, his tone shifting to something more somber, the smile fading as fast as it came.

"Wrapped around her... No. It's not like that," I corrected him, but my protest sounded feeble even to my ears. Maybe there was truth in his jest. Maybe Luka did have me ensnared, but not in the way he thought; she was about a decade younger than me after all. It was her potential, the raw untapped power she contained that had me tied in knots.

Nate leaned against the stone wall, his arms crossed as he watched me with a mix of concern and caution.

"Hey," he said, the word soft but carrying weight. "Remember when you were new to this whole Genesi thing? It wasn't easy for you either."

I slumped onto my throne, the cold of the mountain stone seeping through my clothes. His reminder was a punch in the gut—one I needed.

"Yeah, I remember," I admitted with a sigh. The memories of my own struggles were still fresh after a decade.

"Back then, you had to fight tooth and nail just to get recognized," Nate continued, his voice gentle but firm. "You didn't exactly take it slow, did you?"

"Taking it slow doesn't always keep you alive," I muttered, thinking back to how I'd found the encampment, a rogue desperate for a place. The leader at the time—a brute named Raziel—had laughed in my face, denying me entry. So, I'd challenged him. Fought him. And when his body hit the ground, there was no question left. I became the leader, by blood and right.

After that, I dedicated the next several years to climbing through the ranks, starting as leader of one encampment and eventually rising to commander over all thirteen Genesi encampments.

"True," Nate conceded, "but sometimes pushing too hard breaks more than it builds. Luka needs to find her way, not be forced into it."

"Doesn't change the fact that we're running out of time," I grumbled.Before Nate could respond, the sound of hurried footsteps echoed through the cavernous room. A scout, breathless from urgency skidded to a halt before us. He extended a hand offering a small data chip.

"Message from Lars," he panted. "He managed to pull more footage before... before..."

"Before our spy got caught," I finished for him taking the chip.

My heart sank like a stone in water. Another loss another innocent whose fate was sealed by my father's merciless hand.

"Let's see it," Nate said moving to the console set against the wall as the scout vacated the throne room. We gathered around the flickering screen as he inserted the chip. The image that came to life sent shivers down my spine.Rows upon rows of cryogenic tanks filled the screen each one holding a still figure within. Thousands of them a dormant army just waiting for the signal to wake.

"Genesi soldiers," I breathed, my voice barely above a whisper. "Cain's been busy."

"Too busy," Nate added grimly "When they wake up..."

"They'll come for us." I stated the words tasting like ash in my mouth. My eyes locked onto the screen where cold silent ranks of potential destruction lay in wait.

Chapter 3

Luka

"So in a nutshell, time's running out and I need a way to delay Cain's forces," I finished, my voice steady despite the tremor of urgency that underpinned each word. The four of us stood on the edge of the training grounds, the air thick with the scent of sun-baked earth and the distant clank of metal from genesi soldiers honing their skills in the early morning light. Sam's morning briefing had left a bitter aftertaste; less than a month before Cain's army would be at our doorstep.

"Less than a month," Liz echoed my thoughts, her eyes narrowing as she processed the information, her fingers absentmindedly pulling at the cuff of her sleeve.

The ground felt cold beneath my feet, a stark contrast to the tension that simmered in the air.

I watched Troian and Skai a little ways off, their heads close together in quiet conversation, embodying an odd sense of peace that felt out of reach for the rest of us. Troian's dark hair shone in the morning sun, her features sharp and determined as she spoke. Skai listened intently, her brown eyes focused and serious. They were a strange pair, but somehow they managed to balance each other out.

Focus Luka.

Turning my attention back to my friends, I saw the worry etched on their faces. Liz's usually bright green eyes were clouded with concern, her tanned cheeks paler than usual. Ren stood tall and still, his unruly black hair falling into his face as he gazed off into the distance. He always seemed to be lost in thought these days.

My gaze landed on Harvey, who was now staring at me expectantly. "So what do you suggest?" he asked.

I took a deep breath before answering. "We need to find a way to slow them down," I said firmly. "If we can delay Cain's army long enough, maybe we'll have a chance."

Harvey nodded in agreement while Liz and Ren exchanged doubtful glances. "But how?" Liz questioned.

"We could sabotage their weapons," Ren suggested hesitantly.

Harvey shook his head. "That would only anger them further," he pointed out.

I wanted to confide in them about Sam's plan, the bio weapon he believed could tip the scales in our favor. But the words snagged on the threshold of my lips as I glanced at Harvey. His moral compass was steadfast, unyielding, and I knew the mere suggestion of using such a weapon would spark immediate conflict.

Harvey caught my gaze, his brows knitted in concern, "Luka, you look like you're carrying the weight of the world. Anything else Sam said that we need to know?"

"Nothing more for now," I lied smoothly, averting my eyes. I hated the deception, but some truths were too heavy to share without caution. I felt Liz's gaze burning into me and instead, I turned to Ren, noting the shadows that played across his sharp features. If anyone could understand the necessity of harsh decisions, it was him. He had grown up with Sam, seen sides of him I couldn't fathom. Maybe Ren could help me make sense of this gnawing doubt, help me navigate through the murky waters of what was right and what was necessary.

"Ren, can we talk later? In private?" My words were barely above a whisper, meant only for his ears.

He nodded once, understanding flickering in his eyes. His past with Sam stretched back further than any of us, and if there was a chance he could help me persuade Sam to consider alternatives—or, at the very least, help me accept the grim reality of our situation—I had to take it.

"Sure, Luka. We'll talk." Ren's voice was low and steady.

Harvey, ever watchful, had sensed the shift between us, and the hurt that clouded his grey blue eyes was a dagger to my conscience.

Distractions can wait, survival can't.

With a deep breath, I pushed the looming thoughts of the bio weapon aside. It was a bridge I'd cross soon enough. For now, there were plans to be made, defenses to be bolstered, and an encroaching army to hold at bay.

Ren and I had come to an unspoken agreement, a truce of sorts since we made our alliance with Sam and the Genesi. Our romantic entanglements were a luxury we couldn't afford, not with Cain's forces breathing down our necks. It was time to focus on the war, not the confusing tangle of emotions that threatened to derail us. It hurt, pushing aside what might have been with Ren, but watching Harvey's strained smile made it clear—it was necessary.

"Okay, let's think tactics," I said, breaking the silence. "We need a game-changer, something to throw Cain off our scent. Something to keep Cain distracted."

"Distraction." Liz's voice cut through my thoughts, her eyes alight. "I disabled the forcefield back at Delta Force when we escaped remember. Bought us precious seconds."

"I remember." I said. The idea was forming, growing into a tangible plan in my mind. "But imagine doing that on a larger scale. If we disrupt the power grid, take down the forcefields city by city…"

"It would be chaos," Ren murmured, his gaze meeting mine. There was a glint of admiration in his eyes. This was more than chaos; this was strategy.

Cain would be forced to redirect his attention, to control the uproar in his own domain rather than marching on us. It was risky, but it could work. I could almost see the dominos falling, each city plunged into darkness and confusion, their cries drowning out the drums of war.

"Wouldn't we be exposing innocent people though?" Harvey's brow creased with concern, the moral compass that guided him never faltering even in the face of annihilation.

"Short term pain for long term gain," I countered, though my stomach clenched at the thought. "We're trying to save them too, Harvey. Sometimes you have to crack a few eggs to make an omelet."

Great, now I sound just like Sam.

"Lewis might know how to execute it from a tech standpoint," Ren suggested, always one step ahead, already moving on to logistics.

"Right." My voice was steady, despite the whirlwind of thoughts. "We'll need to move fast. Harvey and I will go find

Lewis."

"Then you'll be headed to the computer lab," Liz said, determination etched into her expression.

Ren and Liz began to discuss their own plans for fortifying our defenses and rallying more support from other genesi encampments. I turned to Harvey, ready to leave and track down Lewis, but he hesitated.

"Are you sure this is the right thing to do?" He spoke softly, his concern evident. I nervously chewed on my bottom lip in response. "I'll only go through with it if we can ensure no innocent people will be harmed," I reassured him. He nodded, satisfied with my answer.

We set off, the soles of our boots crunching against the gravel as we made our way back inside the mountain and toward the computer lab. Harvey walked beside me, his steps measured and deliberate. The urgency of our mission propelled us forward, but I couldn't help but let my gaze wander over the Genesi encampment.

The mountains rose tall and mighty, their peaks like jagged fingers reaching towards the sky. Each one was a different shade of gray and brown, with patches of green vegetation clinging to their sides. The tallest mountain, our rebel home, stood proud and resilient, providing a protective shelter for the Genesi. The cluster of mountains that cradled our rebel home was more than a strategic hideout; it was a living, breathing entity. It had become a sanctuary in this blasted world. Around the body of water at the heart of the camp, life persisted in stubborn defiance.

"Thinking about the plan?" Harvey's voice broke through my reverie, each word laced with the burden he carried. His eyes, searched mine for doubt or fear.

"Always," I replied, tearing my gaze away from the fighting ring in the valley where disputes were settled with sweat and steel. "But we need Lewis to make this work."

"I know." Harvey nodded, his jaw set. "He's brilliant. If anyone can hack into the power grid, it's him."

Once inside the mouth of the mountain we navigated the maze of tunnels, our footsteps echoing off the walls. The air was cooler here, the weight of the mountain pressing down around us, a silent reminder of the strength it represented. Here we had food, water, and shelter—all the essentials for survival, all hidden from the prying eyes of Cain's army.

"Once we disrupt their forcefields, Cain will have his hands full," I said, trying to sound more assured than I felt. "It'll give us the time we need to strengthen our position."

"Let's hope so," Harvey murmured. He paused, placing a hand on my shoulder. "Luka, you know we're all in this together, right? It's not all on you."

I met his gaze, seeing the resolve in his eyes. "I know, Harvey. And I'm grateful—more than you can imagine."

With a nod, we continued in silence, the rhythmic tapping of our boots against the stone floor filled the narrow corridor as we made our way toward the computer lab. Harvey's shadow danced against the walls, stretching and shrinking in the flickering light from the overhead lamps.

"Hey," he said suddenly, breaking the silence that had settled between us. "How are you holding up with… you know, being Genesi?"

I hesitated, caught off guard by the question. The truth was a tangled mess inside me, but I couldn't deny the struggle. "It's…" I started, then sighed, unsure how to explain the whirlwind of pride and fear that came with the revelation of my transformation. "It's overwhelming. There's this power within me, Harvey, a part of who I am, but it feels like an ocean I've only dipped my toes into."

He nodded thoughtfully, his expression softening. "And Thorn?" he pressed gently, knowing full well the storm that name stirred within me.

"Thorn," I whispered, feeling the weight of the memory, the finality of my actions. "I did what I had to do, but Harvey, I can't shake this feeling…" I trailed off, grappling with the confession that clawed at my throat.

"What feeling?"

"That maybe I need to let go of some part of my humanity if we're going to win this war." My voice was barely audible, a confession meant only for the safety of the shadows around us.

Harvey stopped walking, turning to face me fully. His eyes searched mine, looking for the girl he knew amidst the turmoil. "Luka, if you lose your humanity, what are we fighting for?"

"I know, but maybe it's not about what we're fighting for, but what we're fighting against." I met his gaze squarely, my resolve hardening. "Cain won't hesitate. Thorn didn't. If I have to become something else to protect everyone, is that worth the cost?"

"I don't want you to become like them," he said firmly, a note of desperation creeping into his voice.

"Neither do I," I admitted, my heart aching. "But I'm afraid of what it'll take to stop Cain. And what that'll make me."

We stood there, two silhouettes locked in a silent battle of wills and fears, until the unspoken understanding passed between us—a nod to the complexity of the war within and without.

"Let's find Lewis," Harvey said finally, motioning toward the computer lab with a tilt of his head. The concern lingered in his eyes, but he respected my space, my need to navigate the treacherous waters of my own thoughts.

"Right, Lewis." I forced a determined step forward, putting distance between myself and the doubts that threatened to consume me.

"Ready?" Harvey asked as we reached the entrance.

"Ready as I'll ever be," I replied, reaching out to push the door open.

Chapter 4

Luka

We stepped into the vast space of the computer lab. It was a sight to behold—a fusion of nature's raw beauty and the pinnacle of futuristic technology. Monitors, sleek and numerous, lined one entire wall, each displaying a different location. I could see the twelve other genesi encampments blinking with activity, their inhabitants unaware of our watchful gaze.

"Think Lewis is in here?" Harvey asked, his voice bouncing off the cavern walls with a hushed echo.

"Where else would he be?" I responded, my tone laced with the impatience that often crept into me when urgency clawed at my insides. "He practically lives in here."

It always struck me how they'd managed to carve out such a functional space inside an otherwise uninhabitable mountain. The equipment was state-of-the-art, humming with life, its screens casting a kaleidoscope of colors onto the rough rock surfaces. Every terminal, every interface was designed for efficiency and discretion—a necessity for our survival.

"Look at this," I murmured, more to myself than to Harvey, as I approached the surveillance wall. "It's like we're literally a fly on the wall."

From a city intersection to the grim exterior of a military base, the footage rolled, seamless and silent. The rebel genesi, a resourceful bunch, had dispatched drones under the veil of night to plant these hidden cameras. As a former city-dweller, it amazed me how even with my trained senses, I'd been oblivious to their presence.

"Can't believe we never noticed them before," Harvey commented, leaning in closer to examine a feed from a bustling market square.

"Neither did they," I said, pointing to a pair of uniformed guards on one screen who were too preoccupied with their mundane patrol to sense the technology capturing their every move.

This was our advantage—our ability to see without being seen. But finding Lewis was crucial; he was the key to turning what we watched into actionable plans.

"Let's find Lewis," I said, scanning the room for the familiar disheveled mop of dark blond curls. A spark of resolve ignited within me. With Lewis and his brilliance combined with what we had here, we could do more than just watch—we could act.

My boots echoed softly against the stone floor as Harvey and I wove between aisles of humming machinery that seemed out of place within the stark natural beauty of our cavernous hideout. The contrast never ceased to startle me, this fusion of the primitive and the futuristic, a necessary union in our struggle against Cain.

"Keep an eye out for Lars as well," I murmured, my eyes

scanning for the telltale sign of Lewis's partner-in-tech. It was strange to think of gruff, solitary Lars willingly sharing his space with anyone, let alone forming what seemed like an amicable partnership. But then, Lewis could coax a smile from a statue with his earnest enthusiasm for all things technical.

Thinking of them holed up in here, surrounded by monitors and the steady thrum of processors, felt oddly reassuring. Lars usually treated his lab like sacred ground, tolerating no one's presence unless it served a purpose he deemed worthy. Yet, there they were—two tech heads united by their passion for innovation and a shared respect that transcended Lars's usual disdain for company.

Lewis had quickly become indispensable to him, I suspected, not only for his adeptness with code but also because he challenged Lars without encroaching on his territory. It was a delicate balance, one that Lewis navigated with an almost intuitive grace.

As we approached the far end of the lab, my gaze fell upon the wall of surveillance screens. They flickered with life, each frame a window into the world we hoped to free. And behind this intricate web of information pulsed the digital heart of our operation: VIKI.

The artificial intelligence was a marvel in itself, a silent sentinel weaving through our networks, overseeing communications, and keeping a watchful eye on Cain's every move. When Lewis first stumbled upon her existence, his face lit up like the console before him—a beacon of possibilities in our dimly lit cave.

"VIKI is the nerve center," he had said, awe lacing his voice. "She's… incredible."

But for all of VIKI's advanced capabilities, she offered

little comfort when it came to preparing us for war. Her cold, calculated logic could analyze patterns, predict enemy movements, even outsmart some of Cain's own systems. Yet, she lacked the human element, the visceral understanding of fear, hope, and desperation that fueled us. She couldn't comprehend the cost of bloodshed or the weight of sacrifice.

"Advanced doesn't always mean helpful," I had admitted under my breath, watching Harvey nod in silent agreement.

"Especially when it comes to matters of the heart and soul," he had added solemnly.

"Exactly," I had replied. Our war wasn't just about circuits and data streams. It was about people, about lives hanging in the balance, about the future we were desperate to claim. Despite her sophistication, VIKI could never truly grasp the stakes we played for, the fire that burned within us.

In a way, it was a reminder of our humanity—our greatest strength and most profound vulnerability.

We found Lewis hunched over a cluttered workstation, his fingers deftly manipulating a minuscule object under the magnifying arm. The lab hummed with the low purr of machines and the rapid-fire clicking of keys. Harvey and I exchanged a glance before approaching.

"Hey, Lewis," I started, my voice echoing slightly off the cavern walls. "We need to talk about Cain."

He didn't look up, but his hands stilled momentarily. "Give me a sec," he muttered, still tinkering with the minuscule object. Finally, he set aside his tools and turned to face us, wiping his hands on his pants. His gaze flickered between Harvey and me, a silent invitation to continue.

"Sam and I met earlier," I said, leaning against the edge of a desk. "We're trying to figure out how to delay Cain's forces.

Is it possible to disrupt his power grid? Maybe disable his forcefields?"

Lewis's brows knitted together as he leaned back in his chair, considering the implications. "The forcefields are there for civilian safety, Luka. Taking them down could leave people exposed."

"Those forcefields aren't for the civilians, they're to keep us out. The genesi. But we both know we're not the threat Cain's made everyone believe. If we take them down, it's not the people inside we're putting at risk—it's Cain's hold on power."

"Is that justification enough to potentially put innocent lives at risk though?" Lewis asked, his voice tinged with skepticism. He wasn't just our tech guy; he was the conscience of our group sometimes.

"Think about it, Lewis." I locked eyes with him, willing him to understand. "Cain has manipulated the truth, twisted it to create fear. We're not the monsters he's painted us to be. Our fight is with him, not with the people." My heart raced with the urgency of our cause, and I could see Harvey nodding out of the corner of my eye.

Lewis exhaled slowly, his moral compass warring with the logic of our strategy. "If we do this… we have to be absolutely sure no one gets hurt because of it."

"Agreed," I affirmed. "That's why we need your help—to make sure we do this right."

He ran a hand through his curls, pushing them back from his forehead in an all-too-familiar gesture of frustration mixed with resolve. "Okay, let's figure out how to do this without causing harm. It won't be easy, but… if we're lucky, we might just pull it off."

We needed that luck. And Lewis's brilliance. Because sometimes, to dismantle a dictator's empire, you had to start with the barriers he puts up—not just the physical ones, but the lies that support them.

Lewis squinted at the holographic schematics floating above his workstation, lines of code cascading down like digital waterfalls. "We might need Lars for this," he admitted, with a reluctant edge to his voice that told me he knew how that conversation would go.

"Then get him over here," I said, my tone leaving no room for doubt. We were racing against time, and every second counted.

He nodded, sending a quick message through his wrist com before turning back to the screens. Moments later, Lars loomed in the doorway, his bulky frame nearly filling it. His eyes, sharp under bushy eyebrows, immediately found Lewis.

"What's so important that you're interrupting my work?" Lars grumbled, but there was an underlying note of respect in his voice reserved only for Lewis.

"We need to figure out a way to safely take down Cain's forcefields," Lewis explained without preamble. "Luka's idea— she believes it's possible."

"Possible? Maybe." Lars crossed his arms, his expression dubious. "Advisable? That's another debate. You do realize those forcefields are tied into the city's entire power grid?"

I stepped forward. "Yes, but if we can isolate the frequencies—"

"Isolating frequencies is child's play," Lars cut me off. "It's the biometric feedback loop that's the real headache. The system's designed to react to unauthorized tampering—could fry the whole network, or worse, hurt someone."

"Which is why we need your expertise," Lewis interjected before I could respond. "Without dismantling those barriers, we'll never have a chance at getting close enough to Cain."

"Alright." Lars sighed, "Let's dive deeper into these 'biometrics' then. But I'm not promising miracles."

"Thank you," I said, offering him a nod of appreciation I wasn't sure he saw.

Before we could delve further into the complexities of the task, VIKI's voice sliced through the tense atmosphere. "Attention: Genesi operatives Delta-Three and Echo-Five currently within proximity. Probability of assistance in current objective: high. Communication request dispatched."

"Operatives?" I echoed, surprised. Two more genesi here could mean reinforcements or complications.

"Who are they, VIKI?" Lewis asked, the question laced with curiosity and caution.

"Delta-Three: Specialist in energy manipulation. Echo-Five: Expertise in biometric engineering," VIKI replied, her voice devoid of inflection.

"Energy manipulation could be key," Lars mused aloud, already wheels turning behind his eyes as he considered the possibilities.

"Biometric engineering too," Lewis added, a spark of excitement igniting in his gaze.

"Let's hope they're as good as their titles suggest," I said, feeling a mix of relief and unease ripple through me. Allies were good, but every new player added to the game meant another variable in an already uncertain plan.

The hum of machinery and the soft glow of monitors filled the air as we waited. Harvey leaned against a console, his arms crossed as his eyes flicked between the screens and me.

"Bringing more people into this feels like we're stretching ourselves thin," he murmured. "What if they're not on the same page?"

I bit my lip, my mind racing with the same concerns. "We need their expertise, Harv. But I can't shake off the feeling that Sam's keeping too much from us."

"Sam has his reasons, Luka," Harvey said, trying to reassure me, though his gaze held traces of doubt.

"Doesn't mean I have to like it," I replied, the frustration evident in my voice. Trust was a currency running scarce these days, and Sam withholding information about these genesi operatives felt like a betrayal.

"Echo-Five and Delta-Three, huh?" I mused aloud, trying to distract myself from the annoyance prickling at my skin. "Sounds like they've walked straight out of one of those old spy holovids."

Harvey let out a soft chuckle. "I bet they don't have code names as cool as ours."

"Please," I scoffed playfully, "no one tops 'Nova-One.'"

A silence settled between us, comfortable yet charged with anticipation. The wait gnawed at me, each minute stretching longer than the last. From somewhere deep within the cave, the sound of approaching footsteps began to echo, growing steadily closer.

"Showtime," Harvey whispered, pushing away from the console and standing up straight.

"Finally," I muttered, standing taller myself. "Let's hope VIKI's calculations are correct," I added, stealing a glance at the screens where her presence seemed to loom, just as the footsteps reached the entrance of the computer lab.

Chapter 5

Luka

The hum of the computer lab was a familiar symphony to my ears as I leaned against a cold metal table, my gaze fixed on the doorway where two silhouettes stood, backlit by the sterile glow of the corridor. VIKI's voice, smooth as glass, broke the silence.

"Attention. Delta-Three and Echo-Five have arrived."

Heads turned in unison toward the newcomers as they stepped into the fluorescent light.

"Welcome," I said, pushing off the table to stand upright. My voice carried a hint of authority, tempered by genuine curiosity. "I'm Luka Foster."

The man, with hair the color of rust and eyes sharp as flint, nodded at me. "Pleasure's ours. Names Fox." His voice was low, carrying a rumble that resonated slightly within the small space. There was an ease about him, as if he'd walked through a hundred labs just like this one and remade them all in his image.

Beside him, his female companion gave a reserved smile, her black hair pulled back in a neat ponytail that swung as she surveyed us. "Stef Grier," she introduced herself, her tone more measured than Fox's, but no less confident.

Harvey stepped forward next, his posture relaxed yet somehow still full of the quiet strength he always seemed to carry. "Harvey Montgomery," he said, extending a hand. The corners of his mouth lifted in a half-smile meant to reassure, a silent promise that here, they were among allies.

Lewis was already halfway across the room, unable to contain the spark of excitement in his eyes. He extended his hand, which held the faintest tremor of eagerness. "Lewis Kingston, resident tech guru," he declared, an infectious grin spreading over his features. He barely waited for Stef's handshake before rattling off, "Can't wait to hear your ideas on energy manipulation. I've got theories—"

"Save it, Lewis," Lars interjected gruffly from his spot by a bank of monitors, not bothering to move. "Lars Fenton," he simply stated, his eyes flicking to Stef and then away, as if acknowledging that pleasantries were necessary but not particularly his style.

"Team introductions complete," VIKI chimed in, her voice a calm presence that seemed to wrap around us.

"Thanks, VIKI," I said with a nod. This was it – the beginning of something that could change everything.

Fox stepped forward, the overhead lights casting angular shadows across his sharp features. He had an aura of charged energy about him that made the hairs on my arms stand at attention. "My specialty is energy manipulation," he said, voice crackling with a confidence. "VIKI thought I might be able to lend a hand—or rather, a spark."

Stef followed, less flamboyant but no less assured, her gaze analytical, dissecting the room like she could see beneath the surface of things. "And I focus on biometric engineering. It's... intricate work," she admitted with a hint of pride, "the kind that can turn the tide if applied correctly."

I nodded, my mind racing with possibilities and uncertainties. The idea that these two might have had their hands in creating Sam's bio weapon was a splinter in my thoughts. Should I ask? Or would revealing my suspicion only fracture the fragile trust we were trying to build?

"Alright," I started, clearing my throat as I sought to redirect my focus. "Here's the lay of the land." I paced a little, gesturing towards the holographic displays that flickered with blueprints and schematics. "We've been working on a plan to disrupt Cain's energy grids. Without power, the forcefields around his cities drop." I glanced at them, ensuring they grasped the gravity of our aim. "It's only a distraction—a way to buy time—but it's vital."

"Sounds like a full system blackout," Fox mused, already lost in thought.

"Exactly," I continued. "Lewis and Lars are wizards with the tech side, but the biometric feedback loop has been a sticking point."

"Feedback loop?" Stef perked up, stepping closer to the display. Her fingers danced in the air as she traced the flow of data. "That's where I come in, then."

"VIKI mentioned your expertise could make all the difference," I said, watching the gears turn behind their eyes. There was a rhythm to their thinking, a harmony of ideas that began to buzz between them and us.

Fox and Stef huddled over the central console with Lewis

and Lars, their fingers flitting across the interactive screens as they pored over the city's power grid. I hovered at the edge of the group, watching the exchange of complex equations and rapid-fire technical jargon.

"Redirecting the flow here," Fox pointed out, "would cause a cascade effect…"

"Right, but we need to ensure it doesn't backfeed into the residential blocks," Stef countered with a furrowed brow.

"Minimal collateral," Lewis nodded in agreement, his eyes alight with the challenge. "We've got to keep the civilians safe."

As the four of them dove deeper into the problem, a new thought wormed its way into my mind. Our communications had been spotty at best, and as this war between Cain and us progressed, we'd need a foolproof way to talk to each other. The last thing we needed was for Cain to get wind of our plans because of a weak signal or a hacked line.

"Hey," I interrupted, waiting for a pause in their brainstorming. "What about our comms? If we're doing this, we need a more secure network."

Lewis glanced up, processing the request, but it was Lars who responded first, irritation creasing his features. "Luka, we're trying to disable an entire city's defense system here," he snapped, gesturing broadly at the hologram that now showed a red thread weaving through a maze of blue lines. "We can't just drop everything and—"

"Relax, Lars," Lewis cut in before Lars could work himself up further. His curls bounced as he turned to me, a spark of determination in his gaze. "I'll take a look at our comms. VIKI can help me sort out something more secure."

"Thanks, Lewis," I said, offering him a grateful smile.

"VIKI," Lewis called out, already shifting his attention from forcefields to frequencies, "let's run diagnostics on the current communication systems and start drafting some encryption protocols."

"Understood, Lewis," came VIKI's calm, omnipresent voice from the speakers above us. "Initiating diagnostics now."

I stepped back, allowing them to return to their heated discussion. With each passing moment, the plan grew more tangible, the hope we all carried flickering brighter against the encroaching darkness.

The hum of the computer lab blended with the occasional beep and click of keys as we all settled into our roles, each of us a cog in a larger machine gearing up for rebellion. Fox and Stef, their faces set with intense concentration, huddled over schematics that sprawled like veins across multiple screens. They pointed and gestured, their hands dancing in the air as they traced the pathways of energy that sustained the forcefields.

I leaned closer to the holographic display, observing Fox manipulate the model with deft fingers. "If we can reroute the power here and there," he said, his voice a low murmur, "we could create a cascade failure without triggering any alarms."

"Biometric feedback loops are tricky," Stef added, her brow furrowed in thought. "But I think we can simulate a maintenance request from inside the system. It'll buy us time before they realize what's happening."

Lewis was a step ahead, VIKI assisting him in running simulations, his fingers a blur as he tested firewall after firewall. The soft glow of the screen painted his face in shades of blue and green, a silent testament to countless hours spent in the digital trenches.

"VIKI, cross-reference these algorithms with known security protocols," he instructed, his voice steady as he navigated through lines of code.

"Processing, Lewis," VIKI responded, her voice devoid of strain or impatience.

Meanwhile, Lars had commandeered another terminal, his crankiness forgotten as he threw himself into the work, his hands moving with a fervor that betrayed his underlying excitement. He was building something, piece by piece—a framework that would either be our salvation or our downfall.

"Got it!" Lars exclaimed after hours that felt both eternal and fleeting. "This pattern should be indiscernible to their scanners, even if they're actively searching."

"Good," I said, unable to hide the pride in my voice. "Let's run through what we have."

We gathered around a central table, weary but wired on adrenaline and the gravity of our task. Lewis laid out the communication upgrades first, showcasing the new encryption layers and redundancies. It was complex, far beyond anything I'd seen before, but his explanation made it clear—even to those of us less versed in the technical aspects.

"Any breach and VIKI will automatically reroute the signal, scrambling it to junk data," Lewis assured us, his eyes locking with mine. "They won't intercept anything useful."

"Excellent," I nodded, my mind already ticking through the next steps.

Fox and Stef followed, outlining the energy grid disruption and the precise timing required. Their plan was elegant in its simplicity yet audacious in scope. We would strike at dawn when shifts changed and attention waned—a narrow window, but one we could exploit.

"Every second counts," Fox emphasized. "One misstep and

the whole thing unravels."

"Then we don't misstep," I declared, the words thick with resolve.

We fine-tuned the details, ironing out contingencies and fail-safes, our collective expertise melding into a single, unified strategy. VIKI recorded every decision, her silent vigilance a comfort and a reminder—there was no going back now.

"Tomorrow, it begins," I said, my voice barely above a whisper, yet it carried the weight of our shared determination.

"Tomorrow," they all agreed.

"We should all get some rest," I said, stifling a yawn as I scanned the room. "Tomorrow's going to demand everything we've got."

Heads nodded in weary agreement. The air was thick with the scent of determination and lingering electricity. Each of us knew the gravity of what lay ahead. We were setting in motion events that could change the tide of this war—or drown us in its wake.

"Harvey," I added, catching his eye, "We should go update Sam on—"

"Commander Cain has been informed of today's progress," VIKI's voice cut through the lab, smooth and omniscient. Her cameras blinked from high corners—a silent sentinel in our midst. "A detailed communication has been dispatched to his secure line."

"Thanks, VIKI," I replied, my lips quirking up in spite of the exhaustion clawing at my bones. Trust an A.I. to be one step ahead, even when it came to keeping secrets.

"Of course, Luka," she responded, and I imagined if VIKI could feel, there'd be pride in her tone. She was more than just a system; she was our unseen guardian, the all-seeing eye within these cavernous walls.

"Alright, team," I stretched, my muscles protesting. "Let's call it a night."

As the group began to collect their things, Harvey approached me, his stride confident yet considerate. "Hungry?" he asked, arching an eyebrow. "Mess hall?"

I hesitated, picturing the crowded space, the buzz of conversation, the clatter of trays. "Sure, but only if you promise we won't sit near Ian. I can't deal with another lecture on protein intake ratios tonight."

His chuckle was soft, a brief respite from the tension that had built throughout the day. "Deal," he said, offering a hand. "But you're missing out on his latest bean sprout conspiracy theory."

"Hard pass," I grinned, taking his hand and allowing myself this moment of levity. "Let's go find something marginally edible instead."

Chapter 6

Sam

The walls of my private chamber echoed the soft hum of electricity, a constant reminder of the underground life we had been forced to embrace. I stood at the center of my quarters, gazing into the flickering holograph where Camille's image shimmered with a ghostly blue light.

"Camille," I said, my voice steady despite the weight of the days events on my shoulders, "we need to move the noncombatants—your encampment is the safest bet."

Her image nodded, her expression etched with concern. "I agree, Sam. But we must be cautious. Cain's eyes are everywhere."

"Exactly why it's you I trust most." I paced slowly, each step deliberate as I considered the lives at stake. "Can your people handle the influx?"

"Without question," she affirmed, her confidence reassuring me. "But transporting them... that's the tricky part. We can't risk using the main routes."

"Back channels then," I suggested, running a hand through my hair. "Old smuggling tunnels. They're less likely to be watched."

"Risky, but it could work." Her brow furrowed. "What about Luka's friends? The human ones?"

"Especially them." My lips pressed into a thin line. "They're not fighters, but they're targets all the same because of their association with us."

"Understood," Camille replied, her tone firm. "We'll prepare the safe houses along the way. Send them in small groups, staggered. Less chance of drawing attention."

"Good. And make sure they're equipped with scramblers—in case they stumble upon any surveillance tech." I paused, looking directly at her holographic presence. "We can't afford to have Cain sniffing around, not now."

"Consider it done." Camille's gaze held mine, a silent acknowledgment passing between us—the unspoken bond of leaders shouldering the fate of our people.

"Keep me updated," I instructed, the commander once again taking precedence over the man who couldn't help but feel the pull of her unwavering strength.

"Of course." Her image flickered as the connection grew unstable.

The holograph fizzled out, leaving me with the hollow echo of my chamber and the gravity of our plans.

"VIKI reestablish the comm link." I called into the void.

Alone in the dim light, I allowed myself a moment of raw vulnerability, the faces of those I was sending away flashing across my mind's eye. Their safety was paramount; everything else, including my own unease, paled in comparison.

"Commander, the communication link has been reestablished," VIKI informed me.

I looked up and saw Camille's holographic figure appear again.

"What were we talking about?" I said aloud as I struggled to remember our conversation before the connection was lost.

"Hopefully an update from your spy," she said.

I paced the expanse of my chamber, the jagged walls a silent testament to the world above us that had crumbled into chaos. The cool air brushed against my skin as I recounted the grainy footage we'd managed to extract from Winston's last transmission—a haunting tableau of cytogenetic tanks lined up like sentinels of doom. As I described the footage, Camille's expression turned into a mask of terror.

"Camille, that footage is a game changer. His number of genesi soldiers is far greater than we could have imagined… We need to know what Cain is planning. We must have an exact time for when he will awaken them," I said, my voice echoing slightly in the cavernous room.

"Then we send another spy." Camille's voice was resolute, her holographic image flickering with the connection's instability. "We can't go into this blind."

"Another spy isn't an option," I responded, stopping mid-stride. The weight of command bore down on me, each decision etched with the potential for irreversible consequences. "Winston was Delta Force. He knew how to move, how to blend in. And now he's likely dead because of it."

"Dead?" Her tone sharpened with the word, a jolt of urgency shot through our fading line.

"Presumed." I ran a hand through my cropped hair, a gesture of frustration. "He had a biomimetic eye with a camera, and I… I tore it out before sending him back. If they caught him, if they found it had been altered by us…" My words trailed off, leaving the unsaid horrors to linger in the shadows.

"Sam, there must be someone else we can send," she pressed, the leader in her refusing to back down even as the friend in her understood my reluctance.

"Only one of Luka's human friends, and she'd never forgive me if I put them at risk without her consent." I clenched my fists, the mental image of Luka's determined eyes forbidding any such betrayal of trust. "She's protective of them, and they're not trained for this."

"Damn," Camille muttered, the curse stark against the silence that followed.

I sighed, leaning against the cold stone wall. "We play the hand we're dealt, Camille. No more sacrifices. Not if we can help it."

"Okay, Sam. Okay." Her image wavered, the edges blurring. "We'll find another way."

The cavern's walls were cool against my back, the dim light from the holo-projector casting wavering shadows across the stone. Camille's holographic form paced in front of me; even as a projection, her energy was palpable.

"Can we insert someone else into Delta Force? One of ours? There has to be a way," she said, her voice tinged with both frustration and determination.

"Who?" I challenged, knowing full well our options were limited. "We've got no one else trained for this kind of infiltration."

She stopped pacing and faced me, her brow furrowed in thought. "What about reprogramming one of the bots? They wouldn't suspect—"

"Too risky," I cut her off. "Cain's techs would spot a hack in seconds."

"Then we need another angle, we have to know how many tanks and when they will awaken," she insisted. Her gaze held mine, fierce and unyielding. For a moment, I let myself get lost in the intensity of her eyes, remembering the fire that burned between us during those stolen moments when leadership gave way to something far more primal.

"Maybe…" I began, half-distracted by memories of our last real encounter. It had been months, but the thought of her touch lingered like a phantom on my skin.

"Maybe what?" Her voice pulled me back to the present, the urgency clear.

"Nothing solid yet. Just thinking aloud." My words were vague, but she seemed to understand the need to grasp at any thread of hope, no matter how thin.

"Keep thinking, Sam. We need all the ideas we can get," she encouraged, her voice softer now, a reminder of the connection we shared beyond our official roles.

Before I could respond, the chamber door banged open, and Troian stepped inside. She had a knack for timing, always appearing when least expected or when the situation was at its most dire.

"Sam, I intercepted a comm you need to hear," Troian announced, barely acknowledging Camille's presence.

"Let's hear it then," I said, shifting into commander mode despite the lingering tension in the air.

"VIKI intended this for you, but you were obviously pre-occupied, so I got to it first," Troian said, her face serious. "Luka's planning a cyber attack on the energy grids. She aims to take down the forcefield around Cain's cities. Cause pandemonium, delay the war."

Camille's projection leaned forward, intrigued. "That's bold. Risky, but it could work."

"It could," I agreed weighing the potential chaos against the slim chance of success. Luka's plans were always gutsy, threading the needle between genius and insanity. "It'll buy us time, if nothing else."

"Time we desperately need," Camille agreed, nodding. Her image flickered as if emphasizing the precariousness of our situation.

"Keep your people ready. If this works, things are going to move fast," I instructed her, letting the edge of command seep into my voice.

"Very well," she replied with a nod, and then her projection vanished, leaving me with Troian for the moment as Camille had no doubt stepped away to update her second in command.

My pulse quickened as I processed Troian's update, my brain piecing together the details of Luka's audacious plan. It was then a cold realization dawned on me, chilling despite the warmth of the cavernous chamber.

"Fox and Stef," I muttered under my breath, the names hanging heavy in the air. They were the only ones with the expertise to aid Luka in such a technical endeavor. My mind raced with the implications. If Luka had connected the dots, she'd know they were involved in the creation of my bio weapon—the one secret I couldn't afford her to unearth.

"Sam?" Troian's voice pulled me back from the precipice of my thoughts. "There's something else."

I met her gaze, nodding for her to continue. Troian always had a knack for sensing when the cogs of my mind were grinding too hard.

"About communication," she started, shifting her weight

from one foot to another, an unconscious tell that the news carried weight. "Lewis has developed a new secure comm network, encrypted beyond anything we've seen before. He thinks it'll help us connect all thirteen encampments without fear of interception or constant interruption."

"Interesting," I mused, briefly allowing the significance to wash over me. "That could change everything."

"I know." Troian's lips curled into a rare smile, the kind that said she too believed in the sliver of hope Lewis's work represented.

"Camille," I called out, knowing her projection would still be lingering just out of sight. She reappeared, her form stabilizing into a clearer image than before. "Troian brings good news. Lewis has outdone himself with a new comm network. Secure, untraceable but most importantly, stable. It'll tighten the web between us."

Her face lit up with understanding, and I could almost feel the warmth of her approval. "Brilliant," she praised, her voice tinged with relief. "We've been dancing on the edge of a blade with our communications for years. This could be the steadying hand we need."

"Exactly my thoughts," I agreed, feeling a rare flicker of optimism in the midst of our dire situation. "We'll move forward with implementing it immediately. I'll have Lewis coordinate with your techs first."

"Good," Camille said, her projection giving a firm nod. "Reliable lines might just give us the edge we're clawing for."

"Let's hope." I clasped my hands behind my back, grounding myself in the moment.

"Troian, keep me updated on any progress or setbacks," I instructed, already thinking ahead to the challenges we'd face integrating the technology.

"Will do, Sam," she replied before turning on her heel, her boots clicking against the stone floor as she went to leave.

"Anything else?" I asked, turning to Troian.

"That's it for now. I'm headed to dinner," she said, already moving toward the door.

"Dismissed," I said, nodding to Troian. She flashed me a quick, determined glance and pivoted away, her footsteps echoing down the cavernous corridor that led to the heart of our encampment.

I watched her retreating back, a soldier through and through, until she disappeared from view.

"Camille," I began, shifting my focus back to her shimmering image, "before we end this, just… be careful, okay?"

"Always am, Sam," she replied, her eyes catching mine with an intensity that resonated beyond the cold technology between us. It was hard not to acknowledge the undercurrent that always seemed to spark when we conversed—dangerous, given the world we lived in.

"Keep your people on their toes. Cain's tactics are getting more unpredictable, and I get the sinking feeling he's about to make a move," I added, the edge in my voice softening ever so slightly. I couldn't afford distractions, but the concern I felt for Camille was genuine.

"Understood. And Sam," she hesitated, biting her lip—a telltale sign that she was weighing her words, "stay safe. We can't afford to lose you."

"Likewise." The sentiment hung between us, a silent acknowledgment of the bond we shared. But duty called louder than the whisper of what might have been in another life—one not dictated by survival and war.

"Until next time," she said, her holographic form beginning to waver.

"Until next time," I echoed.

With a flicker, she was gone, and the room felt colder in her absence. I took a deep breath, allowing myself a moment of vulnerability before the walls went up again. There was work to do, battles to plan, lives to save. And I would be damned if I let anything, even my own heart, get in the way of that.

Turning away from where Camille's projection had stood, I made my way to the command console. My fingers danced across the keys, bringing up maps and reports.

"Time to get back to work."

Chapter 7

Luka

The clatter of cutlery against trays provided an odd sort of harmony to the buzz of conversation as Harvey and I made our way into the mess hall. The cavern's interior, a testament to the alliance between humans and the Genesi, sprawled before us—a vast space carved into the heart of a mountain, with walls that shimmered in the dim light like the inside of a geode.

"Over there," Harvey murmured, nodding towards a table where Liz, Ren, Ian, and Skai had already gathered. My gaze flickered to Ian, who threw his head back in laughter, his voice cutting through the din. A knot formed in my stomach—Ian and I had never seen eye to eye, and my reluctance must have shown on my face.

"Come on, Luka," Harvey said, giving me a gentle nudge. "He's not as irritating as his days in Delta Force."

"True," I agreed, though my feet dragged slightly as we approached the table.

"Hey, look who decided to join us!" Ian boomed as we sat

down, but I focused on the others, nodding my greetings.

"Any further update from the training sessions this morning?" I asked Liz, directing the conversation away from Ian.

"Skai's been doing wonders and everyone's showing great improvement," Liz replied, her eyes lighting up. "They're really coming together."

"Good. We need everyone sharp." My words were met with nods of agreement.

I glanced around at the faces of those I'd come to rely on—Ren's thoughtful expression, Liz's eager nod, Skai's unwavering determination, even Ian's grudging respect. This haphazard family forged in rebellion was all we had against Cain's forces. It struck me then, amid the sounds of clinking dishes and overlapping voices, how much had changed since we arrived. These caves, once alien and foreboding, had become a home of sorts—a sanctuary where the seeds of revolution could take root.

"Hopefully by the time Cain's forces arrive we're ready," I said, meeting each of their gazes in turn. There was a steely resolve reflected back at me, a silent pact to stand together against whatever lay ahead.

Harvey leaned forward, his eyes glinting with a mixture of excitement and nerves. "Lewis has outdone himself this time," he announced, breaking the bread between his hands before continuing. "He's managed to build a network so secure that even Cain's tech-heads can't sniff us out."

"Encrypted channels?" Liz asked, eyebrows raised in both surprise and admiration.

"Better." Harvey's voice was a low rumble of pride. "An entirely separate system. It's like we've got our own private cyber network humming beneath their noses."

"Perfect," Liz muttered as a sly grin spread across her face.

"Wait until you hear what Fox and Stef came up with," I chimed in, my eyes dancing with the thrill of the reveal.

"Who?" Liz asked.

Right, I forgot that they weren't present when we had met Fox and Stef this morning. Harvey and I had been secluded with them in the computer lab for the entire day.

"Well," I started, "turns out VIKI can be helpful after all. She set up a meeting with two visiting Genesi—Fox and Stef—who specialize in biotech surveillance and energy weapons which when combined with Lewis and Lars' computer skills we were able to come up with a solid plan to delay Cain's forces."

"So what was the plan," Skai urged, leaning in closer to hear better.

"They've found a way to safely sabotage Cain's power supply," I said, "It could delay their forces, give us the edge we need."

"Delays are good," Skai nodded, absorbing the weight of the plan, understanding that a sabotage could provide the distraction necessary for us to better prepare our own forces and evacuate the children and non fighters.

"Imagine them scrambling in the dark," Ren added, a glimmer of hope flashing in his thoughtful eyes. "We'd have the advantage then."

"Could buy us some precious time," Liz agreed, her fingers tapping rhythmically on the table.

"Time is the one thing we never seem to have enough of," I mused aloud.

"Speaking of not having enough..." Ian interjected loudly, cutting through our hushed strategizing. "Luka, still acting like you don't enjoy my delightful company?" He smirked, elbowing me playfully.

I cast him a sidelong glance, willing myself to keep my cool. "Ian, your 'delightful company' is as pleasant as a sandpaper hug," I retorted dryly, though a small part of me appreciated even his abrasive form of camaraderie.

"Ouch," Ian feigned hurt, placing a hand over his heart. "You wound me, ice princess."

"Let's not forget we're on the same side here," Harvey interjected, giving Ian a pointed look that spoke volumes about unity and tolerance.

"Indeed we are," Ian conceded with a dramatic bow of his head. "I'll be the charming rogue, and Luka can keep pretending she doesn't adore me."

"Keep dreaming," I shot back, unable to suppress a chuckle. His antics, while often grating, were an odd source of levity in our grim reality.

"Focus, you two," Liz scolded lightly. "We've got work to do."

"Right," I said, pulling my thoughts back to the task at hand. "Let's go over the details of the sabotage again. We need to make sure everything's set."

The conversation turned back to our mission, each of us contributing pieces to the intricate puzzle that would hopefully lead to Cain's downfall. As plans were laid and roles assigned, I couldn't help but feel the thrum of anticipation coursing through me. This was it—the beginning of our endgame. And despite the odds stacked against us, I believed in us, in our ragtag alliance of Genesi and humans, bonded by the shared goal of reclaiming our future from the tyranny of Cain.

As Liz spooned another helping of the grayish stew onto her plate, she leaned in closer to me, her voice a low murmur amid the clatter of cutlery and the murmur of voices that filled the mess hall.

"Training's coming along better than expected," she confided, her eyes bright with a mix of pride and exhaustion. "Nate's strategies are really paying off. Everyone's getting sharper, more in sync."

"Good," I said, stirring the stew idly, my mind only partly on the conversation. It was hard to focus on food when there was a war looming over our heads, but hearing progress always sparked a flicker of hope. "And morale?"

"Higher than the mountain we're under," she grinned, gesturing broadly at the cavernous stone walls that enveloped us. "They've been pushing each other, learning from one another. There's real camaraderie forming, Luka."

Good.

"Alright, focus," Skai interjected sharply, redirecting our conversation. "You need to finish telling us the sabotage plan."

The group leaned in closer, the air charged with the gravity of what we were about to undertake.

"Lewis has the comms up," I began, locking eyes with each person around the table. "Fox and Stef have been working on the power supply disruption. We hit them where it hurts—their resources."

"Timing's the critical part," Harvey added. "Cain's forces are already mobilizing. We can't afford any mistakes."

"Once we initiate the blackout, it'll give us the edge we need to shore up our defenses and get the non fighters moved to Camille's encampment," Liz chimed in, her fists clenched with fierce resolve.

"Exactly," I affirmed. "It buys us time to strengthen our defenses and disrupt their chain of command."

As we finalized the details of our sabotage plan, the tension in the room grew palpable. We all knew that this was only the beginning, and much more would be required of us in the days to come. But we were united in our purpose, and that gave us strength.

My eyes flickered across the table, taking in the faces that had become so familiar over these past weeks. They were talking strategy, their voices a low hum of determination and resolve. Amidst the lively chatter of our friends, a familiar voice pierced through the noise. My body tensed at the sound, my heart skipping a beat before settling back into its regular rhythm.

I turned to see Ren's piercing blue eyes fixed on me, his hand holding out a small silver shaker, an offering of salt. I hesitantly reached for it, feeling a slight jolt as our fingers brushed. The longing that always seemed to linger between us was palpable, and I quickly withdrew my hand, grasping onto my mug for comfort. My quiet "thanks" hung heavy in the air, silent questions filling the space between us.

Our interactions were always like walking on eggshells these days, trust being something carefully earned and guarded by both of us. Trust was something we both guarded fiercely, and with Ren's quiet intensity and mysterious past, it was not easily given. We had agreed to move on but it was hard to let go of the underlying feelings that lingered.

Ian's booming laughter filled the mess hall as he regaled everyone with yet another one of his stories. I laughed along with the others, but my mind couldn't shake off the awkwardness of my interaction with Ren.

I was grateful when Skai caught my eye and gestured towards a nearby table, indicating that she wanted to talk. Excusing myself from Ian's storytelling, I made my way over to her and took a seat beside her.

"What's up?" I asked, trying to keep the slight edge out of my voice.

"I just wanted to talk about what happened between you and Ren," she said quietly, her eyes full of concern. "You guys used to be so close, but now it feels like there's this wall between you."

"It's complicated," I sighed, picking at a loose thread on the tablecloth. "Ever since the incident with Thorn, things have been different between us."

"I know," Skai said softly. "But you can't let that come between your friendship."

"It's not just that," I admitted reluctantly. "He keeps pulling away from me and then coming back when he needs something. It's exhausting."

"Maybe he just needs time," Skai suggested gently. "He went through something traumatic too, Luka."

I nodded, knowing she was right, Thorn was his father after all. Just then, Nate stood up at the head of the mess hall and tapped his spoon against his mug for attention.

"Listen up," he called out in his commanding voice. The mess hall fell silent as everyone turned their attention towards him.

"As you all know," he began, "our training has been going well. We are getting stronger and more coordinated every day." There were nods of agreement around the room.

"But we cannot afford to become complacent," Nate continued. "Cain and his army grow stronger every day, and we need to be ready for whatever they throw at us. Our survival depends on our ability to adapt and outsmart them." Nate's voice was firm, his gaze sweeping across the room with a sense of urgency.

I felt a knot form in my stomach as I listened to Nate's words. The weight of our mission, our fight against Cain's tyranny, pressed down on me like a heavy stone. I glanced at Ren, his expression unreadable as usual, but I could sense the tension radiating from him.

Harvey, always the voice of reason in our group, spoke up next. "We need to focus on our strengths and work together as a team. That's the only way we'll stand a chance against Cain and his forces."

Skai nodded in agreement, her eyes gleaming with determination. "We've come this far because we believe in each other. We won't let anything tear us apart."

"Unity. Freedom," the room echoed. All around the table, heads nodded in agreement as people went back to eating their meals as Nate began talking strategy with a group of genesi at a nearby table.

I glanced around the mess hall, observing the groups interspersed between the long wooden tables. It was happening—just as I had hoped. These people, who had once been strangers to each other, now shared jokes, bandaged each other's wounds, and worked tirelessly side by side. They were no longer just a resistance; they were becoming a family united against Cain's oppression.

"Looks like they're not the only ones finding their place here," Liz remarked, her gaze following mine as I retook my seat beside her.

"Unity is our greatest weapon," I said, finally taking a bite of my stew as I echoed Liz's words from this morning.

"Exactly." Liz's smile was fierce and determined. "Together, we'll tear down Cain's empire, brick by bloody brick."

"Brick by bloody brick," I echoed, the words resonating within me like a battle cry. But first, we had to see if our plan would work. If it didn't... I pushed the thought away. Failure wasn't an option. Not now, not ever.

Chapter 8

Sam

The computer lab buzzed with the kind of tension that made my skin crawl, the air electric with anticipation. Troian and Nate flanked me, their expressions mirroring the gravity of the moment as we stood before a bank of screens flickering with streams of data. It was the heartbeat of our resistance, and right now, it was racing.

"Report," I said, my voice cutting through the hum of computers and hushed voices of operators at their stations.

Nate stepped forward, the light from the monitors casting shadows over his bald head. "It's happening, Sam. The cyber-attack is in full force. All systems are go."

I leaned closer to the screen, watching symbols and numbers dance across the surface, each one representing a piece of Cain's once impenetrable defense crumbling under our relentless digital assault. My fingers curled into fists at my sides, the phantom sensation of victory tingling at my fingertips.

"Forcefields are down. The military base, the cities... they're all exposed," Troian added, her voice steady but carrying an undercurrent of excitement. She might have been in a foul mood when she entered the computer lab earlier, but duty had a way of putting personal issues on ice.

"Good," I murmured, eyes not leaving the screens as the reality sank in. Without the forcefields, Cain's people were as vulnerable as newborns. It didn't sit well with me, using civilians as leverage, but war had a way of blurring lines until you couldn't tell right from wrong. I reminded myself this was about survival, ours and ultimately theirs too.

"Electricity grids?" I asked, already knowing the answer but needing to hear it spoken aloud.

"Offline," Nate confirmed with a nod. "It'll be chaos out there, man. No lights, no comms. Cain's forces will be too busy playing fire brigade to worry about us… for now."

"Which buys us time," I said, the plan taking shape in my mind. Time was the most valuable currency in war, and we'd just stolen a healthy sum from the enemy's vault. A smirk tugged at the corner of my mouth. I could almost feel the balance of power shifting, if only by an increment.

"Exactly," Troian agreed, her gaze meeting mine. There was a spark there, a shared understanding. We knew what was at stake.

"Alright," I clapped my hands together, the sound sharp in the quiet room. "Let's use it wisely. Troian, send a comm to Luka. Let her know the attack is underway and we've got Cain on the backfoot."

"Consider it done, Commander," she replied, already moving towards the communications array.

"Keep monitoring the situation," I instructed Nate, who gave me an exaggerated salute before turning back to the screens. His easygoing nature was a balm in times like these, but beneath the jokes and smiles was a soldier as tough as they came.

As the first reports of confusion and disarray started pouring in from Cain's territories, I felt a surge of something like hope. For the first time in a long while, it seemed like we might just stand a chance.

Troian moved to the communications array and I couldn't help but notice the rigid set of her shoulders, a stark contrast to the fluid grace that usually characterized her movements. Her hand hovered over the console, and for a split second, it trembled like a leaf in a storm before she caught herself and pressed down with purpose.

"Everything alright?" I asked, my voice low, trying not to draw attention. Nate was absorbed in the screens, his brow furrowed as he tracked the chaos spreading through Cain's cities.

Troian spared me a glance, her eyes clouded. "I'm fine," she said, but her clipped tone betrayed her words.

"Doesn't seem like it," I persisted. I knew her well enough to recognize the signs. The tension in her jaw was more than just the stress of our current operation; it spoke of a personal storm brewing beneath her composed surface.

She sighed, the sound heavy with unvoiced frustrations. "It's nothing, Sam. Just focus on the mission."

My gaze lingered on her profile, noting the way she avoided looking at me directly. "Did something happen with Skai after dinner?" I ventured, remembering the last time I saw Troian she said she was headed to the mess hall for dinner. Her words had a certain edge to them, a sharpness that I failed to notice at the time but now my mind couldn't help but dwell on the memory.

Troian's fingers paused, mid-air, above the keypad. "Why would you ask that?" Her voice was guarded, a fortress rising around her emotions.

"Because I know you," I said simply. "And whatever it is, it's eating at you. We can't afford distractions, not now." My concern was twofold; for the success of our mission and for Troian herself.

"Skai and I... we disagreed on some things," she admitted begrudgingly, her gaze finally locking with mine. There was a fierceness there, the kind that came from being challenged on something fundamental.

"Disagreed how?" I pushed, knowing full well that a disagreement with Skai was rarely a trivial matter.

"Strategies. Priorities. The usual," she brushed off, but her hand balled into a fist at her side. "I don't need to be coddled, Sam. I can handle Skai."

I nodded, the knowledge of their confrontation settling in my gut like a stone. Skai had such a strong personality, and if she and Troian were at odds, it could spell trouble for our already precarious situation. But pushing Troian further wouldn't do any good; she'd retreat behind her walls.

"Alright," I conceded. "Just remember we're all on the same side here."

"Noted," she affirmed, a trace of the old fire returning to her eyes as she turned back to the task at hand. And with that, she was once again the unwavering second-in-command I relied on, the one who could make or break our fragile rebellion with a single command.

The screens flickered with static before revealing the chaos unfolding at Cain's stronghold. My heart thrummed against my ribs as I watched our invisible digital warriors chip away at their forcefields, one pixelated block at a time to prevent Cain's technology from rebuilding them. The air in the command center was electric, each of us holding our breaths, waiting for the inevitable counterattack that was sure to come once Cain's tech's realized this wasn't a mishap on their end but a strategic attack from us.

"Troian," I began, turning toward her, "I need..."

"Enough, Sam!" she barked suddenly, her eyes aflame with a ferocity that matched the collapsing walls on the screens. "Just stop poking around in my personal life, okay? It has nothing to do with you."

Her outburst sliced through the tension in the room like a blade. Nate shifted uncomfortably beside me, his gaze darting between us.

"Troian," I said, my voice steady despite the surge of concern for her well-being, "you know I wouldn't ask if it wasn't important. But if your head isn't in this fight—if Skai's gotten under your skin—it compromises everything we're working towards."

She clenched her jaw, the muscle ticking visibly. For a moment, I thought she might walk out, but then she exhaled sharply, her shoulders dropping ever so slightly.

"Understood, Commander," she replied, her tone clipped but professional. "It won't affect my duties."

"Good." I nodded, satisfied for the moment. There would be time later to delve into whatever had transpired between her and Skai, but right now, we had bigger problems to deal with.

"Troian," I continued, "I want you to find Luka and give her the update that the cyber-attack was a success. Cain's defenses are down, and they're scrambling over there without power or shields. It's bought us some time just like we hoped."

"Got it. How much time do we have?" she asked, her focus already shifting to the new task at hand.

I sighed, rubbing the back of my neck. "Uncertain. Could be hours, could be days. But it's a delay, nonetheless. Let's make sure we use it wisely."

"Will do," she confirmed, and I could see the gears turning behind her eyes as she calculated our next move.

"Alright then," I said. "Let's keep moving."

Troian gave me a curt nod, her earlier fire now channeled into determination, and headed off to deliver the message to Luka. As her figure disappeared from view, I turned back to the screens, watching as the last remnants of Cain's once-impenetrable forcefield flickered and died for good.

Chapter 9

Luka

The chill of the pre-dawn air bit through my thin shirt as I slipped from the warmth of the blankets, careful not to disturb Harvey who slept on the cot beside mine. The soft rhythm of his breathing continued undisturbed as I dressed in silence, pulling on boots and strapping weapons to my body—my sai at my hips, a knife strapped to my ankle. My fingers moved deftly, numbed by necessity rather than cold.

I cast a final glance at Harvey's peaceful face, his chestnut hair tousled against the pillow, then turned away. In the stillness of the early morning, every scuff of my boots felt amplified, every rustle of my clothing like thunder. But years of living on the edge had taught me stealth, and I moved like a shadow through the dim corridors of our mountain sanctuary.

As I navigated the familiar turns and slopes, my thoughts drifted to the day ahead—dawn was approaching, and with it our cyber attack on Cain's power grid would commence. My hand brushed the cool stone for grounding, but the comfort it once provided eluded me now. I needed something to take my mind off the cyber attack that was no doubt unfolding this very moment.

The passage narrowed as I approached the exit, a subtle crack of light the only indication of the world outside. I paused, listening, letting my eyes adjust to the gradient of dawn. It was then I sensed it—not a sound, not a sight, but an undeniable presence. Someone was following me, and it wasn't Troian.

Instinctively, my hand went to the hilt of my sai, every muscle coiled and ready. I hadn't survived this long without trusting my gut, without knowing when eyes were upon me. Slowly, I turned.

"Who's there?" My voice was a low growl, authoritative yet laced with an undercurrent of caution.

The shadows held their breath, and I waited, watched. Whoever it was, they were good—good enough to make me second-guess my senses. But not quite good enough.

"Come out," I commanded, my words slicing through the tension. "I won't ask again."

A figure detached itself from the shadows, stepping into the dim light. "It's just me," Skai said, her voice steady but her body language betraying a hidden turmoil.

"Skai?" Relief flickered through me, quickly replaced by curiosity. "What are you doing here?"

She shrugged, an attempt at nonchalance that didn't quite reach her eyes. "Couldn't sleep. I didn't mean to scare you."

I studied her closer, noticing the slight droop of her shoulders and the way she avoided my gaze. I knew Skai—confident, assertive Skai—and this was not her typical demeanor. Something was churning beneath the surface. Had something happened after dinner last night?

"Talk to me," I urged, lowering my weapon. "What's going on?"

For a moment, she hesitated, caught in an internal debate. Then, with a sigh, she met my eyes. "It's Troian," she confessed quietly. "I think I have feelings for her. But it's all so confusing, and I'm scared she doesn't feel the same."

The words hung between us, raw and vulnerable. My heart clenched at her admission, both for the ache it carried and the trust it implied. We were comrades bound by shared adversity, but this was different—this was personal, intimate.

"Skai," I started, unsure how to comfort her, "that takes courage, admitting something like that."

"Thanks," she murmured. "I know it's not the best timing to be having a personal crisis," she joked, a hint of her usual swagger emerging.

Skai and Troian had always been close, but I never would have guessed there was something more between them.

"It's not just a crush," Skai continued, her voice trembling slightly. "I know what that feels like. This is different. It's like she's always on my mind, and I can't stop thinking about her."

I nodded sympathetically, understanding all too well the tumultuous feelings that come with falling for someone. But then a thought occurred to me, one that made my stomach drop.

"Does Troian know?" I asked cautiously.

Skai shook her head, her expression pained. "Kind of," she admitted. "I started to bring it up last night after dinner but then chickened out. I don't want to ruin our friendship, and I'm afraid if she doesn't feel the same way it will change everything."

My heart went out to Skai—she was caught in an impossible

situation. On one hand, she didn't want to risk losing Troian as a friend by confessing her feelings. But on the other hand, keeping these emotions bottled up could eat away at her from the inside.

She'd be better off having this conversation with Harvey.

"I can understand your hesitation," I said, placing a comforting hand on her shoulder. "But you won't know how Troian feels unless you talk to her about it."

Skai looked up at me, uncertainty etched into every line of her face. "But what if she doesn't feel the same? What if it ruins everything?"

I gave her shoulder a reassuring squeeze. "You won't know until you try," I reminded her gently.

She nodded slowly, taking in my words. Then determination flashed in her eyes as she straightened up.

"You're right," she said firmly. "I need to talk to Troian."

I took a step closer, my own fears pressing against my ribcage, demanding release. "If we're being honest... I'm struggling too."

"Struggling?" Her brow furrowed in concern, the earlier sadness momentarily forgotten.

"With leadership," I clarified, my voice barely above a whisper. "Every decision feels like a gamble with lives hanging in the balance. If we go to battle..." The words trailed off, the unspeakable outcomes lingering like specters in the chill morning air.

"Hey," Skai reached out, placing a reassuring hand on my forearm. "You've kept us safe this far. You're strong, Luka. Stronger than anyone I know."

"Strength doesn't make the choices any easier," I replied softly. There was a strange comfort in sharing this burden, in knowing I wasn't alone in my fears.

"Nothing about what we're doing is easy," Skai said, a fire igniting in her voice. "But we do it anyway, because it's right. And we'll do it together."

"Thank you, Skai," I breathed, feeling a kinship with her that went beyond our cause. "For understanding."

"Always," she promised, a smile touching her lips—a smile that didn't quite reach her eyes, but it was a start.

My wrist communicator vibrated, and I looked down to see a message from Troian informing me that the cyber attack had begun. I ignored her communication, not wanting Skai to catch me talking to Troian after she had just confided in me about her problems.

"Come on," I said, motioning toward the mouth of the cave that led towards the valley. "Let's head out. We have a lot of planning to do."

She nodded, falling into step beside me. As we walked, I felt a renewed sense of purpose. Yes, the weight of leadership was heavy, but it was a weight I didn't have to carry alone, and I was beginning to understand that.

Growing up, I had only ever had Harvey as my friend. Even at Delta Force, it took time for me to form bonds with Ren and Lewis. Despite the constant threat of war, it was a relief to be able to cultivate relationships that I never thought possible before.

We reached the edge of the sheltering rocks, where the chill of the predawn air bit at my exposed skin. Skai halted beside me, her gaze fixed on the horizon that was just beginning to hint at the morning's light. I could feel her eyes on me before she even spoke.

"How are you handling it, Luka? Knowing you're Genesi...

and about General Thorn," Skai asked, her voice low but carrying the weight of our grim reality.

Her question hung between us like a specter, and I felt the familiar shiver of unease crawl up my spine. The dawn's gentle glow seemed to mock my inner turmoil with its serene promise of a new day.

"Sometimes, I wake up thinking it's all been a nightmare," I confessed, turning away from the rising sun to face her. "That I'll open my eyes to a world where I'm just... me. Not this thing Cain and Thorn made me become."

Skai's brown eyes were pools of empathy in the dim light. She stepped closer, her presence both a balm and a reminder of the truth I couldn't escape. "You are still you, Luka. But I get it—it's a lot to carry. And the urges?"

It was as if she'd reached inside and touched the darkest part of me—the part I fought to keep shackled deep within. "They're there," I admitted, my voice barely above a whisper. "A hunger for violence that I never knew before, waiting to be unleashed."

"Does it scare you?" Her question was direct, unflinching.

"Terrifies me," I said, the words tasting like ash. My hands unconsciously curled into fists, as if readying for a fight against my own nature. "I'm afraid of what I might become if I let those urges take over. Afraid that one day, I won't be able to stop myself."

"Then we won't let that happen." Skai's resolve was a steel blade, unwavering and sharp. "We'll find a way to keep you grounded, Luka. You're not in this alone. Remember that."

"Thanks, Skai." I managed a half-smile, grateful for her steadfastness.

Skai's hand found mine, squeezing firmly—an anchor in the

tumultuous sea of my fears. "We're a team now, Luka. Your battle isn't just yours to fight anymore; we share the load."

"Right," I murmured, nodding as the first hints of dawn began to seep into the sky, painting it a pale blue. "But how do I face this part of me without...without losing myself?"

"Control," she said, the word slicing through the cold morning air. "You need to learn control. And there's only one way to do that."

"Which is?" I asked, though a part of me already suspected her answer.

"Fight. A controlled environment, a practice match. There's no better way to test your limits and learn restraint." Skai's eyes were alight with a strategic fire that I'd come to admire.

"Fight who, though? Who would be willing to go up against a Genesi knowing what could happen?" The question hung between us, heavy with the weight of what I was capable of.

"Sam," she replied without hesitation. Her confidence was infectious, but I couldn't hide the flicker of surprise at her suggestion. "He's strong enough, and brave—or stupid—enough to take on the challenge."

"Sam," I murmured, the idea settling in my chest like a stone. Facing him in a fight felt like an insurmountable task, not for fear of injury, but for the potential damage it could do to our bond. "I don't want to hurt him."

"Then you'll learn to hold back," Skai insisted. "Because if you can spar with Sam without losing yourself to the Genesi bloodlust, then you'll know you can trust yourself out there, in the real fight."

And just like that, a plan began to form—a glimmer of hope that maybe, just maybe, I could learn to wield this darkness inside me without letting it consume me.

Chapter 10

Luka

The first hints of dawn were whispering across the valley where Skai and I stood at the edge of our mountain hideout, the air crisp and biting as it filled my lungs. Skai had just tied her dark hair into a tight ponytail, her eyes fixed on the craggy path that led to the training grounds.

"See you at breakfast?" she asked, her voice carrying the melody of determination that always seemed to surround her.

"Sure," I replied with a small smile, watching her turn on her heel.

But before she could take more than a few steps, the sound of approaching footsteps echoed through the valley. Skai paused, her posture stiffening for an imperceptible moment before she continued walking without looking back. I knew that gait—it was Troian—and I understood Skai's sudden urge to vanish.

"Morning, Luka," Troian called out, her voice cutting

through the silence of the breaking day.

"Troian," I nodded, turning to face her, bracing myself for whatever news she brought with the sunrise.

"The cyber attack on Cain's cities—it worked," she said. "Power grids are down, forcefields are kaput. They're scrambling over there, which means they're not marching towards us. At least not yet."

I exhaled slowly, relief tempering the constant tension in my shoulders. "That gives us time," I mused aloud. The very thing I'd hoped the cyber attack would achieve.

"Time to get our non-combatants to Camille's encampment," Troian added, her gaze sharp as it met mine. "And time for you…" She trailed off, but I didn't need her to finish.

Time for me to master the genesi abilities that surged beneath my skin, unpredictable as the wind that swept through the valley. With each passing day, my control over them grew steadier, yet they still felt like wild streams I could only hope to channel, never fully tame.

"More time to prepare is exactly what we need," I said. "Thanks, Troian."

She replied with a curt nod before moving past me heading back toward the entrance to the mountain, me trailing after her.

Watching her retreating figure, I squared my shoulders against the chill of the morning. There was work to do, and now, thanks to Lewis and the others, we had just bought ourselves a little more breathing room.

Troian's footsteps echoed off the stone walls as we descended deeper into the mountain. My boots found purchase on the worn steps, the rhythmic sound grounding me in a way that the chaos outside could not.

"Heads up, Luka," Troian said, her voice a low rumble in the dim corridor. "There's something Sam and Nate found that you should see."

I nodded, steeling myself for whatever awaited us. As we rounded the final bend, the computer lab sprawled out before us—a cavernous space filled with blinking lights and an incessant hum of machinery. And there, at the heart of it all, stood Sam and Nate, their figures rigid and silhouetted against the glow of the wall of screens.

"Sam?" I called out, striding over to them with a sense of urgency that matched the pounding of my heart. "What's going on?"

They turned, and for a moment, their expressions were unreadable in the half-light. But then I saw it—the footage playing out before us. Hundreds, maybe thousands, of cryogenic tanks lined up in neat rows, each containing a sleeping genesi soldier. A chill ran down my spine as I took in the sight, each tank a promise of destruction waiting to be unleashed.

"What is this?" I demanded, my voice steady despite the turmoil inside me.

Sam's jaw clenched, and he shared a glance with Nate before answering. "We had someone on the inside—Delta Force. They were feeding us intel on Cain's movements. Before we lost contact, they sent us this."

"Sent us... what? An army in waiting?" I asked, incredulous as I gestured to the chilling display.

"Yep," Nate chimed in, his tone grim. "We've been trying to come up with a plan to send another spy in. We need more info on these tanks, and if there's a chance to sabotage them…"

"Before these soldiers can swell Cain's ranks," Sam finished, his blue eyes meeting mine squarely.

I took a deep breath, letting the reality of the situation sink in. This was bigger than any one of us, a threat that could very well turn the tide of our already desperate struggle.

My gaze remained locked on the frozen army behind the glass, a sense of dread creeping into my bones. "Sam," I started, my voice steady but laced with an urgency that betrayed my inner turmoil, "we need to think this through. If we can't stop Cain's forces head-on, we might have no choice but to consider..." My words trailed off, unwilling to verbalize the thought of the bio weapon I had been silently dreading.

Sam's expression hardened, his scars stretching taut over his weathered skin as he considered the implications. "Luka, you know as well as I do that we're running out of options. These soldiers could decimate what's left of us."

"Give me time," I pleaded, locking eyes with him. The weight of the decision hung between us, thick and suffocating. "We don't have to rush into anything... drastic. Not yet."

He exhaled, a gust of frustration that ruffled his close-cropped hair. "Alright, Luka. For now, we hold off. But we can't wait too long."

"Thank you," I said, the relief in my voice mirroring the brief softening of his blue gaze.

Turning away from the haunting image on the screens, I headed towards the exit, my resolve hardening with each step. As the cold air of the passageway brushed against my face, I focused inward, where the seeds of a plan began to sprout.

Later, when I see Sam, I'll bring up Skai's suggestion—a practice fight. It's time I learned the full extent of what these genesi abilities can do.

Safety first, always—Skai would want it that way. But

the reality was, soon enough, I'd be facing more than just a controlled environment. And when that time came, I needed to be ready—for everyone's sake.

I nearly collided with Ren in the dimly lit corridor leading from the computer lab. His silhouette melded with the shadows, a familiar comfort in the uncertainty that churned inside me.

"Hey," he said, his voice steady as ever. "How did the cyber attack go?"

"Sam's confident it worked," I replied, brushing a strand of hair from my eyes. The cool air of the mountain was a stark contrast to the heat of the information I carried. "Cain's cities are dark, for now. But we stumbled upon something… unsettling."

Ren arched an eyebrow, urging me to continue.

"Inside the lab, they were analyzing footage—cyro tanks, Ren. Hundreds of them, all filled with genesi soldiers." My words felt heavy, laden with the dread of what they meant.

His sharp features tightened. "Winston's work?"

It was more than a guess. Winston, who had unwillingly escaped Delta Force with the rest of us, had been Sam's best bet for intel on Delta Force. "Must have been," I muttered, anger seething just beneath the surface. "Sam lied. He said Winston was sent to another encampment for safety."

"Sam plays a dangerous game," Ren said, more to himself than to me.

"I know," I admitted, my fists clenching. "He might play it too far. There's talk of using a bio weapon if we can't find another way to stop those soldiers from waking up."

"Would he dare?" Ren asked, though I could see in his eyes he already knew the answer.

"Ren… he's getting desperate," I confessed, feeling the conflict within me grow. "But using that weapon—it goes against everything we stand for. Everything we're fighting to protect."

"Let's hope it doesn't come to that," Ren said, and there was a gravity to his tone that spoke volumes of the unspoken bond between us.

We started walking again, side by side, toward the training grounds. Ren's gaze held mine, a silent understanding passing between us as we walked through the dimly lit corridor away from the heart of our mountain stronghold. I felt the weight of each step, my mind racing with the implications of what I'd seen in the computer lab.

"Sam might not wait for another way," I said abruptly, my voice barely above a whisper. "He has a bio weapon— something lethal and uncontrollable. Fox and Stef, they had a hand in its creation. If Sam believes for a second that it's our only chance…"

"What?" Ren's question hung in the stale air, but his eyes already reflected the horror of my unspoken words.

"To thin Cain's numbers," I finished, feeling a shiver run down my spine. "I'm scared, Ren. If he uses it, the fallout… it won't just be Cain's forces. It'll change everything."

Ren's jaw tightened, and I could see the cogs turning behind those stoic eyes. "We can't let fear dictate our actions, Luka. Not when so much is at stake." He stopped walking, turning to face me fully. "I'll talk to Sam."

"Can you make him see reason?" My question was tinged with desperation. The idea of a biological nightmare being unleashed was too much to bear.

"I'll do more than talk." Ren's voice was steady, resolute. "I'll help find another solution. We have to stop Cain from waking those soldiers without resorting to measures that betray who we are."

"Thank you," I exhaled, feeling a flicker of hope amidst the dread. I knew the road ahead would be fraught with challenges, but with Ren by my side, I believed we might just find a way through this darkness.

"Let's focus on what we can control," Ren suggested, his tone grounding. "We need a plan—one that doesn't involve unnecessary loss of life."

"Agreed," I nodded, the resolve settling within me like a stone. "We'll find a way to stop Cain... without becoming monsters ourselves."

With our pact silently sealed, we turned away from the computer lab's chilling secrets and made for the training grounds. The sun had begun its climb over the horizon, casting long, angular shadows across the rocky terrain of our mountain refuge. The crisp morning air filled my lungs, offering a brief respite from the weight of what lay ahead.

"Training will be good for us," Ren said, his steps light on the uneven ground. "Keep our skills sharp."

I felt the familiar tug of anticipation at the thought of honing my abilities—a welcome distraction from the gnawing anxiety about Cain's sleeping army. "Yeah, and I need to practice control. If I can master my genesi powers, maybe we'll stand a chance without Sam's bio-weapon."

"Control would be good," Ren agreed, his voice low but firm. "But remember, Luka, don't push yourself too hard. You're still learning the extent of what you can do."

A faint smile touched my lips. Ren, always the voice of caution, yet never doubting my capability. It was that quiet confidence he had in me that often sent flutters in my stomach.

As we approached the training area, I could see others already there, engaged in combat drills or focused on perfecting their aim with makeshift weapons. Their determination mirrored my own—each one of us fighting for a future that seemed as fragile as glass.

"Ready?" Ren asked, his gaze fixed on mine with an intensity that both challenged and reassured.

We joined the fray, moving in sync with each other, our actions a testament to the countless hours we'd spent training side by side. As we moved through our routines, I let the rhythm of the training consume me, pushing aside the looming threats for just a moment.

Chapter 11

Luka

Sam's laughter echoed through the vastness of the throne room, a deep and incredulous sound that bounced off the stone walls and back to where I stood. The absurdity of my request seemed to amuse him greatly, his broad shoulders shaking as he tried to contain it.

"Are you serious, Luka?" he finally managed, wiping a tear from the corner of his eye. "You want to spar with me?"

I crossed my arms over my chest, trying not to let his reaction deter me. "Yes. A practice fight," I insisted, my voice steady despite the nerves clenching my stomach. "I need to test my genesi abilities—properly, in a controlled environment."

His laughter ceased abruptly, replaced by a scrutinizing gaze that seemed to size me up, as if seeing me for the first time. "Or is this some ploy to take me down? A fight to the death to challenge my command?"

I flinched at the implication, even though I knew he had a right to be suspicious. That was how Sam claimed his position after all, by defeating the previous commander in a duel that left no questions about who held power among us. But that wasn't my intention—I wasn't so consumed by ambition that I'd risk our fragile stability.

"No, Sam, that's not it," I said quickly, locking my eyes with his. "This isn't about challenging you. It's about learning—about being better prepared for whatever comes next."

He studied me for a moment longer, those piercing blue eyes searching mine, then nodded slowly as if conceding to an unspoken truce.

I squared my shoulders and met Sam's gaze, the cold stone of the throne room echoing back our silence. "I need to do this," I said, my voice sharper than I intended. "To control the red haze—the bloodlust that always threatens to overtake me in a fight."

Sam's brow furrowed, his stance unwavering as the giant pillars that held up our underground sanctum. "Bloodlust is part of who we are as genesi, Luka. It's not something you tame; it's something you embrace."

"Embrace?" The word tasted bitter in my mouth. "Like it's some kind of gift? I won't let it define me. I refuse to lose my humanity to this war."

"Humanity?" He scoffed, crossing his arms. "We're past the point of clinging to what was. Our very nature now is to survive, to fight. The sooner you accept that, the better."

"Survive, yes. Fight, without doubt. But at what cost, Sam?" I challenged, taking a step closer. "If we sacrifice everything we are, what's left to fight for?"

"Power. Control. Victory." His list was like throwing knives, each word hitting its mark.

"Those are hollow victories if we're just husks of ourselves at the end of it." My fists clenched at my sides, the frustration rising like a tide within me. "There has to be a way to hold on to who we are—to remember that we're still human beneath it all."

"Is that your fear, then?" Sam's voice softened, but there was an edge to it—a challenge. "That you'll lose yourself to the fight?"

"Isn't it yours?" I shot back, searching his face for any crack in his stoic mask.

For a moment, he was silent, and I wondered if I had finally reached something real within him. Then he shook his head, the motion dismissing not only my words but the idea behind them.

"Genesi don't have the luxury of fear," he said firmly. "We do what must be done. And right now, that means preparing ourselves for every threat, from within or without."

"Even if it means becoming the very monsters we're trying to defeat?" I asked, my heart racing with the intensity of our exchange.

"Monsters are a matter of perspective, Luka." Sam's eyes locked onto mine, unyielding. "In the eyes of our enemies, we already are monsters. So, what's one more demon among us?"

"Because it matters to me!" I exclaimed, the passion in my voice echoing against the ancient walls. "It matters that when this war is over, I can look in the mirror and recognize the person staring back. That I can say I fought with everything I had—but I didn't lose myself to the darkness."

He sighed, rubbing a hand over his jaw, where a faint scar traced the line of his bone. "If it means that much to you, we'll do it. We'll have your practice fight. But Luka, remember, control isn't something you find in a single battle. It's a war fought every day."

"Then I'll fight that war every day," I vowed, meeting his gaze with renewed determination. "Starting with today."

"Alright." Sam's mouth quirked up in a half-smile that didn't quite reach his eyes. "We'll see what you're made of, Foster. But don't say I didn't warn you about playing with fire."

"Thanks, Sam." I exhaled, a weight lifting from my shoulders. "I need to know I can hold onto myself, no matter what."

"Then let's find out," he said, giving me a nod of reluctant approval. "Tomorrow morning, we test your limits."

"Tomorrow," I agreed, already feeling the adrenaline igniting in my veins. Tomorrow, I'd face more than just Sam in the ring—I'd confront the very essence of my fears.

"Then it's settled, but you'll need a lifeline," Sam said, his voice echoing slightly in the vast emptiness of the throne room. "Someone to pull you back if you go too far."

I stiffened at his words, considering the implication. The idea made sense; a tether to reality when the red haze threatened to consume me. Yet, it was another admission of how close I danced with losing myself. "Who would that be?" I asked, my voice betraying a tremor I hadn't intended.

"Make your choice—Harvey or Ren." His expression was unreadable, but there was a challenge in his tone. "Decide by dawn."

The insinuation stung like a slap. As if my personal connections could be reduced to mere strategy. But this was no time for pride or hurt feelings. This was about control, survival. I nodded, the weight of the decision settling on my shoulders.

"Very well," I mumbled, and turned away from him, already wrestling with the choices laid out before me.

***

Dawn's first light spread across the training grounds outside the mountain, casting long shadows over the gathered crowd. I arrived, my stomach a nest of vipers, regret gnawing at the edges of my resolve. Why had I thought this was a good idea?

The encampment's people were here, their murmurs and stares washing over me like waves. My hands felt cold, trembling slightly as I flexed them, trying to shake off the nerves.

"Ready to make history, Luka?" one of the onlookers called out, their voice laced with what might have been admiration or mockery—it was hard to tell.

I didn't answer, only tightened the straps of my leather armor—a second skin meant to offer protection, though it felt more like a shroud today. The practical design did little to comfort me as I scanned the faces around me: expectant, curious…hungry for violence.

Remember why you're doing this. To learn, to control, not to conquer. Control the power, don't let it control you.

I shuffled nervously, my boots scraping against the rocky terrain outside the mountain. Harvey's voice was a low hum in my ear, persistent as the morning chill that clung to my skin.

"Think about this, Luka. There's no shame in stepping back."

He was right, but it wasn't shame I feared—it was the monster within me that craved release. Ren stood on my other side, quiet and stoic, his presence a silent pillar of support. In the end, I couldn't choose between them. Both were vital threads woven into the fabric of who I was, who I wanted to be when the dust settled.

"Harvey," I said, my voice clipped with finality, "I need to do this." My eyes flicked to Ren, silently including him in my resolve.

With a sigh that whispered through the rising tension of the gathered crowd, Harvey stepped back. His grey blue eyes held mine for a moment longer, a wordless conversation that ended with a reluctant nod.

I turned away from them, focusing on the ring where Sam stood like a statue carved from the mountain itself—solid, unyielding. He made no move to beckon me forward; he didn't need to.

"Can't believe Nate spent the night playing bookkeeper," I muttered under my breath, half-amused, half-disgusted. The notion that someone would profit off our pain was nothing new, but it stung all the same. "You'd think our lives are some kind of sport to them."

"Maybe they are," Ren murmured, his voice barely audible over the din. "But you're not playing their game—not really."

He was right. I wasn't there for their entertainment or their bets. This was about control, about holding onto the frayed edges of my humanity while the world crumbled around us.

Taking a deep, steadying breath, I stepped out from the protective flank of my lifelines and strode toward Sam. The air seemed to thicken with each step, charged with the electricity of impending conflict.

Sam stood at the center of the ring, twin axes gleaming dully in the morning light. He looked every bit the seasoned warrior, calm and sure. A pang of doubt seized me; what if I couldn't find my way back from the red haze? What if my lifeline wasn't enough?

"Scared, Foster?" It was a taunt wrapped in concern, a test of my resolve.

"Terrified," I admitted, because lying now served no one. Fear was a blade held at my throat, sharp and unwavering. But wasn't facing fear the point of all this?

"Good," he replied, offering a nod that bordered on respect. "It means you're still human."

The fight loomed before us, a test of wills and a dance with darkness. And as I took my place opposite Sam, I knew one thing for certain: I had to emerge from this ring not as a victor, but as myself. I was Genesi, yes, but I was also Luka Foster, and I wouldn't let the bloodlust define me.

"Let's begin," I said, my voice steadier than I felt.

A final nod from Sam, his blue eyes scanning mine for any hint of hesitation. "Last chance to back out, Luka. Are you sure you're ready?"

"Never been more ready," I shot back, my voice steady, betraying none of the tumultuous storm brewing within me.

We stood there, facing each other, our figures clad in the supple leather armor that hugged our forms like a second skin. The dark material was designed for flexibility and ease of movement rather than ostentation. The light gleamed off Sam's broad shoulders, accentuating the scars that laced his arms—each one a testament to battles fought and survived. My own gear felt tight across my chest, a constant reminder of the reality I was about to face.

"Looks like it's time then," Nate declared, his voice betraying a hint of concern beneath the usual lighthearted tone. With deliberate movements, he handed me the twin ebony sai, their familiar weight grounding me. In contrast, Sam wrapped his hands around the shafts of his twin axes, the muscles in his forearms tensing in anticipation.

I clasped the sai, feeling the cool metal against my palms. Blades were the Genesi's choice—close, personal, and deadly. You couldn't hide behind a trigger with blades; every strike, every cut borne of your own force. They demanded intention, a conscious application of lethal skill. And that's why I needed them—to learn control, to ensure my intentions remained pure even when stained by the red haze of bloodlust.

Remember, this is about mastery, not murder.

"Begin!" Nate's voice echoed through the valley.

Sam and I faced each other across the dusty ring, our breaths slow and measured. I could feel every set of eyes upon us, but my focus narrowed to the man before me—my commander and, for now, my opponent.

He stood still as the mountain itself, those piercing blue eyes sizing me up, trying to predict my first move. I mirrored his stance, my sais gripped firmly, recalling every spar between Nate and Sam that I'd watched, every feint and dodge Sam favored. My mind whirled with possibilities, strategies forming and dissolving in the span of a heartbeat.

We circled each other, predators locked in a dance of death, though neither of us would aim to kill today. The tension writhed between us, a living thing seeking to unsettle, to provoke. But neither of us gave in; not yet.

"Come on," Sam taunted, shifting his weight. "Show me what you've got."

I lunged, faster than thought, sai slicing through the air towards his side. He parried with an axe, metal ringing against metal, and I retracted only to strike again. Our movements were a blur, the clashing of blades a rhythm pounding in time with my racing heart.

"Is this it, Luka? Is this all your genesi abilities amount to?" he goaded, his axes spinning in a deceptive dance, forcing me back step by step.

The edge in his words was designed to unnerve, to push me closer to the brink. And it was working. A crimson veil began to tinge the edges of my vision, the bloodlust whispering promises of power and dominance.

"More than enough to handle you," I retorted, gritting my teeth as I parried a blow meant to disarm.

I felt it then—the red haze creeping closer, threatening to engulf my senses. It was the beast within, clawing at the confines of my control. I had to prove I could beat it, that I could remain myself even as I wielded these deadly extensions of my will.

"Let's see how long you can keep it at bay," Sam growled, relentless, pushing me further, wanting to draw out the monster he thought lurked within.

With every strike, every narrowly avoided slash, the red haze grew thicker, more insistent. But I fought it, fought him, fought the very nature of what I had become. Because if I succumbed, what would be left of Luka Foster when the dust settled?

The red haze flared, wrapping its tendrils around my consciousness as I sidestepped another of Sam's powerful swings. My breath came out in ragged gasps, the sounds of the encircling crowd fading to a distant murmur. In the periphery of my awareness, a voice called out—a beacon trying to pierce the fog. "Luka!" it cried, desperate and clear. But I was sinking, losing myself to the instinctive rage that fueled my genesi abilities.

"Come on, Luka! Show me what you're really made of!"

Sam taunted, his axes glinting with a challenge I could no longer resist.

Something primal within me snapped. I lunged forward with an intensity that even I hadn't known I possessed. My twin sai became extensions of my will, each movement more forceful than the last. Sam's usual deft counters began to falter as I pressed my advantage, relentless in my assault.

"Lu—ka!" The voice grew more insistent, but I pushed it away, focusing only on the clash of metal and the feel of Sam's defenses crumbling under my onslaught.

Then, it happened—a strike too fierce, a block too slow. Sam stumbled, and I saw my opening. With a howl of triumph, the bloodlust surged, driving my arm forward. I barely registered the shock in Sam's eyes as the tip of my sai hovered a hair's breadth from his throat.

"LUKA!" Harvey's voice finally shattered through the haze, as sharp and jarring as ice water.

I froze, the world snapping back into focus with startling clarity. Sam lay beneath me, wounded and vulnerable, a thread of crimson trickling down his temple where my weapon had grazed him. The horror of what I'd nearly done coiled in my stomach, a cold and suffocating dread.

"Sam," I whispered, my voice trembling. I dropped my sai, the ebony blades thudding dully against the ground as if to mark the weight of my guilt.

"Get him to the infirmary before he passes out," I heard someone say, their words muffled as though spoken through cotton.

Others rushed to his side, hoisting his large frame with strained effort. They carried him off, disappearing into the mountain's shadowy maw, leaving me to grapple with the monster I feared dwelled inside me.

"Ren," I said, turning to my friend, my voice barely above a whisper. "What happened? When I... when it took over?"

Ren met my gaze, his expression somber. "You were like nothing I've ever seen, Luka. It was terrifying—and incredible. You had complete control until... until you didn't."

I nodded, unable to muster any words of comfort or explanation. I was still catching my breath, the pounding of my heart loud in my ears, when Harvey's fingers wrapped around my wrist, pulling me away from the crowd's murmurs. "Luka," he said sternly, his grip firm but not unkind, "lets get you out of here."

His grey blue eyes bore into mine, reflecting a storm I knew all too well. There was an urgency in his gaze that made my stomach twist with guilt. I had almost killed Sam, and it was Harvey's voice that had reeled me back from the edge.

"Okay," I managed to say, though it felt like swallowing shards of glass. We walked side by side, our footsteps echoing against the stone as we made our way through the labyrinthine corridors. The chill of the mountain pressed against my skin, yet I couldn't shake the heat of bloodlust that lingered like a second skin.

"Are you going to tell me 'I told you so'?" I asked, trying to keep my voice light, but it cracked under the weight of my emotions.

"Would it make any difference?" Harvey replied quietly, and there was no missing the worry that creased his brow.

We reached the corridor to the infirmary, a sterile room carved deep within the mountain, and I slowed my pace. Guilt constricted around my chest like a vice.

"Hey," Harvey said softly, slowing his pace to meet mine. His hand found mine, squeezing slightly. "You didn't go through with it, Luka. That's what matters."

"Because you stopped me," I replied, my throat tight with emotion. I looked down at our entwined hands, finding solace in his touch.

"Maybe," he conceded, "but ultimately, it was you. You're fighting it, Luka. And that makes you more human than any of us."

I wanted to believe him, to cling to the idea that I wasn't lost to the darkness within me. Could I really control this power? Or would it eventually consume me?

Chapter 12

Luka

I renewed my walk down the sterile corridor, my boots echoing off the stone walls, Harvey a silent shadow at my side. We were almost at the infirmary doors when Nate's voice cut through the clanging of my heart in my ears.

"Luka! Wait up!"

I slowed, turning to see Nate's muscular figure jogging toward us, his bald head gleaming under the harsh lights. His eyes, always so full of mischief, now flickered with something more serious.

"Let's give Sam an hour, huh?" Nate suggested, hands on his hips as he caught up, breathing easily despite the run. "He needs time to come around."

My chest tightened, and I tried to swallow the lump that had formed in my throat. The memory of the shock in Sam's eyes as the tip of my sai hovered a hair's breadth from his throat. I could still feel the electric surge of adrenaline, the way my muscles tensed, ready to continue the fight, even though it was over.

"Sam's tough," Harvey said, his voice steady. He reached out, placing a hand on my shoulder, grounding me. "He's survived worse."

I nodded, barely registering the warmth of Harvey's touch. My mind was a whirlpool of guilt, each thought crashing into the next: Sam's blue eyes wide with shock, the gasps from the onlookers, the sickening thud of his body hitting the ground. I knew Harvey was trying to reassure me, but the image of Sam, hurt because of me, clawed at my insides.

"Fine, I'll wait," I told Nate, forcing the words out. I hoped the break would blur the sharp edges of the incident, make it easier to face Sam later. But deep down, I knew an hour, a day, or a week wouldn't change the fact that I'd lost control. And if I couldn't trust myself not to hurt my friends, then what was I?

Harvey squeezed my shoulder, pulling me back from the edge of my spiraling thoughts. "Come on," he said gently. "Let's grab some water, sit down for a bit. You need to breathe, Luka."

I let them steer me away from the infirmary door, the weight of my own actions pressing down on me like a physical force. We settled on a bench a short distance from the infirmary, Harvey handed me a bottle of water, and I took an absent sip, my mind still reeling.

"Okay," Nate said, squatting in front of me to meet my gaze. "I saw what happened out there. Right before... you know."

His voice trailed off, but his eyes held mine, steady. A part of me didn't want to hear it, afraid of what truths might spill from his lips. But another part, the part that demanded answers, leaned in.

"You were holding your own, Luka. Then Sam landed that hit on your shoulder—the one that should've been parried." Nate's hand mimicked a deflecting motion, a shadow of the fight we all wished to forget.

"Your eyes changed then," he continued, softer now, as if the memory itself was fragile. "It was like watching a storm roll in—sudden, inevitable."

I swallowed hard, trying to recall that moment. The pain in my shoulder had been real, sharp. But after that? There was nothing but fragments—a red mist, flashes of movement, a roar in my ears that might have been my own voice.

"I don't remember much after that," I admitted, my confession barely above a whisper. "Which scares me, Nate. What if next time, I don't stop? What if Harvey isn't there?"

My hands trembled, gripping the water bottle tight enough to make the metal protest.

"Hey." Harvey's voice was the anchor in the storm Nate described, grounding me. "I was there this time, and I'll be there next time. We'll figure this out together."

He reached out, enveloping my shaking hands with his own, halting their tremor. His touch was warm, solid—real in a way my fragmented memories weren't.

"Remember how you came back to us?" Harvey asked, his eyes locking onto mine. "I called out to you, and you fought through it. That's not nothing, Luka. You're stronger than whatever this is."

I wanted to believe him, to take comfort in his words and the certainty with which he spoke them. I clung to his assurance like a lifeline, hoping it would be enough to keep the fear at bay.

"Thanks," I said, finally meeting his gaze. His presence was a reminder of the strength I had, not just within myself, but in those I chose to surround myself with. I tugged at Harvey's sleeve, a silent plea for privacy. Nate caught the hint, his expressive eyes softening with understanding.

"I'll give you two a minute," he said, stepping back, his playful nature tucked away beneath a veil of concern.

Once Nate's footsteps faded, I turned to Harvey, my voice barely above a whisper. "Every time it happens, this red haze just…swallows me whole. I can't see past it, can't think. It's like I'm not even there."

"Like a storm in your head?" Harvey murmured, understanding coloring his tone.

"Yeah. A storm so wild it could tear down everything we've built." My fingers knotted together, the memory of that power, uncontrollable and fierce, clawing at the edges of my mind.

Harvey's hand found mine, untying the nervous knot. "We've faced storms before, Luka. Together."

"Sure, but this is different. It's inside of me, and if I can't control it…" The sentence hung between us, heavy with unspoken dread.

"Then we find a way," he said resolutely. "We train harder, dig deeper. We don't let fear dictate who we are or what we become. You're Luka Foster. You don't bow to the storm—you break it."

His words were a balm to the raw edges of my anxiety. He was right. I wasn't about to be consumed by something I couldn't understand—not without a fight.

"Okay," I agreed, nodding slowly. "We'll work on it. Together."

Before we could delve any deeper into strategies and fears, Nate reappeared. "Sam's awake," he announced, a relieved smile playing on his lips.

"Thanks, Nate," I said, steeling myself for the confrontation ahead.

Chapter 13

Sam

Consciousness clawed its way back to me, dragging my senses out of the abyss. My eyelids fluttered open, but the world refused to sharpen into focus. Shades of gray and murky silhouettes danced before me as if I was peering through a thick fog. Panic gnawed at my insides; my vision had never betrayed me like this before. Was I going blind? The thought sent a shiver coursing through me, disorienting me further.

I was lying on something hard and cool, the cool surface pressing against my back. The infirmary, I realized—a cave carved deep within the mountain. The damp smell of earth mingled with the tang of antiseptic used to clean wounds.

"Easy, Sam," I muttered to myself, trying to quell the rising tide of dread. With deliberate movements, I began to assess the damage to my body. My fingertips gingerly traced over my torso, feeling for breaks or gashes. There were bruises, tender and swelling, but nothing felt broken. My ribs ached with each shallow breath—probably cracked but not shattered.

The real test came when I reached up to touch my head. A sharp stab of pain greeted me, confirming at least one thing: I had a concussion. That would explain the disconcerting loss of vision. I tried to remember the practice fight with Luka, but details slipped through my mind like water through fingers.

Closing my eyes, I tried to focus on the sensation beneath my skin. The genesi healing abilities were kicking in, a slow but relentless force. I imagined the tiny fibers of my flesh weaving themselves back together, cell by cell mending the unseen injuries. It was a peculiar feeling, like an internal itch I couldn't scratch, accompanied by the warmth of regeneration spreading through the affected areas.

"Come on, heal faster," I coaxed silently, willing my body to repair itself. It obeyed, albeit at a pace that tested my patience. I needed my strength, my sight, and my wits about me if I was going to lead and protect my makeshift family in this forsaken place.

But even as my body worked to heal itself, I couldn't shake the sense of vulnerability that being visually impaired brought upon me. In a world where power and control meant survival, any weakness could be a fatal flaw. And yet, there I lay, defenseless in the dimness of the infirmary, dependent on my other senses to alert me to any approaching threat—or ally.

"Stay alert, Sam," I reminded myself, drawing in a deep breath and exhaling slowly to steady my nerves. "This is just temporary." But the unspoken question lingered in the air, heavy as the darkness that veiled my eyes: What if it isn't?

The scent of moss and damp earth mingled with the sterile tang of antiseptic as I heard the cadence of purposeful footsteps approaching. I assumed it was Lina, her sudden presence a comfort in the haze of my uncertain recovery.

"Sam, how are you feeling?" Her voice was a blend of concern and clinical detachment.

"Like someone's put a blindfold on me that I can't rip off," I replied, trying to sound more annoyed than afraid. "Vision's all shadows and fog."

"Let me have a look," she said, her hands deftly checking my pulse before moving to examine my pupils. I felt the cool touch of her fingers lifting my eyelids, the probing beam of a flashlight that I could only sense as a change in warmth on my face.

"Your pupils are reacting slowly, but they're reacting," Lina confirmed with a hint of relief. "It's the concussion. Your sight should return, but we need to give it time."

"Great," I muttered, the sarcasm in my voice a thin veil for my frustration. As she continued her examination, my mind couldn't help but wander back to the cause of this whole mess—the practice fight with Luka.

She had moved like a force of nature, each strike precise and powerful. But then there was a shift, a flicker in her eyes that spelled trouble. The bloodlust had taken hold, sending her into a frenzy that was nearly my undoing.

It was clear that she hadn't yet mastered the darker aspects of our genesi abilities. And if she couldn't keep that beast at bay, it would spell disaster for us all. However, Luka was not willing to navigate the delicate balance between maintaining control and embracing chaos like I did.

"Maybe what Luka needs is a different approach," I mused silently, acknowledging the danger but also seeing an opportunity. If I could help her harness that wild energy, we'd have a formidable asset on our side. But it wouldn't be easy. It would take patience, trust, and a willingness from both of us to confront the monstrous parts of ourselves.

"Training her one-on-one might be the key," I thought, envisioning sessions where we could push the boundaries of our abilities together. "Control is everything. Without it, we're no better than the monsters we're fighting against."

"Sam? You're frowning. Does something hurt?" Lina's voice pulled me out of my reverie, her concern palpable.

"Nothing new," I assured her. "Just thinking about... training routines."

"Take it easy for now," she advised, her tone leaving no room for argument. "We need you in one piece."

"Understood," I conceded, though my resolve remained unshaken as I listed to Lina's retreated footsteps. Helping Luka find balance within herself was crucial.

I closed my eyes for only a moment before I jerked upright at the sound of footsteps, my heart thumping erratically. The beat was familiar—Nate's confident stride—but the other two were enigmas, their rhythms unrecognizable. Fighting the panic of my blurred vision, I feigned nonchalance, not wanting to expose my vulnerability.

"Hey, Sam," Nate's voice came first, a steady presence in the dimness of the infirmary cave. "How's the head?"

"Seen better days," I grunted, aiming for casual while straining my ears for any telltale sounds that might betray the newcomers' identities.

"Sorry, this is all my fault," another voice broke in, tinged with regret. Luka. At her words, a taut string inside me loosened slightly. With her came Harvey, his presence as silent as always.

"Should've controlled it," she continued, and I could imagine her furrowing her brows, the weight of guilt pressing down on her athletic frame.

"Could've happened to any of us," I replied, keeping my tone even. It felt important to reassure her, despite the throbbing in my skull reminding me just how close she'd come to ending me. "The red haze—it's a tricky beast."

Luka shifted uneasily, the rustle of fabric loud in the silence. "Before it took over, everything turned crimson. Like I was looking through a blood-soaked lens," she confessed, her voice barely above a whisper.

"Sounds like what happens when I snap," I said thoughtfully, probing the shadows of my memory. "The gene coding your father used on you—do you think it might be the same?"

Luka sucked in a breath, her shock palpable even without sight. "You mean... I might be..."

"More similar to me than we realized," I finished for her. A chill skittered down my spine at the implications. If Luka's genes held the key, then understanding her might be our best shot at unraveling Cain's twisted plans.

Harvey's voice cut through the hush of the infirmary, a scalpel of skepticism. "So what does that mean for Luka? Is she not a true genesi then? Is she the same as you? As one of Cain's genesi?"

I propped myself up on my elbows, ignoring the dizziness that swam in my skull, and squinted in the direction of his voice. "It means," I started, pausing to let the gravity of my suggestion sink in, "we might want to have Jon and Lina run some tests."

"Tests?" Luka echoed, her tone sharp with apprehension.

"Nothing invasive," I assured quickly, aware of how my

words must have sounded. "Just... to understand better. They're practically our medics here."

"Sam," Harvey's voice took on a harder edge, "you don't do anything without a reason. What are you thinking?"

The room seemed to hold its breath, waiting for my response. "Let's just say I'm curious about your father's work," I said carefully, feeling my way around the truth.

There was a pause, and I could sense Luka piecing it together, her mind always racing ahead. "You're talking about the video," she stated flatly, the realization evident in her voice. "You think there's something in my blood. The cure my father mentioned."

I remained silent, a nod useless in my current state. Her ash blonde hair would be falling over her face now, her sharp eyes boring into me even if I couldn't see them.

"Sam's got a point," Nate chimed in from somewhere to my right. "If there's a chance to understand this—"

"Understand or exploit?" Luka shot back, her defense rising like a shield.

"Understand," I said firmly, forcing conviction into my voice despite the uncertainty gnawing at my gut. "Only understand."

The silence stretched on, I could feel their eyes on me, Luka's especially, probing for the truth I had yet to fully unveil. The air in the infirmary felt charged, thick with unspoken words and possibilities that could alter the course of our lives.

"Look," I started, my voice rough as gravel, "I haven't been entirely straight with you all." My fingers clenched into the thin blanket covering me. This was it—the moment of truth. "Luka, your blood... it might hold the key to reversing what we've become."

There, I'd said it. The weight of my confession hung heavy

in the room, an anchor sinking into the depths of uncertainty. I waited, bracing myself for her reaction.

"Reversing?" Her voice was quiet, but there was a tremor of hope I hadn't expected.

"Yeah. If there's a cure in your genes, we should know. After the war, it could mean freedom for any genesi who wants it."

"Freedom," she whispered, the word lingering between us like a fragile promise.

My gut twisted with worry. What if Luka decided to take the cure now, abandon the fight? She was pivotal, her strength, her leadership. We needed her. But the risk of not telling her—the betrayal—felt worse.

"Sam," Harvey interjected, his strategist's mind always analyzing, "you think she's a flight risk, don't you?"

He wasn't wrong, but admitting it out loud would only feed the tension. Instead, I shifted the focus. "Regardless, we need to be prepared. Luka, I want to help you control your abilities better. Personal training, just you and me."

"You're going to train me?" There was skepticism in her tone, but also curiosity.

"Yes. And Harvey," I added, sensing his protective instincts flaring up, "you'll be there too. To pull her back from the edge if we get too close."

"Damn right I will," he muttered, and I could almost see him crossing his arms, that strategic brain already planning contingencies.

"Fine," Luka agreed, and I could practically hear the steel in her spine as she accepted the challenge. "We do this your way, Sam. But remember, we're in this together. No more secrets."

"Agreed," I said, feeling a strange mix of relief and apprehension. Whether this was the right move or not, only time would tell.

I rubbed at my eyes, but the world persisted in its newfound blur—a stubborn fog that clung to everything I looked at. My fingers brushed against the rough fabric of the infirmary cot, gripping it as if it could anchor me back into clear sight.

"Still feeling like you're in a cloud?" Nate's voice held a teasing edge, but concern underscored each syllable.

"More like swimming through murky water," I quipped, forcing a chuckle despite the unease coiling in my gut.

"Ah, so that's why you've been acting off." Luka's remark cut through the room, her tone light but not without a sharpness that matched the glint I knew would be in her eyes. "Here I thought the concussion gave you a personality change."

"Ha," I shot back, trying to match her levity and ignoring the pang of vulnerability. "If I'd known getting knocked on the head would make me more charming, I'd have let you wallop me sooner."

"Charming isn't the word I'd use," Nate interjected, his voice a low rumble. "More like disoriented puppy than battle-hardened warrior."

"Hey, even puppies have their day," I retorted, finally sitting up straighter, testing my body's limits.

"Sure they do," Nate chuckled, "just maybe not on the training mat."

"Watch it," I warned, grin audible in my voice, "or next time I might mistake your foot for a chew toy."

Their laughter filled the space, easing the tension that had tightened around us like a vice.

"Alright, 'Puppy Sam,'" Luka said, amusement lacing her words, "let's see how well you train once those eyes of yours decide to focus again."

"Let's hope it's soon," I replied, "because I'm starting to think this whole clear vision thing might actually be useful."

"Who knew?" she teased, and I could almost picture her sly grin and determined eyes.

"Definitely not me," I admitted, and despite everything, I found myself smiling too.

Chapter 14

Luka

The infirmary's door creaked open with an apology, admitting my shadow into the sterile glow of the dimmed lights. I had left Sam alone for just a few hours, but guilt clawed at me with every stealthy step I took closer to his cot. Sam's steady breathing filled the dimly lit infirmary as I perched on the edge of his cot. The smell of antiseptic was sharp in my nostrils, almost masking the metal and sweat scent that clung to us both.

"Thought I smelled trouble," Sam's voice cracked the silence, a playful tone laced with sleep.

"Guess I'm not as sneaky as I thought," I managed a wry smile. The dim light caressed his features, softening the usual hardness of his rugged face. His piercing blue eyes, clear now from the fog of concussion, met mine with an ease that sent a wave of relief through me.

"Looks like you can see me without the double vision now," I teased, trying to keep the mood light.

"Unfortunately," he quipped, and we shared a chuckle that

didn't quite reach our eyes.

The laughter died quickly, smothered by the memory of our practice fight. I saw it all again—my fist connecting with his jaw, the red haze clouding my vision, the sharp taste of fear when I realized what I'd done.

"Sam, I—" My voice faltered, choked by the guilt that had taken root in my chest.

"Hey," Sam interrupted, his hand finding mine, rough and warm. "You've got nothing to apologize for, Luka. It was a spar. Things got... intense. Happens to the best of us."

"Intense?" I repeated, the word feeling inadequate for the fury that had possessed me. "I could have killed you."

"But you didn't," he said firmly. "And that's because you're not like them, Luka. You're fighting this...this thing inside you. Every day, you fight it. That's what matters."

His words should've been comforting, yet they felt like a coat too heavy on my shoulders. I was teetering on the edge, between the leader I needed to be and the monster I feared becoming.

"Sam, I don't know if I can control it," I whispered, the confession scraping against my pride.

"You will," he said, his grip tightening. "Because you're the strongest person I know, Luka Foster. You'll beat this, like you've beaten everything else. And I'll be right here, helping you through it."

I looked into his unwavering gaze, letting his confidence seep into the cracks of my own doubt. It wasn't enough to repair them, but it was enough to make me believe, even for a moment, that maybe I could hold on to the person I still hoped to be at the end of this war.

"Camille's preparing for the first batch," he said suddenly, his voice low enough that it blended with the hum of the medical equipment. "Non-combatants. They're moving at dawn."

"Good," I replied, my gaze wandering over the empty cots in the room. "They'll be safer there." But even as I spoke, a knot formed in my stomach, an unspoken fear taking shape.

"Harvey's going to go with the last batch," Sam stated matter-of-factly, watching my face for a reaction.

My head snapped back to him, my eyes narrowing. "No," I said sharply, more to the universe than to Sam. "He won't want to leave. Not now."

"Maybe not," Sam agreed, tilting his head to study me. "But Luka, he has to. You know Cain's forces are coming. And Harvey... he's your anchor, yeah, but he's also human. Vulnerable."

I felt my fists clench involuntarily. Harvey was more than just my best friend; he was my conscience when the red haze threatened to swallow me whole. We've never been apart before.

"Then I'll protect him here," I shot back, standing up. My shadow loomed over the cots like a silent guardian.

"By convincing him to go," Sam continued, unfazed by my defiance. "If he stays because you can't let go, he will get hurt. You'll both know it was because you couldn't bear to part ways, even if it meant his safety."

"Sam, he's stronger than you think," I argued, but my voice cracked, betraying the fear that maybe he wasn't.

"Of course, he is," Sam conceded, his blue eyes piercing through the darkness. "But strength isn't always about holding on, Luka. Sometimes, it's about letting go."

"Letting go," I murmured, the words tasting bitter. I sat

back down, deflated. "Do you think I haven't tried? Every plan, every move—it all leads back to him. He's a part of me as much as I'm a part of him."

"Then you need to change the pattern," Sam said gently. "You've got time now before they march thanks to your delay tactic. Use it. Talk to Harvey. Make him see reason."

"Reason," I scoffed, a hollow laugh escaping my lips. "In a world gone mad, where's the reason in abandoning your friends?"

"Survival," he countered softly. "It's not abandonment. It's strategy. Your kind of strategy." He reached out and squeezed my hand, a silent reminder of our shared purpose.

"Okay," I breathed out, allowing myself the briefest moment to accept the possibility. "I'll try, Sam. I'll try to make him understand."

"Good," he said, his grip firm. "Because we can't force him, Luka. That would break something inside him. And you."

My mind instantly thought of fractures and fissures, of bonds strained to their limits. Of choices that cut deeper than any blade.

"Promise me, Luka," Sam urged. "Promise me you'll convince him."

I nodded, the weight of the promise anchoring me to reality as much as it threatened to drag me under. "I promise."

"Good." Sam relaxed against his pillows. "Now, tell me about the changes you've made since the cyber attack and the... practice fight."

I pulled up a chair and sat down, leaning forward with my elbows on my knees. "We've reinforced our firewall, thanks to some code tweaks. It should hold if Cain decides to counter our cyber attack. And after our practice fight..." My voice trailed off, the memory of red haze and uncontrolled rage still vivid in my mind. "Now that I have a better understanding of the behavior and abilities of Cain's genesi soldiers, I've come up with some new ideas for strategies to implement."

Sam listened intently as I detailed each new plan, asking questions and making suggestions along the way. As we talked, I felt my mind clearing, the fog of worry and fear lifting just slightly.

We discussed potential weaknesses in our current defenses and ways to strengthen them. We also talked about how to exploit Cain's reliance on his genesi soldiers and how to use that against him.

But despite the progress we were making, I couldn't shake off the dark cloud that hung over me. My thoughts kept drifting back to Harvey and how I was going to manage convincing him to leave with the others.

I knew Sam was right – I needed to convince him to go for his own safety. But every time I thought about it, my heart clenched with pain.

"Do you think he'll understand?" I finally asked, voicing my doubts out loud.

Sam gave me a sympathetic look. "He's your best friend, Luka. He knows you better than anyone. He'll see reason eventually."

"But what if he doesn't?" I pushed, almost desperate for reassurance.

"He will," Sam said firmly. "You just have to keep trying."

I nodded, taking a deep breath to calm my racing thoughts. A silence fell between us as we both let our minds wander.

"We're going to win this war," Sam suddenly said, breaking the quietness.

I looked at him, surprised by his sudden declaration of optimism.

"How can you be so sure?" I asked skeptically.

"Because we have something they don't," he replied with a small smile. "We have hope."

I considered his words for a moment before letting out a bitter laugh. "Hope? What good does hope do against an army of genetically modified soldiers?"

"Hope gives us strength," Sam countered calmly. "It keeps us fighting when everything else seems hopeless."

I couldn't argue with that logic. Hope had always been my driving force, even in the darkest of times. I just hoped it wouldn't fail me now.

"Speaking of hope," Sam interjected, shifting slightly, wincing from the movement, "you've got that meeting with Jon and Lina tomorrow, right? I asked VIKI to schedule it."

"First thing in the morning," I confirmed with a nod, thinking back to the comm I'd received at dinner. "Blood tests and all sorts of poking and prodding to see if there's any truth to the idea that my DNA holds the key to a cure."

"Your father believed it. And Jon's got a good head on his shoulders," Sam mused, his gaze steady. "It could change everything for us."

"Or it could be a dead end." I couldn't mask the skepticism in my tone.

"Either way, we need to know." Sam's hand found mine, his grip firm yet gentle. "You carry a lot on those shoulders, Luka. It's okay to lean on others sometimes."

"Thanks, Sam." I squeezed his hand back, grateful for the connection. "I'm not used to being the one on the exam table, though. I prefer being in control, you know?"

"Control is good," he agreed with a hint of a smile, "as long as you know when to let go."

"Letting go isn't exactly my forte," I admitted, thinking about Harvey, about the red haze, about every decision that led me here.

"Which is why you'll have me," Sam said firmly, his blue eyes locking onto mine. "Once I'm out of this bed, we'll start your personal training. We'll tackle that bloodlust together."

His resolve was contagious. I felt it seep into my veins like a promise—a vow that I wouldn't have to face my demons alone.

"I'll hold you to that," I told him, determination seeping into my voice. "And when you're better, we'll make sure I never lose to the red haze again."

"Deal." Sam's smile was a rare sight, like the sun peeking through storm clouds. "We'll start as soon as I'm back on my feet."

"Promise me you won't push yourself too hard," I countered, standing up and looking down at him, the ghost of a smile on my lips.

"Wouldn't dream of it," Sam replied, though we both knew it was a promise he'd struggle to keep.

Chapter 15

Luka

My hand hovered over the panel beside the door, palm slick with sweat. The sterile scent that seeped from the seams of the metal entrance did nothing to ease my nerves. Inside this cave, lay answers that could change everything—or cement my fate as a weapon I never chose to be.

"Come in, Luka," a voice called from the other side, muffled but unmistakable. I pressed the panel, and the door slid open with a hush that seemed too gentle for the heavy slab of steel. In the threshold, I stood frozen for a moment, taking in the sight of the lab—a cavernous space filled with equipment that gleamed under the artificial lights, a sharp contrast to the rough stone walls.

"Welcome." The woman who had beckoned me, Lina, stepped forward, her fiery curls reflecting the light like molten copper. She extended a hand that felt steady and capable. "We've been expecting you."

"Thank you," I said, grasping her hand, trying to mirror her calm.

"Jon, this is Luka Foster," she introduced warmly, guiding me further into the lab.

"Ah, yes," Jon murmured, turning away from a console lined with screens. His graying hair gave him an air of wisdom, his eyes were pools of empathy as they met mine. "It's good to finally meet you, Luka. Sam speaks highly of you."

"I doubt that," I muttered.

Lina's gaze remained fixed on me, searching, perhaps, for a sign of the strength everyone seemed to believe I possessed. "We'll do everything we can to help you," she assured me, the promise shining in her green eyes. "Shall we begin?"

Before I could respond to Lina's question, the steel door swung open with sudden urgency. Harvey burst into the room, chest heaving from what must have been a sprint from the training grounds.

"Sorry I'm late," he panted, running a hand through his tousled chestnut hair. "Lost track of time at drills."

I felt a rush of relief at his presence, thankful not to face this alone. His gaze locked with mine, an unsaid promise of unwavering support conveyed in his steady grey blue eyes.

"It's okay," I said, offering a nod that I hoped conveyed more confidence than I felt.

"Good to see you, Harvey," Lina greeted him with an understanding smile. She gestured toward a sleek machine that looked out of place against the rugged cave walls. "We're just about to start. Luka, we will conduct a series of non-invasive scans to analyze your genetic make-up. It should be painless."

"Should be?" I echoed, my voice steadier than I expected.

"Will be," Jon corrected with a reassuring smile, stepping

up beside Lina. "The technology is quite advanced. You won't feel a thing."

"Advanced" was an understatement. The machines around us hummed with a silent promise of secrets to be uncovered—secrets that lay dormant within me. I swallowed hard, trying to push down the knot of apprehension in my throat.

"What exactly are you looking for?" I asked, turning to face them squarely. My hair fell into my eyes, and I brushed it aside impatiently.

"Your father reported a unique mutation in your gene sequence," Jon explained, his tone patient and clear. "One that doesn't align with typical genesi traits. It's our hope to isolate this mutation."

"For what purpose?" I pressed. "To understand or to alter?"

"Both, potentially," he admitted. "If there's truth to the cure your father believed he had embedded in your DNA, it could change everything for our kind."

I glanced at Harvey, whose composed expression didn't falter, though I sensed his mind racing behind those dark eyes. We both understood the implications—a cure could mean the reversal of what had been forced upon me, a chance to reclaim all the lives stolen by the genesi code.

"Then let's find this cure," I declared, determination setting my jaw firm. It wasn't just about me. It was about all of us—the transformed, the lost, the hopeful.

"Let's begin," Lina said, motioning me toward the scanning platform.

As I stepped up, I felt Harvey's hand brush against mine briefly—an anchor in a sea of uncertainty. With a deep breath, I looked into Jon and Lina's earnest faces and prepared to dive into the unknown depths of my own genetic blueprint.

Jon was telling the truth when he said the scan wouldn't hurt. Lina efficiently attached electrodes to my head and chest, and then I found myself surrounded by a machine that whirred as it scanned for something, though I wasn't entirely sure what it was looking for.

I stepped down from the scanning platform, muscles coiled with a tension that wasn't solely from the examination. Harvey's question sliced through the humming silence of the room.

" So what happens next?" His voice was calm, but I could hear the undercurrent of concern. "Once you discover what's in Luka's DNA—what's the plan for that information?"

Lina exchanged a fleeting glance with Jon before answering. "We're not at liberty to discuss the intentions behind the research," she said, her green eyes apologetic yet firm. "That's beyond our authorization."

"Isn't that convenient," I muttered, allowing my sly grin to surface despite the frustration bubbling inside me.

Jon's kind eyes flickered with something that might have been admiration or maybe just shared rebellion. "Perhaps," he began slowly, "we should focus on the task at hand. You see, Cain once captured a genesi named Hawkins and coerced him into replicating a version of the genesi code."

"Replicating?" I echoed, my heart pounding as I recalled the brief story Sam had told me about how Cain's genesi army had been created.

Harvey's hand found my shoulder, a silent reminder he was with me.

"More than that," Jon continued. "Hawkins allegedly created other... tools for Cain. Mind control drugs, among other horrors." He paused, gauging my reaction. I straightened up, refusing to show any sign of weakness.

"However," Jon added, "when your father, Dr. Christopher Foster, constructed his iteration of the Genesi code, he did so without access to any genesi blood or DNA. He used something else—a unique mutation within your own genes. It's eerily reminiscent of the original genesi genesis."

My breath hitched. My father had never mentioned Hawkins, but the weight of his legacy pressed onto my shoulders anew, a mantle I was learning to bear. "So he did use my mutation?" I asked. I struggled to wrap my head around everything Jon had just told me. It was even more than what my father had revealed in the video he left for me.

"Correct," Jon confirmed, his demeanor patient. "Your genetic blueprint could hold the key to understanding the origins—and potentially the undoing—of the genesi transformation."

If there was even a sliver of hope to be found within me, I wouldn't rest until we unearthed it. For everyone's sake.

Lina's gaze locked onto mine, a flicker of uncertainty in her otherwise unwavering demeanor. "The truth is, we're not sure if the cure will be specific to you or if it has broader applications," she confessed, her hands clasped tightly together as if holding onto the hope she offered. "Your genesi code... it's unique. We need to explore this further, run extensive tests."

"Tests?" I pressed, my voice barely above a whisper.

"Comprehensive ones," Jon chimed in, his eyes alight with the spark of scientific curiosity despite the gravity of our situation. "And we'll need time—"

"Which is precisely why we asked to be transported with the non fighters to Camille's encampment," Lina cut in, her tone steady. "Away from the battlefront, we can continue our research without the constant threat looming over us."

I nodded, understanding the necessity of their safety for the sake of all genesi. But another question gnawed at me, one that haunted the fringes of my mind. "How can there even be a cure? To become a genesi," I hesitated, the memories swirling like dark clouds, "you have to... die."

"Not permanently." Lina's voice was soft but firm. "The transformation only requires your heart to stop momentarily. That brief cessation allows the dormant coding to activate. It's during that fragile threshold between life and death that the heart is restarted, injuries healed by the awakened genesi code."

A shiver ran down my spine. Death had always been the gatekeeper to our rebirth, a price paid in full each time. Yet, Lina proposed a different narrative—one where the finality of death was but a mere pause in an eternal cycle.

Harvey's voice cut through the sterile silence of the lab, pulling me back from my spiraling thoughts. "Is there anything we can do about Luka's bloodlust?" he asked, his eyes flickering with contained urgency.

I caught a glimpse of myself in the polished surface of a metal cabinet—pale and drawn, the weight of my own nature bearing down on me. The bloodlust was a relentless hunter, lying dormant until the scent of violence awoke its ravenous appetite.

Lina exchanged a look with Jon, her brows knitting together slightly. "We can certainly investigate," she said, her tone not quite masking her skepticism. "But realistically, Luka, it might be more about learning to manage it rather than eliminating it entirely."

"By learning to control it," I said, the words tasting bitter on my tongue. Control had always been what I struggled with most. Maybe the training sessions with Sam would be beneficial. Although I wasn't excited about our upcoming lesson later this morning, especially after he was still recovering from yesterday.

"Let's focus on what we can do right now," Jon suggested, setting aside philosophical debates for practical action.

They led me to a chair that looked more like a relic from an ancient torture chamber than medical equipment. Straps dangled ominously from the armrests, but they went unused as I offered up my arm willingly.

Lina prepared a series of vials, her movements precise and practiced. She swabbed my inner elbow with a cold antiseptic, the sharp smell stinging my nostrils.

"Sharp scratch," she warned, and then the needle pierced my skin—a brief sting.

Blood, dark and rich with secrets, filled the first vial. Lina's fingers were deft as she swapped it out for another, her green eyes focused intently on her task. Beside her, Jon scribbled notes onto a holoscreen.

"Good," Lina murmured, more to herself than to us as she filled the last vial and carefully labeled it. "These samples should give us plenty to work with."

"Will you be able to isolate the mutated gene from these?" I asked, watching my life force divide into glass prisons.

"Hopefully," Jon replied, not looking up from his notes. "It'll take some time to analyze the sequences and match them against known genesi markers. But we'll do our best, Luka. You have my word."

"Thank you," I said, the gratitude genuine despite the knot

of anxiety in my stomach.

"Take it easy for the rest of the day," Lina instructed, pressing a small bandage over the puncture wound. "The body is resilient, but it needs care too."

I doubt Sam will let me take it easy.

As I hopped off the chair, feeling the comforting pressure of the bandage against my skin, I knew their work was only beginning. A mountain of data awaited them, each piece a potential key to unlocking the mystery of my existence.

"Will you keep me updated on any progress?" I asked, trying to sound casual but feeling anything but.

Jon exchanged a look with Lina before responding. "You'll need to discuss that with The Commander," he said, his voice neutral but firm.

The response sent a chill through me, prickling at the back of my neck. Why would updates about my condition be restricted? My mind raced, concocting scenarios I didn't want to entertain, yet couldn't ignore.

"Thanks," I muttered, my suspicions gnawing at me as I turned towards the exit.

Harvey was right behind me, his presence a steadying force. We stepped out of the lab, the door shutting with a quiet thud that echoed down the cavernous hallway. I grabbed Harvey's arm, pulling him into an alcove shadowed from the flickering lights.

"Something's not right," I whispered, my words laced with urgency. "Why would Sam need to control the flow of information about my own blood?"

Harvey's eyes, deep pools of concern, met mine. "What do you want to do?"

"Sam's hiding something." I clenched my fists, my determination hardening like the rocks surrounding us. "I need to find out what it is."

"And how do you plan on doing that?" His voice was low, cautious, but I could tell he was with me—no matter where this path led.

"I'm going to ask Lewis for help," I declared. "If he can hack into Cain's network, maybe we can find out if there's any information on a cure… or if Cain has developed one himself."

Harvey nodded slowly. "That's dangerous, Luka. If Sam finds out—"

"He won't." My hair fell over my eyes as I shook my head, brushing it away with a swift hand. "We need answers, Harvey. And I'm tired of being kept in the dark."

"Okay," he agreed, his loyalty a beacon in the murky uncertainty. "You know I've got your back."

"Thank you," I breathed out, the weight of my secret fears slightly lifted by his solidarity.

We navigated the maze of the encampment, my mind racing as fast as my feet. The cold, stone walls pressed in on us, echoing with the sound of our hurried steps. Harvey kept pace beside me, his presence a steady pulse amid my rising storm of thoughts.

"Sam's hiding something, Harvey," I said, breaking the silence. "There's more to this cure, and whatever it is, I'm going to uncover it."

Harvey's eyes met mine, reflecting both determination and concern. "Luka, if there are secrets, Sam's not going to let them go easily. You've got guts, but you'll need more than that to face him."

I stopped abruptly, causing a small cloud of dust to rise from the ground. "I know. That's why I can't do this alone." My voice echoed off the cave walls, carrying my resolve with it.

"Then we should get Ren involved," he suggested after a moment, his tone serious. "He's got a way with Sam. He can get through to him, maybe even understand what he's planning."

"Alright," I conceded. "We bring Ren in." The idea settled in my stomach like a weight, solid and undeniable. I'd speak with Ren before I met Sam for my training.

Chapter 16

Luka

The morning sun was peaked high over the craggy peaks of the valley that cradled our hidden training grounds. I stood there, feet planted firmly on the dew-kissed grass, facing Sam.

"Remember," he said, his voice a low rumble, "control is everything."

I nodded, keenly aware of Harvey's gaze from the sidelines, his eyes tracking every move with that protective intensity he reserved for moments like these. Ren leaned against a nearby tree, arms crossed, his presence a silent reminder of the line we weren't supposed to cross.

I glanced at Sam, there was a subtle wince when he moved, so minute you'd miss it if you weren't looking for it. And I was always looking. The practice fight from the day before had been rough, and I suspected a concussion still haunted him, though he'd never admit it. I hoped that Lina had given him the green light to start my training, although she never mentioned it to me earlier this morning when I was at the lab.

The training grounds were unrecognizable from the day

prior. Overnight, the open space had transformed into a landscape designed for my specific training needs. It felt strange, standing here in a place that seemed as familiar as the back of my hand, yet now looked like foreign territory.

"Let's begin," Sam finally said, breaking me out of my reverie.

"Okay," I replied, rolling my shoulders back and shaking out the tension in my limbs. My heart thrummed with a mix of nervous energy and anticipation; today would be a test of not just my physical abilities, but my ability to quell the storm within.

"You've got this, Luka," Harvey called out, his voice steady and reassuring. I gave him a quick nod, grateful for his watchful eye, ready to step in if the bloodlust proved too much.

"Thanks," I shot back, a half-grin tugging at my lips. But I wasn't grinning because this was fun; it was a cover for the gnawing worry nipping at the edges of my mind.

Could I really master this beast inside me?

The earth was uneven beneath my boots as I surveyed the training ring, now an obstacle course carved into nature itself. Huge logs were embedded into the ground at odd angles, meant to be vaulted over or crawled under—a test of agility and strategy. A network of ropes stretched from tree to tree, creating a web that demanded grace and balance to navigate.

"Looks like someone got creative," I muttered, eyeing the layout.

How had Sam managed all these changes overnight?

"Everything here serves a purpose, Luka," Sam's voice was laced with that knowing tone he often used. "You'll see."

My gaze followed the trail of obstacles until it landed on the large boulders randomly placed throughout the course. They varied in size; some were as tall as me, others just high enough to serve as a step. Their smooth, rounded surfaces seemed out of place among the roughness of the natural setting. What role they played, I couldn't guess, but I was certain Sam had his reasons.

"Control isn't just about suppressing your strength, Luka," Sam started, pulling me back to the task at hand. He stood before me, arms crossed, his blue eyes sharp even beneath the shadow of doubt I saw lingering there. "It's about understanding it—mastering it."

"Easy for you to say," I retorted with a hint of bitterness. "You don't fight the bloodlust like I do."

"Actually, I did. Once." His admission caught me off guard. Sam, always so composed, had grappled with this too? "But I learned quickly. You find a middle ground where control and instinct coexist. It's delicate, but not impossible."

"Middle ground," I echoed skeptically. Yet, as I looked around at the meticulously designed training ground, I realized that was exactly what this was—all carefully balanced between pushing limits and ensuring safety.

"Precicely," he said, as if reading my thoughts. "Now, let's get you to find yours."

Sam placed the weight of the boulder in my hands, its gritty texture pressing into my skin. "Focus. Break it in half," he instructed, his voice firm yet encouraging.

I narrowed my eyes, trying to channel the strength that surged within me. I envisioned the rock splitting, but when I squeezed, the stone crumbled under my fingers, dust and fragments cascading to the ground. I had crushed it entirely.

"Again," Sam said, unfazed by my overexertion. He handed

me another boulder, this one larger and more daunting.

My heart raced as I wrapped my hands around it. The familiar red haze crept into the edges of my vision, a warning sign of the bloodlust that lay coiled inside me.

"Concentrate, Luka," Sam's voice cut through the fog of my impending frenzy.

I glanced at Harvey, standing off to the side with arms folded, his face an unreadable mask. Beside him, Ren's nod was subtle but steadying—a silent message of support. Their presence was a tether, grounding me.

Drawing in a deep breath, I focused on the sensation of the earth beneath my feet, the cool mountain air filling my lungs. The red haze retreated slightly. With every ounce of control I could muster, I tightened my grip on the boulder and applied pressure. A sharp crack echoed through the valley as the boulder split evenly in two.

"Good," Sam said, a hint of pride lacing his words. "Now keep it up."

The next attempts were a dance with danger, the red haze flirting with my concentration, but each time I managed to push it back and break the boulder cleanly. My confidence grew, alongside my understanding of the balance Sam spoke of.

"Let's see you break it into smaller pieces," Sam challenged after several more successful splits.

This task demanded precision, a finer edge to the blunt force I was accustomed to wielding. Each strike had to be measured, calculated—a test not just of strength but of finesse. The red haze lurked, but I was learning to keep it at bay. Learning to recognize the signs, to anticipate the surge, to stay one step ahead of the bloodlust that sought to define me.

And with each fractured piece of stone that fell to the ground, I felt a shard of my old self shed away, leaving room for the person I was becoming—someone capable not only of great power but of great control.

The sun climbed higher, its rays turning the valley into a sweltering forge as I split one boulder after another. Sweat streamed down my face, each drop stinging my eyes and reminding me of the monotony of the task at hand.

"Sam," I called out, pausing to wipe my brow with the back of my hand, "can we try something else? This is getting old." My muscles ached for a different challenge, my mind for a change of pace.

He stood stoic, his arms crossed over his chest, but his blue eyes held a stern message. "Control isn't just about strength, Luka. It's about patience, too. Keep going."

I sighed, knowing arguing was futile. The rhythm of breaking rock into smaller and more precise fragments continued, each snap and crackle testing my resolve.

"Enough," Sam finally said after what felt like an eternity. He stepped into the training ring with me, his presence commanding even in silence. "Now, hit me."

"Are you sure?" I hesitated, my fists clenched at my sides. The memory of the red haze still fresh, the fear of losing control and hurting him hung heavy in the air between us.

"Stop worrying," he chided, a ghost of a smile pulling at the corner of his mouth. "Just hit me."

My hands moved almost of their own accord, aiming for his shoulder. But the thought of my power crashing into his flesh made me pull back at the last moment, turning the strike into little more than a tap.

"Again," Sam instructed, unfazed by my reluctance. "And

mean it this time."

Finding the balance between holding back and unleashing my full force was like threading a needle with shaking hands. Each blow I landed was either too soft or teetering on the edge of too hard. Frustration bubbled inside me, blending with the fear that simmered just beneath my skin.

"Focus," Sam said, catching my fist mid-air with ease. "It's not just about hitting—it's about knowing you won't break everything you touch."

His words were a beacon, guiding me through the murky waters of doubt. With every controlled strike, I began to understand the true nature of my strength, not as a curse, but as a tool that I could wield with precision.

"Good, Luka," he praised as I finally managed a hit that was firm yet restrained—a perfect balance.

"Thanks," I panted, feeling a mix of pride and relief wash over me. The sweat trickling down my back felt like the only thing keeping me grounded as I squared up against Sam again. My fists, now somewhat controlled, found their targets with enough force to matter, but not enough to cause real damage.

"Come on, Luka, hit me like you mean it," Sam taunted, his grin sharp and his eyes glinting with a challenge. "Show me that fiery spirit."

I knew he was trying to push me, to test the limits of my restraint, but understanding his motive didn't douse the anger.

"Sam—" I began, my voice tight, but he cut me off.

"Prove to me you're not just a ticking bomb waiting to go off," he continued, his tone edged with something darker than before.

My fist clenched, knuckles whitening as I drew back, aiming for a punch that would surely cross the line between sparring and actual combat. The red haze at the edge of my vision started to creep forward.

"Enough!" Harvey's voice cracked through the tension, sharp as a whip. He strode forward, positioning himself between Sam and me, his eyes laced with disapproval. "You're taking this too far, Sam. It's her first real lesson."

Sam's gaze flicked to Harvey, the hardness in his blue eyes never wavering. "She's in complete control," he shot back, though his body language softened ever so slightly at Harvey's intervention.

I took a measured breath, fighting back the tide of blood-lust that threatened to swallow my hard-earned composure. Harvey's presence was like a beacon, reminding me of why I needed to master this power—why we were all here, risking everything.

"Can we try another spar?" Sam asked, turning back to me, his expression serious now. "I promise it'll go differently than yesterday's practice fight."

I hesitated, studying the earnestness in his rugged features. Harvey still looked skeptical, but there was a trust in Sam's eyes that I couldn't ignore. With a nod, more to myself than anyone else, I stepped around Harvey, ready to face Sam once again.

"Let's do it," I said, letting my determination shine through the doubt. "But if I start seeing red, you better be quick on your feet."

"Wouldn't have it any other way," Sam replied, his brief smile reassuring me that this time, we'd both find the balance we were seeking.

I circled Sam, my fists raised, every muscle coiled and ready to strike. His eyes tracked me with an intensity that made the air between us electric.

"Come on, Luka," he taunted, a smirk playing at the edge of his lips. "Show me what you've got."

His words were like sparks to kindling, igniting a fury within me. I lunged forward, throwing a punch aimed at his shoulder. At the last second, I reined it in just enough to make contact without causing harm.

"Is that all?" Sam's voice cut through the tension, goading me further.

I could feel the red haze creeping into my vision, a warning siren in the back of my mind. It beckoned, promising power, but I knew better. I took a deep breath, focusing on the rush of cool air filling my lungs, pushing the crimson tide back to the edges of my consciousness.

Sam came at me then, feinting left before striking right. I parried the blow, our dance of controlled aggression a testament to our respective wills. Each time he prodded, each jest a thinly veiled attempt to push me over the edge, I managed to pull back, keeping the beast at bay.

"Getting tired yet?" he asked, his tone light, but his eyes never losing their sharpness.

"Nope," I shot back, allowing a small grin to flash across my face. My response was a deflection, a mask over the effort it took to maintain my composure.

We continued, the sound of our sparring the only noise in the valley, until finally, we stepped back from each other, both breathing heavily but unharmed.

"Good," Sam said, nodding with respect. "You're learning."

I closed my eyes for a moment, letting the world fall away as I centered myself. With clarity, I understood the delicate balance I held within me—the red haze was a sentinel, not an enemy. It rose from the depths when provoked by anger or fear, a visceral response to perceived threats. But it was mine to command, not the other way around. If I kept my emotions in check, if I acknowledged the warning without succumbing to it, I could wield this power without becoming its puppet.

Chapter 17

Sam

Sweat trickled down my spine, a cool contrast to the sun's relentless heat as I made my way across the compound headed inside the mountain. The morning's training with Luka had been intense, her genesi abilities like a wild current we were learning to tame together. I could still feel the thrum of energy in the air, a restless reminder of the power she held within her veins.

The med lab loomed ahead, its sterile scent seeping out as I pushed through the doorway. Inside, past the rows of metal surfaces, Jon and Lina huddled over a microscope, their focus as sharp.

"Any news?" My voice cut through the silence like a knife, urgent and edged with the weight of our collective hope.

Jon looked up, his gray hair falling into his eyes before he pushed it away. "We've found something," he began, his tone cautious yet tinged with excitement. "It's just like you said, something in Luka's DNA might very well hold the key to a cure."

Lina nodded in agreement, her green eyes alight with the fire of possibility. "But we need test subjects—other genesi to confirm our findings. It's risky, Sam. We can't just…"

"I'll handle it," I interjected quickly, feeling the gravity of what I was about to promise. Their gazes locked onto mine, searching for reassurance where I had none to give. "I'll find us test subjects. Don't worry about that part."

Their relief was palpable, but it was shadowed by the unspoken question in their eyes—where would I get these genesi from? I held their gaze steadily, letting them see the resolve etched into every line of my face. I'd do whatever it took to protect Luka and our people, even if it meant crossing lines that were never meant to be blurred.

"Focus on the cure," I told them, my words firm. "Leave the rest to me."

Lina's fingers danced across a holoscreen with an expertise that belied her youth, her brow furrowed in concentration.

"Sam," Jon said, drawing my attention away from the whirring machines and blinking lights. "Luka's genetic structure—it's unlike anything we've seen before. It's as if she's a living blueprint of the original genesi code."

"As I suspected" I murmured, struggling to keep my voice steady.

"Her father," Lina chimed in, her voice laced with reverence and a hint of fear, "Dr. Christopher Foster… he created something purer, closer to the source. Cain's version is altered, flawed—like a distorted reflection."

My fists clenched involuntarily at the mention of Cain. The thought of my father's meddling hands crafting the very essence of who I now was…

"Which means," Jon continued, unaware of the storm brewing inside me, "the heightened level of bloodlust Luka battles with—the struggle for control—it's likely due to the discrepancies between her coding and the variant strain Cain developed."

I turned away, my gaze fixing on a scratch in the wall, a token from a past patient's outburst, no doubt. My mind raced. If Jon and Lina were right, then Luka wasn't just valuable. She was irreplaceable—a singular anomaly in a twisted experiment gone awry. And that would make her a target—a prize my father would go to great lengths to recapture. Not for any affection, but for the untold scientific breakthroughs her genes promised. The power to shape the future of the genesi lay within her, within the very blood coursing through her veins.

Cain would want her back. Desperately. And the thought chilled me to the bone.

"Did the data files I brought help at all?" I asked, watching as Jon and Lina hunched over their microscopes. The steely edge of concern in my voice was hard to mask.

"Immensely," Lina replied without looking up, her fingers deftly manipulating a slide. "It's given us a new perspective on the possible pathways for a cure."

I nodded, but my mind churned with heavier thoughts. If my father was truly seeking a cure, why? It contradicted everything he'd preached, his war strategy that painted the original genesi as vermin to be exterminated. Yet here I stood, contemplating the possibility that he was plotting an end to the very genesi code he had manipulated and spread.

"Sam?" Jon's voice cut through my reverie, gentle yet insistent.

"Sorry," I said, shaking off the grim musings. "It's just… if Cain is searching for a cure, it doesn't add up. His war drums have been sounding relentlessly, focusing on the threat outside his city walls."

Jon exchanged a look with Lina, concern etching their faces.

"Overpopulation," I continued, my words gaining momentum as the pieces fell into place. "His resources are stretched thin; food supplies can't keep up with the vast numbers within his cities. He wants casualties from the war—thinning out the numbers, especially in the poorer districts."

"Genocide masked as warfare," Lina murmured, her green eyes darkening with understanding.

"Exactly," I said. "But there's something else…"

My mind flashed back to Luka's piercing gaze, the intensity of her plea resonating deep within me. She wanted a solution, one less barbaric than the war looming over us. I recalled the spy footage, the cyro tanks lined up like tombstones in a silent white graveyard, filled with sleeping soldiers awaiting their call to arms.

"Cain has cyro tanks full of sleeping genesi soldiers," I began, watching their expressions shift from curiosity to alarm. "Those soldiers… we need to make sure they don't wake up to join Cain's ranks. Any ideas on how to disable the tanks?"

Lina bit her lip, pondering, while Jon rubbed his chin thoughtfully. "There might be a way to disrupt the stasis protocols," Jon suggested after a moment. "But it would require precise timing and expertise."

"Let me worry about that," I assured him. "I'll speak with Nate and Troian. They're good with hatching schemes—could be our best shot at pulling this off without setting foot inside enemy lines."

"Be careful, Sam," Lina warned, her freckles standing out against her pale skin tinged with concern. "If Cain discovers what you're planning—"

"He won't," I interjected, my voice laced with a determination that felt more like hope. "We'll stay under the radar. Keep working on that cure; it's our only chance to end this without bloodshed."

"Sam," Jon said, his voice steady but laced with an undercurrent of worry. "We're concerned about moving to Camille's encampment now that we're focusing on a cure. The transition could disrupt our research."

"Camille's place is secure," I said, clapping him on the shoulder in reassurance. "You'll have everything you need there, including your equipment. We've got it planned out so you can continue working without missing a beat."

Lina nodded, her green eyes searching mine for certainty. "And what about our safety during the transfer?"

"Got it covered," I replied with more confidence than I felt. "We're not taking any chances when you leave with the next batch—there will be an armed escort."

"Good to know," she murmured, tucking a strand of rebellious red hair behind her ear.

I leaned against the cool metal frame of a workbench, my gaze fixed on the pair. "But remember, we need to keep this cure business quiet. Just between us three."

"Luka's already been asking for an update. Wouldn't people feel hopeful knowing there's a potential cure?" Jon asked, his brow furrowing. "It might ease the tension, give them something positive to focus on."

"Hope can be as dangerous as despair in times like these,"

I countered. "If word gets out, it could spark panic or false expectations. We need to maintain order until we're ready."

Jon's expression tightened, and I knew I had their full attention. "Cain's forces might be at our doorstep any moment now, and we won't have this cure ready in time to prevent a confrontation."

"Sam, surely if Luka knew about her potential..." Lina began, but I cut her off with a raised hand.

"Listen to me," I said, my voice hard as steel. "Luka can't know. If she understands just how badly Cain wants her for her unique genesi code, she might do something drastic, like turn herself over to save us all."

The thought alone sent a shiver down my spine, the mere possibility igniting a protective fire within me. Luka was impulsive when it came to protecting her loved ones, and I couldn't risk her making the ultimate sacrifice.

"Her selflessness could lead to disaster," I continued, locking eyes with each of them in turn. "We need to keep her out of Cain's clutches at all costs."

"Are you threatening us?" Jon asked, his voice barely above a whisper yet carrying an edge of disbelief.

"Consider it a promise," I replied evenly. "For Luka's sake, for all of our sakes, this stays between us. No one else hears about what you found in her blood."

They both nodded, the severity of the situation sinking into their bones. The silence that followed was heavy, brimming with unspoken vows.

"Let's focus on getting you safely to Camille's encampment," I added, softening slightly. "Once there, you can continue your research without the constant threat looming over our heads."

As I walked away, the weight of every secret I carried pressed down on me like a physical burden. But it was a load I would bear willingly if it meant keeping Luka—and our fragile chance at peace—alive.

Chapter 18

Luka

I pushed through the heavy makeshift door, its creaks lost in the buzz of conversation that filled the cavernous mess hall. It was dinner time, and the space hummed with life. My friends were huddled at our usual spot, their laughter echoing off the sculpted walls. I noticed Ren's head tilted back in amusement, Liz's hands animatedly moving as she spoke, and Skai's intense gaze fixed on whoever held the floor.

"Hey," I greeted, sliding onto the bench beside them. The warmth from their bodies was a welcome reprieve from the chill of the caves.

"Hey, Luka," Skai replied, scooting over to make room. "How did it go today?"

"Sam's really putting you through the paces, huh?" Liz chimed in, her eyes bright with curiosity.

I nodded, picking at the coarse bread on my plate. "It's... intense." I flexed my fingers, feeling the unfamiliar strength coiling beneath my skin. "Each day, it's like I discover something new I can do—things I never thought possible."

"Like what?" Liz asked, her voice steady but her interest evident in the slight lean forward.

"Strength, for one," I began, remembering how I had effortlessly crushed a boulder that would have taken four men to move. "And I'm getting better at managing the bloodlust."

"Seriously?" Ian interjected, a hint of skepticism laced in his tone. I shot him a glance, choosing to ignore the undertone and focus on the positive progress.

"Sam says it's about mental discipline, connecting with that primal part without letting it take over," I explained. "It's not easy, but I feel like I'm finally starting to get a handle on it."

"Good," Liz nodded, her sharp features softening slightly. "We're going to need every advantage we can get."

"Speaking of advantages…" I trailed off, turning towards Lewis at the far end of the table when Ian's voice cut through the warm haze of the conversation like a shard of ice.

"Sounds to me like you need all that training and then some," he quipped, tearing into his piece of meat with unnecessary force. "Wouldn't want our fearless leader losing control and stabbing one of us, now would we?"

The table fell into an uncomfortable silence. A few uneasy glances darted my way, as if expecting me to bare fangs I didn't possess. Heat crept up my neck, and I clenched my jaw to keep my cool.

"Very funny, Ian," I said, my words laced with a forced calmness. The muscle in my cheek twitched, betraying my irritation.

"Can't help it, Luka. It's not every day you dine with a ticking time bomb." His smirk was infuriating, but I refused to give him the satisfaction of seeing me riled up.

"Tick tock," he added under his breath, eyes glinting with mischief.

"Enough, Ian," Liz interjected, her tone brokering no argument. Her disapproving look seemed to squash his amusement as effectively as a boot on an ant.

"Sorry," he muttered, not sounding sorry at all.

I drew in a deep breath, trying to dispel the sting of his words. My hands steadied, and I shifted my focus back to my friends, their faces a mix of concern and support.

"Give me a sec," I murmured as I stood and weaved my way towards the other end of the table, my boots scuffing against the stone floor. I reached Lewis's side just as he was about to shovel another spoonful of the gray mush we called dinner into his mouth.

Before meeting with Sam for my training, I had bumped into Lewis and took the opportunity to discreetly request any information he could find on a potential cure for the genesi code.

"Hey, Lewis," I leaned in, keeping my voice low. "Any luck with hacking back into Cain's data stream today?"

He paused, spoon midway to his lips, and his eyes darted around the room before settling back on me. "Oh, you know, the usual firewalls and encryption stuff. It's like hitting a brick wall with a toothpick." He chuckled nervously, setting the spoon down.

I studied him for a moment, noting the way his fingers tapped against the table, an erratic rhythm that didn't match his casual tone. "But did you find anything? Even a small lead could help us."

His gaze flickered away, focusing on something over my shoulder. "Nothing worth mentioning, Luka. Just more of

Cain's propaganda and empty threats. Same old, same old."

I leaned back, crossing my arms. The forced nonchalance in his voice set off alarm bells in my head. Lewis was too eager to dismiss the topic, too quick to smother it under a pretense of triviality. And if there was one thing I knew about Lewis, it was that no piece of information was ever 'nothing' to him.

"Right," I said slowly, letting the word hang between us. Sam had been unusually quiet since we parted ways after training. If he'd found something, something significant enough to keep from me, I had to know.

"Okay then," I continued, forcing a smile that felt as genuine as the food on our plates. "Just let me know if anything pops up. You know how these small things can sometimes lead to big revelations."

"Of course, Luka. You'll be the first to know." His reply came out too quickly, the words tripping over each other like clumsy dancers.

"Thanks, Lewis." I gave his shoulder a firm, reassuring squeeze, but my mind was already racing ahead. There was a secret here, buried beneath layers of deflections and half-truths. I needed to uncover it before it was too late—for all of us.

I moved back to my seat, the mess hall buzzed with the clinking of utensils and the low hum of voices—a symphony of normalcy in our anything-but-normal world.

Across from me, Liz was laughing at something Skai had said, but her eyes were sharp, too focused on Lewis, who now sat fiddling with his food. No doubt she had been watching my entire exchange with Lewis, her eyes missed nothing.

Harvey's gaze was also locked onto Lewis, unblinking and intense. The air around him seemed to tighten, like an

149

invisible noose drawing closed. Liz mirrored that scrutiny, her lips pressed into a thin line. It wasn't just me then; they all noticed Lewis' odd behaviour.

"Speaking of upcoming plans," I said, aiming for casual but feeling my heart thrum like a caged bird against my ribs, "Harvey, have you thought any more about accompanying Lewis, Ren, Ian, and Skai with the elders and kids to Camille's encampment? Before things get... messy here?"

It was a loaded question, one that hung heavy in the air between us. I watched Harvey's face for any sign of agreement, any indication that he'd take the safer route. But I knew Harvey—knew that his loyalty was as much a part of him as his steady heartbeat.

"Hasn't crossed my mind," he answered after a pause, his voice betraying none of the conflict I knew roiled beneath his calm exterior. "You know me, Luka—I'm not one to sit out when I could be making a difference."

"Of course," I nodded, trying to mask the surge of both admiration and fear that pulsed through me. This was Harvey, ever the protector. I knew he would stay to protect me and be my lifeline back to myself. Yet, the thought of him in the thick of war, where strategy met chaos, sent a shiver down my spine.

"Besides," Harvey continued, locking his eyes onto mine with an intensity that always seemed to read my thoughts, "I wouldn't be much of a friend if I left you to face the fire alone. You're not packing Ren off to safety either."

A hush fell over the table as heads turned subtly in our direction. They sensed the tension, an unspoken conflict playing out in the flickering shadows cast by the cavern's dim lights. Across the table, Ren's gaze met mine. His eyes, sharp and knowing, offered no judgment, only an unspoken acknowledgment of the bond we shared. A silent pact of solidarity.

The moment stretched between us, taut like a bowstring, before I broke away, my attention drawn back to Harvey.

"Ren is different," I tried to argue feebly, but even as the words left my mouth, I knew they rang hollow. We were all in this fight together, each of us with our own role to play.

Harvey simply smiled, that cautious optimism of his undiminished by the grim reality we faced. "We protect our own, Luka. That's what we do."

As dinner wrapped up and conversations ebbed into silence, I found myself alone with my thoughts. My friends dispersed, carrying their plates to the wash bins, their laughter and chatter a stark contrast to the turmoil inside me.

I needed to uncover whatever Sam was hiding from me. But how? Sam was careful, meticulous even in his deceit. I rose from the table, my movements automatic as my mind raced through possibilities. As I walked through the cavernous halls, echoes of my footsteps a lonely cadence, I made a silent vow. Whatever Sam was now keeping secret—whatever it took, whatever the cost, I would protect my friends, my family.

Chapter 19

Luka

I skulked through the dimly lit corridors, my steps silent against the cool stone floors.

"Ren?" I called out softly, pausing at the entrance to the quarters he shared with Lewis. The door creaked open under my touch, revealing Ren's tall, shadow-like figure hunched over a stack of ancient books and maps spread across a makeshift table. After dinner, Lewis headed off to the computer lab and I knew he would probably end up spending the entire night there, falling asleep at one of the desks.

"Hey, Luka," Ren greeted without looking up, his voice carrying that measured intensity that always made me listen a little closer. "Something on your mind?"

"Have you talked to Sam about the bio weapon?" I asked, crossing the room in three swift strides. I didn't bother with pleasantries; time was not a luxury we could afford.

Ren finally lifted his gaze, those piercing eyes locking onto mine. "Yeah, I did," he said, his tone serious. "He's agreed to shelve the idea for now."

A sigh escaped my lips, the tension in my shoulders easing ever so slightly. But we weren't out of the woods yet—far from it.

"And the soldiers in the cryogenic tanks?" I pressed on, needing to know more.

"We're working on it," Ren admitted, brushing a hand through his dark hair. "Sam's been digging into alternatives to investigate the cryo tanks without alerting Cain. The goal is to stop him from waking them without resorting to bloodshed."

"Good," I replied. "We can't become what we're fighting against."

"I know." Ren nodded, a rare flicker of agreement lighting up his features. "We find another way. There's always another way."

"Ren," I said, the urgency clear in my voice, "I need to know what's going on with the cure. Jon and Lina, they've clammed up completely. It's like Sam's ordered them to keep me in the dark."

His eyes narrowed slightly, the shadows casting a severe look across his face. "You think Sam's keeping secrets about your bloodwork?"

"Every time I ask for an update, they dodge the question. Even Lewis is acting weird." I paced the cold, stone floor, the echo of my boots bouncing off the walls. "It doesn't add up. Why involve me and then cut me out?"

"Perhaps he's trying to protect you from something," Ren offered, though the skepticism in his tone told me he wasn't convinced by his own suggestion.

"Or control the narrative," I countered, stopping to stand before him. My hands were balled into fists at my sides, a physical manifestation of my frustration. "Either way, it's not right. And now, with Jon and Lina preparing to leave with the next batch of non-combatants to Camille's encampment…"

"Time is running out," Ren finished for me, standing up. His body language spoke of decision, the set of his jaw telling me he was with me. "Let's go find Sam."

We moved together, my stride matching Ren's as we navigated the labyrinthine corridors. As we approached the throne room, the heavy wooden door loomed before us like a barrier to the answers I so desperately sought. Ren reached out and pushed it open without hesitation, his confidence bolstering my resolve. The room beyond was vast, the high ceilings lost in shadow, but it was Sam who commanded the space, standing tall and solitary before a table strewn with holographic maps and reports.

"Sam," Ren's voice cut through the silence like a scalpel, precise and probing. "Luka has concerns about the cure. She thinks you're keeping us in the dark."

I stood beside him, my arms folded across my chest to hide the tremor in my fingers. My eyes never left Sam's face, searching for any flicker of deceit.

"You think I'm keeping secrets?" Sam's tone was flat, his expression unyielding as he faced us. "There are no secrets here, only strategies that need to remain confidential for our safety."

"Strategies that involve my blood," I countered sharply. "And yet somehow, I'm excluded from knowing how it's being used?"

"Your blood is part of a larger plan," Sam said, his words measured. "But not everything can be shared openly—"

"Openly? Or at all?" The air in the room seemed to thicken

with tension, pressing against my skin.

"Sam," I pressed, my voice rising, "if there's something about this cure or those tests—"

"Nothing is being kept from you out of malice, Luka," he shot back, frustration edging into his voice. "I'm trying to protect—"

"Protect, or control?" The accusation slipped out, sharp and barbed. A mistake. Suddenly, a red haze crept into the edges of my vision, an ominous warning sign. It threatened to engulf me, to unleash the raw energy that I fought so hard to keep in check.

"Control yourself, Luka," Ren murmured, his presence a steady force at my side. But I didn't need his reminder; I knew the stakes.

Control it Luka.

I closed my eyes briefly.

Breathe in, breathe out. Breathe in, breathe out.

Slowly, the red receded, replaced by the stark reality of the throne room.

"Forgive me," I said, opening my eyes to meet Sam's concerned gaze. "That was uncalled for."

"Good work, Luka," Ren's voice was steady, a quiet affirmation that cut through the lingering tension.

I nodded, my pulse still racing from the effort it took to quell the storm inside me. Sam's scrutiny felt heavy, but his nod of approval came as an unexpected comfort.

"Looks like you're getting a handle on your bloodlust," Sam said, his blue eyes meeting mine with a hint of respect I hadn't seen before.

"Yeah. Now, enough with the pep talk," I said, brushing off the praise. "We need to focus on what really matters here.

What are you keeping from us, Sam?"

His jaw clenched, and for a moment, I thought he'd revert to his obstinate silence. But Ren stepped forward, his gaze locking onto Sam's.

"Sam, Cain's maneuvers are becoming more unpredictable, and Luka's part of this fight. She deserves to know everything," Ren stated, his voice carrying the weight of unspoken secrets between them.

Sam exhaled slowly, the internal battle clear in his eyes. Finally, he relented, turning his gaze to the cold stone floor before lifting it back up with a resigned sigh.

"Alright," he conceded, "We require test subjects for Jon and Lina's cure," said Sam. My mind raced, trying to decipher the implications of his words, but Ren spoke up before I could.

"You want to use the soldiers in cryo tanks, don't you?" he demanded.

Sam's expression twisted in pain; it was obvious he didn't want us to know about the fate he had planned for those sleeping soldiers. Ren and I had pleaded with Sam to find a more humane solution to prevent them from joining Cain's forces. Now it seemed that Sam's answer was to turn them into experimental animals for testing the cure.

"But that's not all," Sam murmured quietly, as if he couldn't hold back the full truth any longer.

"Cain has been working on a cure—a supposed 'cure' for our kind." His words hung in the air like a loaded weapon.

"Wait, Cain has a cure?" My voice sharpened with suspicion. "And you didn't think to tell me?"

"It's not that simple, Luka," Sam said, his tone edged with defensiveness. "I believe Cain's only making it seem like they're searching for a cure. He wants to unleash this war, let it ravage both sides, then play the savior with a too-late miracle."

"That's convenient," I spat out, anger flaring once more. "You're telling me you knew about this and said nothing? What, do you think I'll run at the first sign of trouble?"

"Luka…" Sam's voice held a warning, but I wasn't having any of it.

"No, I want to hear why you kept me in the dark!" I demanded, my hands balling into fists at my sides.

"Because I can't afford to take chances—not with you. I don't know if you might break under pressure, if you might be a flight risk," Sam admitted, finally saying the words aloud. "I'm not used to being this… open. It's hard to let people in when you've only ever relied on a trusted few."

His confession hit me harder than I expected. There was vulnerability there, beneath the layers of command and control, a flicker of doubt that even Sam Cain could not easily extinguish.

"Is this some twisted form of protection, then?" I asked, my anger cooling into something more akin to understanding. "Protecting your plans by isolating yourself?"

"Maybe," he muttered, almost to himself. "But now you know. And knowing is half the battle we're facing."

I locked eyes with him, seeing the fissures in the fortress he had built around himself.

"Fine," I said after a heavy silence. "Now that I know, we fight together. No more secrets, Sam. We can't afford them."

"Okay," Sam nodded, something like relief passing over his features. "No more secrets."

Nodding, I paced the length of the cold, stone floor, my boots echoing in the empty chamber as I grappled with the gravity of Cain's scheme. It was a devious ploy—a war to eradicate his own creation, only to emerge as the savior of the surviving few. He had forged a new strain of genesi, a weaponized generation designed to annihilate their predecessors and, in doing so, cull the population. His soldiers, shackled by mind control, wouldn't even remember the blood on their hands.

If we couldn't find a cure before all hell broke loose, I would have no choice but to face Cain's army. The thought of sacrificing those who didn't even know they were pawns made my stomach churn.

"Have you gotten through to Harvey yet?" Sam's voice cut through my silent turmoil, pulling me back to the present.

I stopped pacing and faced him. "No," I admitted, feeling the sting of failure. "He won't leave. He's as stubborn as the rest of us."

"Stubborn or loyal?" Sam's blue eyes narrowed, studying me.

"Both," I snapped, more sharply than I intended. Then, softer, "He doesn't want to abandon what we're fighting for, even if it costs him everything."

I caught Ren and Sam exchanging a look, their silent communication an unnerving reminder of how much went unsaid between us. "What are you two plotting now?" I demanded, crossing my arms.

Sam glanced at Ren before answering. "We're just making sure we're prepared for every possibility, Luka. That includes keeping our people safe—"

"Even if it means going against their wishes?" I interjected, knowing full well the lengths they would go to protect the cause.

"Especially then," Ren added, his voice steady but his gaze sharp. "Sometimes leadership means making the hard choices for the greater good."

I sighed, as much as I hated to admit it, they were right. We had to be ready for anything. And sometimes, that meant facing the prospect of losing more than just a battle.

Ren's hand found my shoulder, a firm grip that halted my restless pacing. "Luka," he said softly, the word barely more than a whisper in the dimly lit cavern, yet it sliced through my thoughts with the precision of a blade.

I turned to face him, his eyes holding mine with an intensity that always seemed to see right through me. "What is it, Ren?"

"When we leave for Camille's encampment," he began, his voice carrying the weight of unspoken promises, "I'll take Harvey."

I blinked, confusion momentarily muddling my thoughts. "You'll what?"

"Take him. By force if necessary," Ren clarified, his tone devoid of doubt. "It will keep him safe, and you won't have to bear the brunt of ruining your relationship with him."

His words settled like stones in my stomach. It was the solution I hadn't dared to consider, a sacrifice made on my behalf that I wasn't sure I could accept. "But our friendship—"

"Will endure," Ren cut in, his conviction unwavering. "Or it will crumble under the weight of what must be done. Either way, Luka, you cannot let your connection to Harvey endanger him or distract you from the fight ahead."

"Ren's right," Sam chimed in from where he stood, arms crossed, his posture as solid as the mountain that encased us. "Tough calls are part of this war. We all know that."

I knew they were right, each in their own merciless way.

Yet, the thought of Harvey, taken against his will, unaware of the looming threat, trusting us to the very end—it brought a tightness to my chest that I struggled to breathe through.

"Okay," I conceded, the word brittle. "Do what you must. But I don't have to like it."

"Nobody's asking you to," Ren replied, releasing my shoulder as he stepped back.

As they left, the silence of the throne room pressed in around me, punctuated only by the distant drip of water echoing through the caverns.

Harvey—sending him away was like severing a limb, yet I couldn't shake the terror that gripped me at the thought of him caught in the crossfire.

As I stood there in the quiet, surrounded by stone and shadow, my heart waged its own silent battle. The cost of keeping Harvey safe was etched in stark relief against the backdrop of my fears. It was a price paid in trust and friendship, a currency far more valuable than any weapon or strategy.

In this war, pawns were sacrificed without a second thought, but Harvey was no pawn. He was a king in his own right, and yet, I had to let him be taken off the board. The irony was not lost on me; in trying to protect him, I was betraying the very essence of our bond.

Chapter 20

Luka

I snapped awake, the chill of panic frosting my skin before I could even register why. There was a shadow in our quarters—another presence that hadn't been there when I had surrendered to sleep's heavy embrace. My hand instinctively reached for the knife under my pillow, but it relaxed when the figure stepped into the dim light.

"Troian?" My voice was a gravelly whisper, heart pounding against my ribs like it wanted out. "What's going on?"

"Sam sent me," she said, urgency lacing her tone. "You both need to get to the computer lab now. Cain's made his next move."

Any remnants of sleep evaporated. I nudged Harvey, who lay in his cot beside mine, still lost to the world. "Harvey, wake up. We've got trouble."

His eyes fluttered open, and he sat up with a start, instantly alert. "What is it?"

"Get dressed," I told him, already throwing off the covers and reaching for my combat gear. "Troian, talk. Now."

161

As I yanked on my boots, Troian paced, her words tumbling out with haste. "Cain bombed one of the genesi encampments. VIKI caught hovercraft activity on satellite—multiple units. They've confirmed at least one hit, but there could be more."

My hands moved deftly, strapping on thigh holsters and securing my weapons as her news sank in like bullets through armor. "We didn't think he knew where any of them were, exactly," I muttered, fury and fear tangling inside me.

"Neither did we," Troian said grimly. "But he does, and it changes everything."

"Damn it." The last clip snapped into place, and I stood, ready for battle but hating the necessity of it. My mind raced, trying to align this new reality with the plans we'd laid, the hope we'd nurtured.

"Let's go," I said, leading the way out with Harvey close behind. The weight of my gear was familiar, almost comforting, but my thoughts were chaos, whirling with the implications of Cain's attack.

How did he find them?

As we dashed toward the computer lab, I felt the sharp edge of responsibility cut through me. Lives had been lost tonight, and if we didn't act fast, there would be more blood on our hands. More than ever, I understood the enormity of what we were facing—a foe who was always two steps ahead, leaving us scrambling in his wake.

We sprinted, the soles of our boots slapping against the cold earth in a frenzied rhythm. Harvey's breath was hot on my neck as we raced towards the computer lab, our hearts pounding louder than the alarms that screeched through the hallways. Troian, with her lithe figure, darted ahead like a shadow flitting through the darkness.

Bursting into the lab, the scene before us struck like an icy blast. The room buzzed with urgency, illuminated by the glow of countless screens. Genesi worked feverishly, their fingers dancing over keys and their eyes wide with disbelief. Along the back wall, a tapestry of horror unfolded on the massive display—a mosaic of destruction and despair.

"Sam! Nate! Lars!" I called out, my voice barely rising above the chaos.

Sam turned, his blue eyes locking onto mine for a brief moment. His face, usually stoic, was etched with lines of concern. "Luka," he acknowledged, his voice low but carrying through the turmoil. "Harvey. Two encampments have been hit."

My gaze snapped to the screens. Billowing smoke obscured the sky in one frame, while another showed Genesi scrambling amidst rubble, their faces contorted with shock and pain. My chest tightened as I watched a small group helping one another from the debris, their bodies silhouetted against the flickering flames.

"Two?" Harvey echoed, the word hanging between us like a death sentence.

Sam nodded grimly, his jaw clenching. "Cain's hovercrafts came out of nowhere. They were precise, calculated."

I felt a surge of anger, hot and bitter. How many lives had been snuffed out in an instant? It wasn't just an attack—it was a message. Cain was showing us how vulnerable we really were.

"Show me," I demanded, stepping forward. My hand balled into a fist at my side. This was more than a battle; it was a war for our very existence.

As the screens flickered with images of destruction, my

mind reeled. I remembered when Sam had first told me about the genesi encampments – once teeming with life and hope, dozens in number. Now, reduced to thirteen scattered havens, hiding from Chancellor Cain's insatiable hunger for power. How could he have discovered their locations? We'd been so careful, believing our current camp was the only one he had a rough idea about.

"Sam, how is this possible?" Troian's voice cut through the hum of computers and hushed whispers like a blade. "How did Cain know where to strike? There must be a traitor among us."

I felt a chill creep up my spine at the thought. *A spy here?* The betrayal seemed as poisonous as the bombs themselves.

Sam's eyes, hard as stone, met mine before he addressed Troian. "VIKI detected the hovercrafts entering the airspace too late," he said, his voice tinged with frustration. "She sent out warnings, but there wasn't enough time."

"Damn it," I muttered under my breath, watching another screen as VIKI's interface attempted to reconnect with the far reaches of our network. If the AI system couldn't get through in time, what chance did we stand?

"VIKI's trying to reestablish her network across all en-campments," Sam continued, his gaze now fixed on a display showing lines of communication stuttering back to life. "We're blind without it."

My hands clenched into fists, useless against an enemy that could strike from the skies without warning. We needed more than hope; we needed a way to fight back. And fast.

"We've sent an alert. Every encampment is to go under-ground until they receive further instructions," Sam's voice was steady, but his hands, clenched at his sides, betrayed the tension coursing through him.

Underground.

My mind raced as I processed his words, images of my human friends flitting across my consciousness. They were counting on us to get them to Camille's—safety in numbers, we had said. But now, with Cain's eyes seemingly everywhere, what safety could we promise? I could almost feel the walls of our sanctuary closing in.

Think, Luka.

"Sam," I blurted out, my voice slicing through the unease that had blanketed the room. "What about creating our own forcefield? Lewis, Lars, Fox, and Stef—they dismantled Cain's during the cyber attack. Can't we use the same tech to protect our own people?"

His piercing blue gaze locked onto mine, a spark of something—hope, perhaps—flaring briefly. "That's not a bad idea, Luka." His voice had regained some of its usual command. "We need them here. Now."

"Someone find Lewis, Fox, and Stef, and get them to the lab pronto!" he barked at the nearest set of ears. Without hesitation, a figure darted out of the room, their mission clear.

I watched them go, my heart hammering with a mix of fear and fierce determination. This was it—the kind of solution that could tilt the scales back in our favor. Or plunge us deeper into chaos.

A shrill siren pierced the air, halting every conversation and causing my heart to skip. VIKI's voice, usually so calm and collected, carried an edge of urgency that left my veins ice cold.

"Alert: Incoming attack on Northern Encampment Theta. Warning has been issued, but time is insufficient for evacuation."

The room stilled, breaths held hostage by the unfolding nightmare on screen. My eyes were glued to the live feed, showcasing our brethren scrambling in vain as the ominous shadow of Cain's hovercrafts blotted out the sky above them.

"Brace for impact," came the soft murmur from Sam beside me, almost drowned by the whirling chaos onscreen.

The first explosion ripped through the encampment, a bloom of fire and debris that clawed its way into the sky. Screams, distant and digital yet harrowingly real, echoed through the lab. One by one, structures that had stood for centuries crumbled like sandcastles before the tide. I felt Harvey's hand squeeze mine—a lifeline in a sea of helplessness.

I can't watch this.

"VIKI," Sam growled, his usual stoicism cracking under the strain. "Casualty report. Now!"

"Processing," the AI responded. The screens flickered as she attempted to compile data amidst the destruction. "Preliminary estimates indicate... severe structural damage, casualties... high."

"Wait. Stop." The word was not loud, but it cut through the tumult with sharp precision. "Don't waste resources on the dead. Focus on saving the living. Can you track more incoming attacks?"

"Realigning satellite feeds. Prioritizing threat detection and forcefield feasibility analysis."

"Good. Keep us updated—every second counts."

Sam's orders were met with swift action, the team rallying around the command. The weight of leadership rested heavily on his broad shoulders, but he shouldered it with a grim resolve, his blue eyes fierce and unyielding.

"What should we do?" I asked Sam, noticing his eyes flick towards me as if he had just remembered Harvey and I were present in the room.

"There's nothing you can do, unless you happen to know how to create a forcefield," he replied with a hint of frustration. Of course, I didn't. In the aftermath of Cain's attack, I felt completely useless standing here, unable to help in any way.

Harvey's hand tightened around mine, pulling me away from the barrage of terrible images that flickered relentlessly on the screens. The room felt like a heartbeart that had gone erratic, every pulse a reminder of the chaos we'd just witnessed. I stumbled slightly as he led me through the maze of consoles and operators who were too engrossed in their desperate tasks to notice us leave.

"Come on," Harvey murmured, his voice barely audible over the hum of machinery and low murmurings of strategy and despair. We navigated through the corridor, his presence beside me both a comfort and a call to reality. The coolness of the walls brushed against my fingertips as we moved, a stark contrast to the heat that flushed my cheeks, the rage and sorrow brewing inside me.

Once outside the lab, the silence hit us like a wave receding after a storm. Harvey didn't let go of my hand. He didn't need to say anything; his grip said enough—it told me he understood the tangled mess of fear and fury in my gut. It was the same turmoil that shadowed his eyes, usually so sharp and calculating, now clouded with something dark and heavy.

We found ourselves at our usual spot, a secluded alcove with a view of the steel-grey sky through a narrow crack. We sank to the floor, backs against the cold stone, our breaths syncing in the quiet.

"Harvey..." I started, but words felt futile, meaningless in the face of what we had just seen.

"I know." He cut me off, nodding once as if confirming an unspoken truth. "I know."

We sat there, side by side, lost in our own thoughts yet bound by a shared grief. In the stillness, my mind replayed the scenes of destruction, the flames engulfing everything we held dear. Cain's ruthlessness wasn't new, but each attack chipped away at the hope I clung to so fiercely.

"Can we...?" I couldn't finish the sentence, but Harvey understood.

"Can we stop him?" He filled in the blank, turning to look at me. "We have to try, Luka. It's not just about survival anymore. It's about standing up for who we are, for our right to exist."

"Even if it feels like we're fighting shadows," I whispered, leaning my head against his shoulder. "Shadows armed with fire."

"Especially then," he said, his arm wrapping around me, pulling me close. "Because when you fight shadows, you become the light."

I closed my eyes, letting his words sink in.

"Let's rest," Harvey suggested softly. "Sam will send word if anything changes."

"Okay," I murmured, closing my eyes once more, allowing myself the luxury of leaning on someone else. For a moment, just a fleeting moment, I let go of the leader within and allowed myself to be just Luka—scared, tired, but never defeated.

Chapter 21

Luka

"Sam should have sent word of an update to us by now," Harvey whispered, his voice low but laced with an edge of frustration. He brushed his messy chestnut hair from his eyes, revealing that intense gaze that could cut through steel.

I nodded, trying to keep the worry from my face. "He will. He's probably just busy dealing with the aftermath of Cain's attack." My words were meant to reassure us both, but the silence that hung between them felt heavy, burdened with unspoken fears.

We sat in the dimness, our breaths slow and deliberate, trying not to think about what news might come. The quiet was almost suffocating, each moment stretching out endlessly, until it wasn't quiet at all. A sound—a soft shuffle—reached my ears, so faint I doubted anyone without Genesi hearing could detect it.

"Someone's coming," I said, straightening up and tilting my head to better catch the sound. Harvey tensed beside me, ready to spring into action if needed. But my pulse slowed when I recognized the rhythm of the steps; they belonged to Ren.

The shuffling grew louder, and then Ren's lean figure emerged from the darkness, his movements silent as a cat's. He paused, his piercing eyes finding mine in the gloom. "Sam figured you'd be here," he said, his voice carrying that characteristic intensity that always seemed to hint at deeper layers of thought.

"Ren, have you heard anything new about the attack?" I asked, my voice barely louder than a whisper. The urgency in my tone was palpable, even to my own ears.

Ren's face remained impassive, but his eyes betrayed a hint of concern. "Nothing since the last update," he admitted with a slow shake of his head. "We're still in the dark, still on lockdown."

I clenched my fists at my sides, fighting the surge of disappointment that threatened to overwhelm me. "Damn it," I muttered under my breath.

Suddenly, my ears picked up the sound of rapid footsteps echoing down the cavernous hallway. I held up a hand, signaling Ren and Harvey to be quiet. My heart raced as I tried to count the number of approaching footsteps—more than one person, less than a group.

"Who is it?" Harvey whispered, his eyes narrowing as he searched the shadows that clung to the walls.

"Wait for it…" I said, straining to listen.

The footsteps grew louder and more distinct until finally, the familiar faces of Ian and Skai burst into view, their expressions taut with worry and anger.

"Tell us what's going on, Luka!" Ian demanded, his voice echoing off the stone walls. "We deserve to know!"

Skai's brown eyes bore into mine, echoing Ian's demand without a single word. They wanted answers, needed them, just like the rest of us. But what could I tell them when I knew so little myself?

"Look," I began, trying to keep my voice steady, "we're all in the same boat here. As soon as Sam provides an update, we'll—"

"Will that be before or after we're all dead?" Skai cut in sharply, her frustration clear.

I met her gaze squarely, feeling the weight of our shared fear. "Before," I promised, though the certainty of that promise felt as hollow as the cavern around us.

I clenched my fists, the grit from the cavern floor embedding into my skin as I faced Ian and Skai. "Cain's forces—they bombed three of our encampments overnight," I said, the words heavy with the weight of lives lost. "They struck before we could even finish raising an alarm."

The flickering light from the nearby luminescent fungi cast eerie shadows across their faces, but nothing could hide the shock and grief that swept over them. My chest tightened; we'd been playing a dangerous game thinking we could stay hidden forever.

"Is there any plan for defense?" Skai's voice was low, almost a whisper.

"Lewis and some others are trying to put together a force-field," I admitted, hoping that our best team members could pull off a miracle. "If they succeed, it may just buy us the time we need to protect what remains."

"Time..." Ian echoed bitterly, pacing back and forth like a caged animal. He stopped abruptly, turning to face me with fire in his eyes. "And what about the non-fighters, Luka?

What if war reaches us before we're evacuated to Camille's safe haven?"

I met Ian's gaze, feeling the sting of his accusation. It was a question with no good answer, one I'd been asking myself in every quiet moment. But uncertainty was a luxury we couldn't afford—not now. I steadied my voice, infusing it with more confidence than I felt. "We're doing everything we can to avoid that scenario. But you know as well as I do, Ian, we might have to fight long before we thought we would."

His jaw clenched, eyes searching mine for something—reassurance, maybe, or a sign of a plan I hadn't yet shared. All I could offer him was a silent promise that I wouldn't give up, not while there was still breath in my lungs and hope in my heart.

Ian's demand hung in the air like a specter, its weight pressing down on us all. I swallowed hard, my mind racing for solutions that refused to materialize.

"Moving everyone now would be more dangerous than staying put," I said, forcing each word out as if they were shields against our shared dread. "Cain's eyes are everywhere. We can't risk it—not until Lewis manages that forcefield."

I watched frustration ripple across Ian's features, his hands balling into fists at his sides. I knew he was scared, we all were, but I couldn't let that fear cripple us. Not when every second counted, not when every decision could mean the difference between life and death.

In the hollow silence that followed, my thoughts churned with the direness of our situation. How could I smuggle my friends—my family—out of harm's way when every path was laced with danger? The caverns' walls seemed to close in around me, a tangible reminder of the suffocating responsibility resting on my shoulders.

I shifted my gaze to the uneven ground, a myriad of plans beginning to take shape only to dissolve into doubt. There had to be a way to keep them safe, to outmaneuver Cain's relentless pursuit. But the more I considered the options, the more each seemed like a thread fraying under the tension of impending war.

"Trust me," I whispered, more to myself than to Ian or Skai. "I'll find a way." But even as I spoke, I wasn't sure who I was trying to convince.

The cavern's meager light cast long shadows on the faces of my friends as I steadied my voice, determined to slice through the tension. "Look," I began, locking eyes with each person in turn—Ian, Skai, Ren, and lastly, Harvey. "I am going to make sure you're evacuated to safety. All of you." The words felt like stones in my mouth, heavy with the weight of promises I wasn't sure I could keep.

"What about you?" Skai's voice cut sharp and quick, but it was Harvey's reaction that snagged my attention.

"Me? Evacuated?" Harvey's tone was incredulous, his gaze boring into me with a mix of betrayal and resolve. "Luka, we've been over this. I'm staying—with you."

"Harvey, I—" I started, but he forged ahead, cutting me off.

"Look at me, Luka. You know I can handle myself out there. We fight better together." His chestnut hair fell into his face as he leaned forward, the intensity in his dark grey blue eyes imploring me to understand.

"Better together or not," I said, my voice rising despite my efforts to keep calm, "it doesn't change the fact that it's my job to protect you—"

"Your job?" His voice rose to match mine. "This is war, not

some task you can check off a list!"

"Enough," I snapped, frustration igniting within me. "This isn't up for debate, Harvey. You will go to safety with the others. That's final." The words came out colder than I intended, but panic had sharpened them, fear for his safety honing each syllable.

"No, I wont," he spat back, the words a verbal slap. He turned sharply, stalking several paces away before stopping short, his fists clenched at his sides. Silence stretched out, thick and suffocating, as the rest of the group exchanged wary glances.

I swallowed hard, feeling the sting of our disagreement. There was no room for argument—not when lives hung in the balance. "We'll figure this out," I murmured, more to myself than to anyone else. But even as I spoke, doubt whispered through the hollows of my mind, questioning if I could truly keep them safe from the storm that was brewing.

Harvey's retreating back was a silent testament to the fracture between us. I stood rooted, feeling every pair of eyes on me, but it was Ren who held my gaze.

There was no need for words, not with him. In the subtle dip of his chin, the faint narrowing of his dark gaze, I saw all I needed. He would stand by me, even if it meant dragging Harvey to safety against his will. The gravity of our silent pact settled in my stomach like a stone. I turned away, unable to bear the weight of Ren's silent promise just then.

***

Two days later, I found myself sitting alone on the cold stone floor of what used to be mine and Harvey's shared quarters.

He had taken his few belongings and moved them into a room with Lewis, forcing Ren to move into my room.

Lewis had worked miracles with the help of Lars, Fox and Stef, bending raw energy into a protective barrier around us all. For now, we were safe, insulated from Cain's wrath. But how long could a shield, no matter how strong, hold against the relentless tide of war?

I drew my knees up to my chest, resting my forehead against them. Harvey's absence was a stark reminder of the lines being drawn, decisions made in haste that would alter the course of our lives. I had promised to keep them safe, but at what cost? Would they forgive the orders given out of love, twisted by fear?

In the quiet, I let myself feel it all—the fear, the doubt, the weary ache of leadership. I mourned the distance growing between Harvey and me, the cost of decisions yet to come, and the uncertain fate of the world I was fighting to save.

Chapter 22

Luka

"Look at it, Luka. It's just a mountain," Sam said, his voice cutting through the thin, cold air like a knife. Today, Sam had promised a unique type of training that would push my abilities to their limits and challenge my self-control.

I followed his gaze, squinting against the blazing sun reflected off the icy peak that loomed above us. "It's not 'just' anything," I murmured, my breath visible in puffs of white. The mountain was a titan, its jagged silhouette a testament to the wild and untamed world we inhabited.

"Your genesi blood means you're more than capable," he insisted, piercing blue eyes locking onto mine with an intensity that made my heart race—a mix of anticipation and fear.

"Easy for you to say," I shot back, though the edge in my voice was betrayed by a flicker of doubt. My abilities as a genesi were undeniable, but they often felt like a distant theory rather than tangible strength I could rely on.

"Stop doubting yourself," Sam urged, his tone softening. "Remember who you are, Luka. You've got power coursing through your veins that others can only dream of. Use it."

His words stirred something within me, kindling a flame where uncertainty had cast a shadow. Still, the thought of scaling the sheer face before us seemed daunting.

"Come on," he said, breaking into my hesitation. "We'll do it together." He extended a hand, roughened from his life of survival, yet steady and sure.

I hesitated for a moment longer, then placed my hand in his. His grip was firm, and somehow, the simple act of intertwining our fingers provided a surge of confidence. "Together," I echoed, allowing the word to fortify my resolve.

Sam released my hand and led the way, finding footholds with an ease that spoke of his experience. I followed suit, the soles of my boots scraping against rock as we began our ascent. Each step upward was a small victory over the voice in my head that whispered of failure.

With each new height we reached, the world below stretched out like a vast, uncharted promise. And as we climbed, shoulder to shoulder, the mountain began to feel less like an adversary and more like an old friend challenging me to rise higher.

"Keep up," Sam called back with a grin, and I realized this was more than a physical journey—it was a climb towards understanding my true potential.

The mountain loomed above us, indifferent to my trepidation. I concentrated on the rhythm of my breath—inhale, exhale, step up. My muscles protested, a stark reminder of the chasm between my potential and reality.

"Come on, Luka, you've got this," Sam's voice broke through my thoughts. His confidence was infuriatingly solid, as if doubt was a concept he'd never entertained.

"Easy for you to say," I muttered under my breath, too low for him to hear. But with every inch we ascended, something began to shift inside me. My limbs moved with increasing assurance, matching the cadence of my heart that thumped loudly in my chest—a drumbeat spurring me onward. With a start, I realized that I was climbing not just a mountain but also the walls I'd built within myself.

"Scared of a little height?" Sam suddenly teased, glancing back at me with that challenging spark in his eyes. The corner of his mouth twitched upward, and I knew what was coming before he even said it. "Bet I can reach the top before you."

"Is that so?" I replied, the fire of competition igniting within me. I pushed off from my perch, my fingers finding purchase on cold stone. The world below seemed to fall away with each new foothold conquered.

"Try and keep up then!" I shouted, surprising both Sam and myself with the boldness of my challenge.

In response, Sam's laugh echoed off the rock face, a clear invitation to the race. He surged ahead with renewed vigor, and I followed suit. We climbed, higher and faster, our movements synchronized and as I climbed, the voice inside me grew quieter, overshadowed by the pounding of blood in my ears and the rush of adrenaline.

For a fleeting moment, I was more than a Genesi grappling with her destiny—I was a force of nature, scaling the impossible, proving to myself that I was as boundless as the sky that awaited us.

My fingers curled around the mountain's peak, a final ledge that gave way under my triumphant pull. With a heave of breath and strength I didn't know I possessed, I swung myself over the edge. Before me stretched an endless canvas of skies and earth—a view unmarred by the chaos below. My heart hammered against my ribs, not from exertion but sheer exhilaration.

I'd done it. I had beaten Sam to the top.

"Ha!" I panted, spinning around to find him just a few steps behind. "I win."

Sam hoisted himself up, a grin splitting his face. "You call that winning? I was merely enjoying the scenery."

"Sure you were," I laughed, rolling my eyes. "Admit it, I was faster."

"Maybe," he conceded with an exaggerated bow, "but who climbed with more style?"

"Style?" I scoffed, raising an eyebrow. "Since when did mountain climbing become a fashion show?"

"Since," Sam said, stepping closer with a mischievous glint in his eyes, "the moment we decided to scale this beast." Then, without warning, he reached out and shoved.

The ground disappeared beneath my feet, and I was falling— air whooshing past, ripping any semblance of laughter right out of my lungs. Panic flared bright and sharp within me as the world spun wildly around.

I screamed, a raw, primal sound torn from my throat as gravity claimed me. My arms flailed, seeking anything to halt the descent, but there was only empty air and the cruel rush of wind. Panic clawed at my insides, icy fingers wrapping around my heart, squeezing until I thought it might burst.

But then, almost as quickly as it had erupted, the terror began to subside. The chaos in my mind stilled, like the eye of a storm. I was a Genesi. Survival was etched into our very DNA. My thoughts sharpened, honed by the immediacy of danger, and I twisted mid-air, angling my body for the least impact. Instincts, long dormant, stirred to life within me.

Focus, Luka.

I quickly recalled every lesson I'd ever learned about falls. Bend your knees, roll with the impact, protect your head. As the ground rushed up to meet me, time seemed to slow, each detail imprinted on my memory—the jagged rocks to my left, the softer earth to my right.

With a last-second adjustment, I aimed for the softer ground, tucking into a roll just as I collided with the unforgiving earth. Pain exploded through me, lightning bolts shooting through my limbs, but it was distant, bearable. I came to a stop, a jumble of limbs and pounding heart, dirt caking my skin, breath heaving in my chest.

And then I lay there, sprawled on the ground, taking stock. It was a miracle—I was alive. Intact, even. A laugh bubbled up, tinged with hysteria and relief. I pushed myself to a sitting position, my body protesting with sharp stabs of pain, but nothing felt broken.

"Sam!" The name tore from me, a growl of anger mixed with disbelief. "What the hell was that?"

The betrayal stung more than the scrapes and bruises blossoming across my skin. Sam, the bastard, had pushed me from a mountain top. Genesi or not, it was insane. My hands fisted in the dirt, the grains embedding beneath my nails as I waited for his answer. The answer better be good, because right now, all I could think was how much I wanted to push him off a cliff and see how he liked the sudden flight.

Peering up through the haze of dust and disbelief, my eyes locked onto a figure silhouetted against the bright sky above. It was Sam, perched on the precipice from where I'd been cast down moments ago. He crouched low, then leaped with the grace of an apex predator, descending towards me in a freefall that seemed both reckless and precise.

He hit the ground with a thud that sent another cloud of dirt into the air, knees bent, one hand pressed to the soil—a superhero's landing if I'd ever seen one. The sheer audacity of it left me momentarily speechless.

"Sam!" I roared, finally finding my voice as he straightened up, brushing off the dust from his clothes. "You pushed me off a mountain!"

"Technically," Sam replied, his tone infuriatingly calm, "I nudged you."

"A nudge?" My voice escalated, incredulous and tinged with residual fear. "That was not a nudge!"

"Come on, Luka." He met my glare with those piercing blue eyes, a flicker of something unspoken passing between us. "You know I wouldn't do it if I thought you'd actually get hurt. You're a Genesi. Your reflexes, your instincts—they're beyond human. I knew you'd figure it out."

"Figuring it out doesn't mean it wasn't terrifying," I shot back, struggling to keep the tremor from my voice. "You can't just—"

"Can't test your limits?" Sam interrupted, stepping closer, his shadow falling over me. "Isn't that what we've been doing this whole time? Preparing for every possible scenario?"

"Preparation is one thing," I said, pushing myself to my feet, standing tall despite the ache in my bones. "But there's a line, Sam. You don't get to decide when and how I cross it."

"Maybe," he conceded, but the edge of a smirk tugged at his lips. "But you did it, didn't you? You survived."

"Surviving isn't enough. Not for me, not for any of us. And especially not when we're talking about the difference between life and death," I retorted, all too aware of the stakes that loomed over us like the mountain itself.

He nodded slowly, the playfulness fading from his expression as the weight of our reality settled back upon us. "We're in this together, Luka. All the way to the top, or all the way to the bottom."

"Fine," I said, meeting his gaze squarely. "But no more surprises, okay? We can't afford them."

"Very well," Sam said, and I could tell by the look in his eyes that this was a promise he intended to keep.

The dust settled around us, and I swiped a strand of hair out of my eyes. "We can't keep reacting, Sam. Cain's hit three of our encampments, and we're just… what? Waiting for our turn?" My voice cracked with the frustration that had been building inside me over the past few days.

Sam's jaw clenched, and he ran a hand through his close-cropped dark hair. "We've got to be strategic, Luka. This isn't just about survival anymore—it's about taking the fight to him."

"Then what's the plan?" I demanded, my hands balling into fists at my sides. "Because from where I'm standing, it feels like we're playing defense while Cain is out there, picking us off one by one. We're running out of time again."

Sam's blue eyes held mine, a storm brewing within them. "Remember the bio weapon I had developed?" he asked, his voice low and steady despite the chaos that surrounded us. "The one we hoped we'd never have to use?"

I nodded, apprehension creeping up my spine as I remembered the argument Sam and I had when he first suggested it to me. The very idea of the weapon—a silent killer designed to target only Cain's Genesi army—had always made me uneasy.

"We use it before they get here," Sam said, determination etched into every word. "We take out as many of Cain's forces as we can. Diminish their numbers so when the battle comes, it's on our terms."

"Sam…" The conflict was clear in my tone. The thought of unleashing such a weapon chilled me to the bone.

"Listen," he continued, stepping closer, the rugged lines of his face set in grim resolution. "It's not an easy choice. But this could give us the advantage we need. If we wait, if we hesitate, more of our people will suffer. We've already lost so many from the bombings, I can't lose any more of my people."

I looked away, the horizon stretching wide and desolate before us. Could we carry the weight of such a decision? Could I? Cain had no qualms about eradicating our people, and the thought of his soldiers sleeping in cryogenic tanks, ready to join his army, made my stomach churn.

"Okay," I finally said, my voice barely above a whisper. Sam's nod was almost imperceptible, but the resolve I saw in him bolstered my own.

We would face this together. Whatever came next, we wouldn't back down—not from Cain, not from the mountain, not from the future that awaited us.

The air turned cold as the sun dipped below the jagged horizon, throwing long shadows across the barren landscape. We had made our decision in the waning light, a decision that could alter the course of this war. As Sam walked away to prepare, I sat on the cold ground, my back against an outcropping of rock, feeling the weight of our impending action settle heavy on my shoulders.

Is it worth it? Or have I made a terrible mistake.

The bio weapon, filled with the potential to save or to

condemn, was now an undeniable reality. I closed my eyes, letting my mind race through the possibilities, the costs.

In my head, I saw the faces of those who had already fallen, I saw the Genesi encampments, the children oblivious to the shadow of Chancellor Cain's tyranny. The innocent lives caught in the crossfire of a battle they never asked to join.

The power to protect them lay within our grasp, but so did the power to become what we despised. To release the weapon would be to unleash death indiscriminately, to reduce humanity to mere targets. It would mean crossing a line that couldn't be uncrossed, dealing in absolutes just like Cain.

Sam believes it'll give us the upper hand.

But belief wasn't certainty, and there was no guarantee of victory even with diminished numbers. What if we won the war but lost ourselves in the process? Was the price of peace truly worth the soul of our rebellion?

Can I live with the consequences?

Could I bear the weight of lives taken by my command, even in the name of freedom? Would the reflection staring back at me tomorrow be one of a leader or a monster?

"Power comes with a cost," I recalled my father once saying in a moment of quiet reflection. "And sometimes," he'd continued, a pained look crossing his features, "the cost is part of your humanity."

With a shaky breath, I stood up, brushing the dirt from my clothes. Every choice carried its own burden, every action a ripple through the future. If we were to use the weapon, we'd have to carry its toll together, share the burden of a necessary evil.

Let it be for the greater good.

I knew the uncertainty would linger, the debate within

myself far from over. But in this desolate world, where shades of gray colored every corner of our existence, perhaps that was the best we could hope for—a chance to fight another day, even if the means tarnished the purity of our cause. And for now, at least, that was enough.

Chapter 23

Luka

I took a breath, the chill of the early morning air biting at my lungs as I quickened my pace toward the computer lab. Somewhere beyond the crumbling walls of our hideout, scouts had whispered through static-filled comms that Chancellor Cain's army was on the move.

Hours after Sam had pushed me off the mountain, his scouts informed us that the soldiers within the cryogenic tanks were being thawed out. Those soldiers quickly joined Cain's forces and now he was finally launching his attack against us.

The knowledge sat heavy in my chest; it was the kind of news that turned stomachs into knots and minds to racing chaos. But there was no time for fear now—Sam and I had set our plan in motion. Today, the bio weapon would be released.

The halls were mostly empty as my boots echoed against the worn floors, each step a steady drumbeat counting down the precious seconds we had left. The past few days had been a blur of scheming and sleepless nights, spent huddled over screens and vials with Sam and his team. We had poured over every detail, every variable, ensuring that once Cain's forces crept within our reach, the bio weapon would be ready to deploy.

The responsibility gnawed at my conscience, but the alternative, allowing Cain's iron grip to squeeze the life out of us all, was something I could not accept. Every test, every simulation had led to this moment, and there was no turning back.

As I approached the lab, I couldn't help but think of the others in the resistance who trusted me—trusted us—with their lives. They didn't know about the bio weapon, about the invisible line we were about to cross. This was the burden Sam and I carried together, a secret that twisted in my gut like a blade. But if it meant saving them, saving any chance of a future free from Cain's tyranny, then it was a burden I'd bear. It was what leaders did, wasn't it? Make the hard calls, even when they threatened to split your soul in two.

The hallways were empty, save for the echo of my own footsteps as I continued my way to the lab. Everyone had been ordered to report to the infirmary for a vaccine—mandatory protocol—that's what Sam had told them. No questions, no hesitations. It was for their safety, we had assured them, though the lie sat heavy on my tongue. They didn't need to know that it was a safeguard against our own weapon. They trusted me, and I exploited that trust, telling myself it was all in the name of survival.

I rounded a corner, the sound of my breaths amplified in the silence of the corridor. That's when I heard it—a faint shuffle, almost imperceptible, like a shadow flitting just out of view. I tensed, slowing my pace, listening.

There it was again—the soft scuff of rubber soles on stone,

the hushed exhale of a breath not quite in sync with my own. Someone was tailing me—and doing an excellent job at it.

I came to a halt, my hand inching toward my sai secured at my waist. The shuffling stopped too, a beat of silence hanging between us. Then, stepping from the shadows with a raised eyebrow and a posture devoid of threat, was Harvey.

"Going somewhere important?" he asked, his tone light but his eyes searching. I relaxed marginally, sliding my hand away from the weapon.

"Harvey," I breathed out, a mixture of relief and frustration. "You shouldn't sneak up on me like that."

"Sorry," he shrugged, but the casualness didn't reach his eyes. "I wanted to talk."

"Can it wait?" I asked, though I already knew the answer. With Harvey, it was always something significant. Something that couldn't be shelved for later. I knew what he wanted to ask.

"Is it true?" Harvey's words were a blunt instrument, striking with an unexpected force that had my mind reeling.

"Harvey, I—" The confession tangled on my tongue, knotted with fear and a desperate need for him to understand.

"Did you and Sam create a bio-weapon to use against Cain's forces?" His voice was steady, but the undercurrent of disbelief made my insides churn.

I hesitated, my heart thudding a chaotic rhythm. The truth lay between us, stark and unforgiving.

"Yes," I admitted finally, the word tasting like ash in my mouth. My brain scrambled for footing, skittering over thoughts of condemnation and conflict. Harvey's gaze felt like it could slice through all my defenses, laying bare the turmoil within me.

"Damn it, Luka." He ran a hand through his hair, a gesture of frustration I knew all too well. "You know we should be finding a cure for the Genesi, not plotting their annihilation."

"Harvey, please," my voice broke, pleading for him to see reason. "Cain's army is advancing. We don't have the luxury of time on our side. I bought us as much as I could and it still was not enough."

"Not enough time?" He scoffed, his eyes darkening. "And what about morality, Luka? Or does the end always justify the means for you?"

"Morality won't protect the innocent from being slaughtered!" I shot back, my hands balling into fists. The weight of lives at stake anchored every word. "We do this, or we die. It's that simple."

"Nothing about war is simple," he countered, his grimace etched deep. "Especially not when you're making decisions that can never be undone."

"Then tell me, Harvey! Tell me how we win this without becoming monsters ourselves!" My chest heaved, each breath a struggle as if the air itself had thickened with our argument.

"By remembering who we are, what we're fighting for." His conviction was a beacon, unwavering despite the storm raging between us.

"Sometimes, to protect who we are, we have to take actions that…" I faltered, unable to finish, the gravity of my plan pressing down on me.

"Actions that what, Luka?" Harvey's voice softened, but the challenge remained. "That betray our humanity?"

"Is it betrayal," I whispered, "if it saves our humanity in the end?"

He shook his head, the disappointment in his eyes a sharper

sting than any reprimand. "The *way* we win matters, Luka. It has to matter."

The chasm widened with our every word, and as I stood there, locked in a war of wills with Harvey, I knew that whatever the outcome, the cost would be etched upon my soul forever.

Harvey and I burst into the computer lab, our argument trailing behind us like a toxic cloud. The sterile hum of machinery filled the room, an eerie backdrop to our heated exchange.

"Using this weapon... it's unconscionable!" Harvey hissed, his face flushed with anger.

"Unconscionable? It's survival, Harvey," I shot back, my fists clenched at my sides. "Cain won't hesitate to wipe us out!"

"Survival doesn't justify—"

"Ah, the passionate debaters arrive," Sam interjected from behind a bank of blinking monitors, his voice cutting through the tension. He didn't look up, but the slight tilt of his head toward us indicated he'd been expecting our arrival, no doubt heard our entire argument.

"Sam, this is wrong, and you know it!" Harvey turned on him now, but Sam remained focused on his screens, typing furiously.

"Harvey—" I began, but it was too late.

"Save it, Luka." He cast me one last pained look before storming out, leaving silence in his wake.

I watched his retreating figure, my heart sinking. I wanted to call out, to mend the rift that had formed between us this past week, but the words wouldn't come. Instead, I stood there, hollowed by the weight of my choices.

"Give him time," Sam said quietly, finally turning to regard me with those piercing blue eyes. "He'll come around. He always does."

I sighed, leaning against a cold metal table, the chill seeping through my clothing. "You don't understand. This is different, Sam. We've crossed a line."

"Maybe," he acknowledged, rising to stand beside me. "But Harvey knows you, Luka. He trusts your heart, even if he can't agree with your methods right now."

"Trusts my heart?" I repeated, a small, bitter laugh escaping. "If only my heart knew what it was doing."

Sam's hand found my shoulder, squeezing gently. "You're doing what you believe is necessary for all of us. That takes courage. And yeah, it might leave scars, but Harvey... he sees the person behind the tough decisions. Your friendship is stronger than this war."

I closed my eyes, letting his words wash over me.

"Thanks, Sam," I murmured, drawing a deep breath as I pushed off from the table. "We should get to work. There's still so much to do."

"Always is," he replied, a trace of a smile touching his lips as we both returned to the task at hand, the ghost of Harvey's indignation lingering between us like a specter neither of us could quite shake.

***

I paced the length of the computer lab, my boots clicking against the cold floor. The relentless hum of machines filled the air, but my mind buzzed louder with thoughts of what we'd unleashed. My fingers itched to fiddle with something, anything, as I turned to Sam. "How effective has the bio weapon been?" My voice was steady, betraying none of the turmoil that gnawed at me.

Sam's eyes met mine, blue and piercing even in the dim light of the monitors. "It's working," he said, his words clipped as he pulled up a series of maps and charts on the screen. "Cain's forces have taken significant hits. We've infected about seventy percent of their front lines. They're disoriented, weakened."

"Numbers," I pressed. It was easier to think of them as numbers, not faces.

"Estimated two thousand neutralized," he responded without missing a beat. "It's bought us time, Luka. Maybe another forty-eight hours, if we're lucky."

"Forty-eight hours..." I echoed, the reality settling heavy like a stone in my stomach. It wasn't just a number—it was life or death for so many.

"And there's more you need to do," Sam added, tearing his gaze from the screen to fix it on me again. "It's time to send Harvey and the others to Camille's encampment. It's safer there, beyond the reach of Cain's retaliation. The last batch will be departing at dawn"

"Harvey won't go willingly," I said, the image of his storming out still vivid in my mind.

"Then you'll have to make him...or have Ren come good on his promise to you," Sam insisted, and I could hear the underlying urgency. "It's the only way to ensure their safety and to ensure Harvey as your lifeline remains out of Cain's grasp."

"Right." The word was hollow, tasting of ash and metal in my mouth. Making decisions for Harvey had never sat well with me, but then again, nothing about this war did.

"Camille's prepared to take them in," Sam continued, unaware of the silent battle within me. "She's reinforced her defenses since Cain's attack. They'll be okay, Luka."

"Okay," I repeated, nodding slowly. This was the cost, the toll of our choices—the will to live against the weight of souls. I steeled myself for the task ahead, knowing full well that each step forward was another thread frayed in the fabric of who we were before the world turned to rust and shadows.

I resumed my pace of the length of the lab, each step echoing like a drumbeat in my head. The screens flickered with data, charts mapping the spread of our weapon—a virus designed to work swiftly and silently. I ran my fingers through my hair, feeling the grit of dried sweat. Sam's voice was a dim murmur in the background, but the numbers he had recited clung to me like a second skin.

"Are we done here then?" My voice was almost foreign to my own ears, strained thin by the gravity of what we had unleashed.

"Mostly," he replied, his eyes downcast. "The initial spread is as expected, you don't have to stay and watch."

"I'll stay," I murmured. We had stopped an army, yes, but at what cost? Lives, too numerous to count, extinguished because we decided they were on the wrong side of this war.

I wish I'd had time to find another way.

I stopped my pacing and leaned heavily against a table, the cool metal offering no comfort. The silence pressed in around us, broken only by the distant hum of generators and the occasional shuffling of feet. I could feel the weight of every life lost bearing down on my shoulders, a burden I would carry long after the war ended—if it ever did.

"Hey." Sam's hand rested gently on my arm, pulling me back

from the edge. "You did what you had to do, Luka. We all did."

His words should have been a balm, but they stung like salt in a fresh wound.

What I had to do.

The phrase churned in my stomach, mingling with the bile of guilt and fear. This wasn't just about survival anymore; it was about the kind of person I was becoming—the kind of world we were shaping.

"Harvey won't understand," I murmured, the image of his pained expression haunting me. "He thinks there's always another way."

"Sometimes there isn't," Sam said, his voice steady but not unkind. "And sometimes the other way is a luxury we can't afford."

Can't afford. It just sounded like defeat.

Harvey believed in us, in a future where the Genesi weren't just a threat to be neutralized but people who needed help. And I had betrayed that belief, betrayed him.

"Listen, I'll handle the arrangements for Camille's encampment," Sam offered, giving my arm a reassuring squeeze. "You've done enough."

It would never feel like enough, not when the cost was etched into the very fabric of who we were. I nodded, granting permission I didn't have the strength to withhold. Harvey would go, even if it meant dragging him there myself. His safety was non-negotiable, even if it meant driving another wedge between us.

I walked out of the lab alone, the once familiar corridors now feeling like a labyrinth designed to trap me with my thoughts. Each step was a reminder of the lives taken and the friendship strained. As I made my way back to the heart of our resistance, to face the ones I had deceived for their own protection, I knew the taste of victory would be ash on my tongue.

This war had changed us all, some more than others. But one thing was certain: the blood spilled today, the souls extinguished by our hands, would forever stain my conscience. We might win this war, but part of me wondered if we hadn't already lost something far greater.

Chapter 24

Luka

Forty-eight hours. That's all we had left before Cain's forces descended upon us, their boots set to trample the fragile peace we'd carved out of chaos. Forty-eight precious hours ticking away like a heart beating against time. And I couldn't shake the image from my mind—the bio weapon, an invisible reaper, sweeping through their ranks with quiet devastation. Over half of them gone. Just... gone.

I trailed my fingers along the crumbling wall as I walked, the texture gritty and real beneath my touch. The weight of what I'd unleashed pressed down on me, heavy as the leaden sky above. Did survival always demand such a grim toll? Our enemy was ruthless, but they were human too. Faces I'd never seen, dreams I'd never know – extinguished because I gave the order. It was a choice made in desperation, the kind that leaves your soul feeling scraped raw. But it was either them or us, and I chose us without hesitation. Yet, every life snuffed out by that silent killer was a ghost in my shadow now, a whisper in the wind that sounded suspiciously like accusation.

I turned a corner, stepping over a tangle of metal that used to be something useful. Once. Harvey would be waiting by the makeshift loading docks, where the rest of our ragtag group had gathered. Ian's restless energy would be a stark contrast to Skai's calm, while Lewis probably tried to hide his anxiety behind a poorly timed joke. And Ren... well, Ren would just be ready, like he always was. Ready to leave, ready to fight, ready to make good on his promise.

"Luka," called a voice, grounding me back to now.

There he was—Harvey, leaning against a rusted truck with that look in his eyes, the one that said he knew exactly what was going on inside my head. He always did.

"Hey," I replied, forcing a smile that felt more like a grimace. "Everyone all set?"

"Yep," Harvey answered, pushing off from the truck. There was no mistaking the tension in his shoulders, though. The same tension mirrored in mine.

"Let's go say goodbye to the others then," I said, motioning towards the small convoy of vehicles that held our friends, my human connection to a world that once was. My steps faltered for just a moment. This was more than a farewell; it was releasing a part of myself, sending it off to safety when every instinct screamed to hold on tighter.

Harvey fell into step beside me, close enough for our arms to brush. "It's going to be okay, Luka," he murmured, so low I almost didn't catch it.

"Is it?" I couldn't help the edge in my voice. The future was a dark road, uncharted and full of perils, and we were sending our friends straight down it. But it was the only way to protect them from the warpath Cain was hellbent on carving through our lives.

The loading docks loomed ahead, it was time to face our

friends, to offer smiles that didn't reach our eyes, and to speak words of encouragement that tasted like ash on our tongues.

"Ready?" Harvey asked, his hand hovering near mine—a lifeline offered.

Ready as I'll ever be to break my own heart.

I took his outstretched hand, feeling relieved that there was an unspoken understanding between us as we said goodbye to our makeshift family.

"Let's do this," I murmured, steadying my breath. My heart drummed an erratic rhythm, each beat a reminder of what was at stake. Of what was coming.

"Hey, Luka," Lewis called out, his voice pulling me back to the present. His face was drawn, etched with the lines of too many late nights in the computer lab as he pulled me in for a hug.

"Take care, Lewis." My voice was steady, but the words felt hollow as I returned the embrace. "Keep your head down out there."

"I always do," he replied with a grin that didn't quite reach his eyes as he released me. Skai stood beside him and looped an arm through his, her expression solemn. I nodded to her, a silent promise that we were doing the right thing and would see each other again.

"I promise we will be okay, Luka. Just make sure to stay safe, alright?" she reassured me.

"I'll do my best," I replied quietly as she pulled me in for a hug.

Ian was next, standing apart with his arms crossed over his chest. We exchanged a terse nod—our version of understanding—and then my gaze slid past him, landing on Ren. His dark eyes met mine, and the world narrowed down to that silent exchange. Everything was said in that look; everything was understood. I needed a moment with Harvey before Ren fulfilled his grim promise.

"Harvey," I called softly, my voice betraying none of the turmoil within. My fingers twitched at my side, resisting the urge to reach for him, to hold on to the promise of a future that was slipping through our fingers like grains of sand.

"Give us just a second?" I asked the group, not waiting for a response as I stepped toward Harvey, whose presence was a beacon of calm in the chaos of my thoughts.

"Of course," Ren answered, his voice low—a thread of steel woven through velvet. He stepped back, granting me this final moment of pretense.

Harvey's eyes, a stormy mix of grey and blue, searched mine for answers. "Luka, I thought you were done trying to convince me to leave with them?" he asked, the lines of his forehead deepening.

"Ten years ago, you promised to stick by me after my father died," I began, my voice steady though my heart thundered against my ribs. "But now... Harvey, I'm releasing you from that promise."

"Releasing me? What do you mean?" His confusion was a tangible thing, a cloud darkening his features.

"Survival is about knowing when to hold on and when to let go," I said, my throat tightening. "And I care about you too much to not let go."

"But—"

Before he could protest, before I could falter, Ren's hand clamped over Harvey's mouth, a cloth pressed firm against his lips. Harvey's eyes widened in shock, betrayal flickering across his face before panic set in.

"Ren, what—mmph!" His muffled voice was a gut punch, but I forced myself to stay rooted to the spot as Harvey struggled, his arms flailing in an attempt to break free.

"Shhh," Ren whispered, almost tenderly, as if his gentle tone could soothe the treachery of his actions. Harvey's fight was fierce, born of desperation and a sense of being utterly betrayed by those he trusted most.

I wanted to cry out, to stop it all and cling to Harvey, to tell him everything would be okay. But lies were the luxury of the ignorant, and I had no such innocence left. My resolve wavered, tears pricking at the edges of my vision as I watched one of the few people I loved in this broken world succumb to the darkness I'd orchestrated.

"Forgive me Harvey," I whispered, the words meant only for me as Harvey's struggles slowed, his body going limp in Ren's unyielding grip. My sly grin and determined eyes were nowhere to be found, replaced with the raw anguish of a girl who'd just betrayed her anchor.

"Take care of him, Ren," I mouthed silently, the weight of power and responsibility crushing me more than any physical force ever could. As Harvey's consciousness slipped away, so did a piece of my soul.

Ren adjusted his hold on Harvey's unconscious form, the weight of his friend both physical and symbolic. With a sharp nod, he signaled to Ian, who was standing nearby with Skai, their faces etched with concern.

"Help me get him to the truck," Ren said, his voice steady yet soft, revealing the gravity of the situation.

Ian and Skai hurried over, taking Harvey from Ren's arms with careful efficiency. Together, they maneuvered his body towards one of the parked vehicles, their movements practiced and precise, a testament to the countless drills we had run in preparation for moments like these. I watched them go, each step they took with Harvey between them widening the chasm inside my chest.

"Once he wakes up," Ren's voice pulled me back from the edge of that abyss, "I'll explain why you did this." His eyes met mine, and in them, I saw the reflection of my own turmoil—a mirror to the storm within. "Because you love him."

There it was, the truth laid bare between us. My heart clenched at the acknowledgment, and suddenly the air felt too thick, too charged with unspoken words and the echo of what might have been.

"Thank you, Ren," I managed to say, the words feeling foreign as they left my lips. "For understanding... for everything."

He stepped closer, the distance closing until I could see the resolve etched into the lines of his face. "I'll take care of him, Luka. And the others. With my life." His vow was a sacred thing spoken in the quiet between heartbeats, a promise from the depths of who he was.

"Ren," I began, but my voice cracked, emotion threatening to spill over. He reached out, his hand brushing against mine in a fleeting touch that spoke volumes.

"Go," he urged gently, his gaze never leaving mine. "They need you to be strong now. We all do."

Swallowing hard, I nodded, knowing he was right. "Be safe," I whispered, my resolve solidifying once more into the armor I'd need for the coming war. Ren gave me a small, almost imperceptible nod, a silent farewell steeped in the promise of a future where we might meet again under different stars.

As he turned away to follow the others, I felt Liz's hand on my shoulder, her presence a reminder that we were not alone in this fight, that together we were stronger than the sum of our parts.

"Tomorrow, we face Cain," Liz said, her voice laced with determination. "And we'll be ready, Luka. For Harvey, for all of us."

I blinked back the sting of tears, clutching at the frayed edges of my resolve while watching Ren's back as he walked away from me. The air hung heavy around us, charged with the unspoken goodbyes and the weight of what lay ahead. My friends—my family—were leaving, and the void their absence would create already gnawed at me.

Ren stopped abruptly and turned around, taking a few steps back towards us.

"Ren!" Ian's voice sliced through the thick silence, sharp and impatient. "Quit dawdling, man. We don't have all day for your sappy farewells."

I shot Ian a glare that could have cut him down to size, but he just shrugged it off, his gaze fixed on the horizon. I understood his urgency; time was a predator here, always nipping at our heels, but his insensitivity grated against my raw emotions.

"Sorry," Ren said quietly, not even sparing Ian a glance. He turned back to me, his eyes somber. "Luka, I—" His voice carried the weight of a thousand unspoken words, each one laden with gratitude and sorrow.

"Ren, you don't have to—"

"I do." He cut me off gently. "You gave me something I thought was lost to me... a chance at freedom, at a life unchained by my father's shadow. For that, I owe you more than I can ever repay."

Our eyes locked, and in that moment, an understanding

passed between us that no words could fully capture.

"Just...keep yourself safe and I'll consider the debt repaid," I managed to say, my voice a mere whisper.

He turned then, striding towards the vehicles that would ferry them to safety, to Camille's encampment. But after a few steps, he paused and looked back over his shoulder. Our gazes collided once more, a silent exchange that sealed our commitment to each other and to the cause that had brought us together.

"See you soon," his eyes seemed to say, and mine answered in silent agreement.

See you soon.

I turned away before the dam of my emotions could burst.

The rumble of engines faded into the distance, leaving behind a silence that seemed to press against my eardrums. I stood motionless, watching the dust settle back onto the cracked earth.

"Hey," Liz's voice was soft, her hand landed gently on my shoulder once more, warm and reassuring. I didn't need to look at her to know her eyes were offering the same comfort.

"Tomorrow..." My voice cracked.

"Yeah," she said, squeezing my shoulder. "Tomorrow we face Cain's forces head-on. This... this is it, Luka."

I closed my eyes, inhaling deeply. The scent of metal and desperation seemed embedded in the air we breathed, a constant reminder of the war that had torn through our lives and the one that loomed on the horizon.

"Are we ready for this?" The question escaped me before I could cage it, betraying the flicker of doubt that danced in the pit of my stomach.

Liz's grip tightened. "We have to be," she stated firmly.

"You've gotten us this far. You'll lead us through whatever comes next."

"Lead us? Or send more of us away to stay safe?" The bitterness in my words surprised even me.

"Survival isn't a betrayal," Liz countered. I felt her move around to stand beside me, her presence a pillar of strength. "It's strategy, and it's necessary. It hurts, but it's the right call. Harvey will understand that, too."

I nodded, though the knot in my chest pulled tighter at the mention of his name. "It's just… what if it's not enough? What if all the sacrifices, the choices—"

"Then we fight harder." She cut me off. "We fight smarter. We are not our doubts, Luka. We're the resistance. Remember that."

"Tomorrow," I murmured, nodding once with determination. "Tomorrow, we go to war."

As the last rays of sunlight dipped below the horizon, casting long shadows across the desolate landscape, I watched the trucks speed into the distance.

"Come on," Liz said, breaking into my thoughts. "Let's get back to the others. There's work to be done before daybreak."

Chapter 25

Luka

Sam's words hit me like a wall of cold air, "Cain's forces will march within the hour."

His voice was as steady as the rock beneath our feet, but I caught the subtle tremor of fatigue that he couldn't quite mask. I glanced up from the holographic map we'd been poring over and saw the weight of impending battle etching deeper lines into his rugged face. Shadows clung to the hollows under his piercing blue eyes, a stark testament to sleepless nights spent in strategic preparation.

As Sam continued outlining last-minute adjustments, my mind momentarily wandered back to the quiet of my room just after dawn. A special suit had awaited me there, its fabric engineered for protection and flexibility—a second skin designed for a day that might be my last. With methodical precision, I had dressed myself, sliding each limb into the armored embrace of the suit. The twin sai, cool and familiar, found their place strapped against my thighs, an extension of my own resolve. The weight of them grounded me, a silent promise that I was ready for whatever lay ahead.

I shifted my attention back to Sam, pushing away the memory of solitude and steel. Now was the time for action, not reflection.

"We won't let Cain break us," I said, my voice carrying the edge of command I had hoped it would. "Not today."

Sam met my gaze, and I saw the flicker of admiration in his eyes before he masked it with his usual stoic expression. Sam's voice, roughened from tireless nights of planning, cut through the hushed murmur of the Genesi gathered at the base of the mountain. "Luka has words to share—words that will steel our resolve," he announced with a firm nod toward me.

My heart stuttered for an instant; no warning had been given of this speech I was apparently prepared to deliver. I swallowed back my surprise and annoyance, feeling the prickle of hundreds of anticipatory eyes upon me. The twin sai against my thighs seemed to pulse in time with my racing heartbeat as I searched within for the right words. This was not the moment to falter. These people, my people, needed hope—a beacon in the storm of war.

"Genesi," I began, forcing strength into my voice as I stepped forward. Sam's gaze never left me, his eyes reflecting a belief so deep it rooted me to the spot. "We stand on the precipice of change. A future where the war between humans and Genesi ends with us."

"Too long have we lived in shadows, feared for the power within us. But today, we fight not just for survival, but for harmony. For a world where we are not hunted or hated, but understood and accepted. Where the walls that divide us crumble under the weight of our unity." My own doubts wavered, the embers of conviction growing with each word.

"Today, we show Cain and his forces that our spirits cannot be broken. We are not anomalies of nature, but its evolution. And together, we will rise from the ashes of this war, not as conquerors, but as guardians of a new era."

A cheer erupted from the crowd, their faces alight with purpose. Their belief in me, in us, surged like electricity through my veins. I let their energy envelop me, allowing it to transform nervousness into the unshakeable will to lead.

"Arm yourselves with courage," I called out over the resounding echo of unity, "for today we reclaim our freedom and our future!"

With those final words, I turned, ready to meet whatever the day would bring, the rebellion's roar in my ears fueling the fire within. Now was the time for action. We were ready.

I turned to face the Genesi who'd followed me this far. "Remember," I said, scanning the sea of determined eyes, "stay hidden until the signal." They nodded, a silent ripple of affirmation.

With one last look, I headed for the mountain, my boots crunching over the rough terrain. The ascent was steep, but my body moved with precision. Reaching the summit, I found a secluded ledge and crouched low, waiting.

The minutes ticked by slowly as I watched the sun rise higher in the sky. I couldn't shake off the feeling of unease that settled in my stomach. This was it—the moment we'd been building towards for weeks. And yet, doubts and fears crept in, sending shivers down my spine.

I took a deep breath and pushed those thoughts away. Now was not the time for hesitation or second-guessing. We had planned every detail of this meticulously, and I trusted in our preparations.

The distant march of Cain's forces was like the drumbeat of an oncoming storm.

"Come closer," I whispered to the wind, my gaze locked on the horizon where dust clouds announced their approach.

As the troops drew near, I checked the detonator clutched in my hand, its cold metal a stark contrast to the warmth from the rising sun. Each explosive had been placed with painstaking care, every calculation double-checked. There could be no mistakes.

"Wait for it…" I muttered, anticipation coiling tight in my chest.

When they were within range, a grim smile tugged at my lips. This was it—the moment of reckoning. I pressed down hard on the trigger.

The first explosion erupted in a fiery bloom, ripping through the frontline of Cain's army. Successive blasts followed, each one a thunderous declaration of our resistance. But I knew we couldn't stop now. We had to keep going until we'd decimated every last shred of their forces. The ground shook violently beneath me, the force of our own weapons nearly as terrifying as the enemy's might.

The edge crumbled where I knelt, sending me sprawling toward oblivion. Instinct took over; I twisted midair, grappling for purchase. Fingers scrabbling against rock, I managed to arrest my fall, my breaths coming in ragged gasps.

"Damn that was close," I panted, adrenaline surging through my veins.

I hauled myself up, muscles protesting, and peered over the ledge. Smoke veiled the chaos below, but through it, I saw the gaps in their ranks—gaps that hadn't been there before. Our plan had worked; we'd weakened Cain's relentless tide.

Dust clouded the air, stinging my eyes as I continued squinting down at the battlefield. The aftermath of the explosions was a jagged landscape of fire and debris. Pockets of flame danced like vengeful spirits among the scattered remnants of Cain's forces. For a moment, I allowed myself to feel pride in the damage we had inflicted. Then the harsh reality set in—this was just the beginning.

"Regroup!" The shout rose from below, barely audible over the ringing in my ears. Cain's soldiers, those who had survived, were pulling together with a discipline that sent a thread of fear through me. My heart hammered against my ribs as they rallied, their movements swift and purposeful. They were like a hive, mindlessly bent on our destruction.

"Dammit," I breathed, watching them reform ranks with relentless efficiency. This was Cain's doing; his cold, tactical mind at work. He wouldn't let a few bombs break his stride. No, he'd use this. He'd make us pay for every inch of ground we'd thought we'd won.

I tasted bile at the back of my throat. Below, the Genesi began to clash with the advancing troops. The sound of metal and cries of combat surged upward, a cacophony of desperation and defiance.

It was time to move. My feet carried me back from the edge, gaining speed as I raced toward the descent. The mountain slope was steep, treacherous, but I knew these paths. Every rock, every turn was etched into my memory. My legs worked on instinct, propelling me forward, every step a silent vow to those risking everything below.

"Forgive me," I said to the wind, thinking of the friends I might be leading to their end. The words tumbled out, lost amidst the roar of the ongoing battle.

The edge approached, a sheer drop-off that promised a swift reunion with the earth. I didn't slow. Couldn't. My body coiled, ready, then I leapt. Air rushed past, a howling gale that tore at my suit and whipped my hair into a wild halo around my head.

For an instant, I was weightless, suspended in mid-air. Then gravity caught up and pulled me down with dizzying speed. I plummeted towards the ground below, my heart pounding in my chest. The adrenaline coursing through me was intoxicating, fueling my body as I prepared for impact.

I hit the ground with a thud, rolling to absorb the shock of the fall. Pain exploded through my side as it collided with a rock jutting out from the ground. But there was no time to dwell on it; I had to keep moving.

I scrambled to my feet and surveyed the battlefield below. The Genesi were holding their own against Cain's soldiers, but just barely. His forces seemed endless and their discipline unrivaled.

Ignoring the pain in my side, I sprinted towards them, dodging bullets and debris along the way.

They seemed to be everywhere at once - climbing over rocks, jumping out from behind trees - like ants swarming towards their prey.

I pushed forward, my heart pounding in my chest as I weaved through the chaos below. The Genesi were fighting with everything they had, but Cain's soldiers were relentless. They seemed to have an endless supply of reinforcements, and their discipline was unmatched.

Bullets whizzed past me, a constant reminder of the danger I was in. But I pushed on, determined to help turn the tide of this battle.

As I reached the frontline, I was met with a flurry of activity. I scanned the huddled forms of my comrades, as they surged forward with weapons drawn, faces twisted in an almost savage anticipation of the fight.

"Let's show Cain we're not going down without a fight!" I roared over the clamor, my voice echoing off the mountains that bore silent witness to our desperation. The rebel genesi responded with a feral cheer, their bloodlust palpable in the air.

The Genesi on both sides were like caged beasts finally set free, muscles tensed and eyes alight with the fire of impending battle. There was no turning back now. Sam, towering beside me, glanced at me with those piercing blue eyes full of unspoken words. He didn't need to say anything; we both knew what was at stake.

In a split second, he shoved me aside with one broad shoulder, a silent command for me to stay back. But this was no time for protective gestures. "Sam, I can—" My protest died on my lips as he charged ahead, taking on the brunt of an oncoming attack with the ferocity of a man possessed.

Around me, the world seemed to shrink down to nothing but the sound of clashing metal, the scent of sweat and fear, and the raw energy of Genesi pitted against Genesi. It was chaos, it was madness—it was revolt. And I was right in the heart of it.

Chapter 26

Luka

The chaos erupted around me like a storm, with the clash of metal and the hiss of energy blades cutting through the thick tension that had amassed before the onslaught. Screams rang out, not just in pain but in the primal exultation of battle, as Genesi rebels clashed with Cain's enhanced army.

"Push them back!" I yelled over the din, plunging headfirst into the fray, my ebony twin sai gleaming in the sporadic flashes of light from nearby blasts.

Everywhere I looked was a blur of movement—bodies twisting and turning in an intricate dance of death. A rebel would surge forward, driving their opponent back with desperate ferocity, only to be met by another of Cain's soldiers, relentless and unforgiving. It was a maelstrom of violence, a whirlwind I couldn't escape.

And then it happened—a coil of red beginning to slither into my vision, tingeing the world with the color of rage. Bloodlust clawed at my senses, whispering promises of power and domination if I surrendered to its embrace. My heart hammered against my ribcage, each beat a drum call to let go and lose myself in the frenzy.

No, I had to fight it. Sam... the rebels...they needed me.

Focus, Luka. Breathe.

With every breath, I pictured the faces of those I fought for, anchoring myself to them, using their memory as a shield against the creeping haze.

One of Cain's soldiers lunged at me, eyes wild and manic, but I sidestepped, letting his momentum carry him past before striking. He went down with a grunt, and I didn't pause to watch him fall—I couldn't afford to.

You can do this.

I urged myself forward as the red mist receded bit by bit, beaten back by sheer willpower and determination.

I threw myself back into the battle, my movements deliberate, carving through Cain's troops, one calculated strike after another. I fought not just to survive, but to protect—to preserve something far greater than myself.

This was our rebellion. This was our chance. And by the steel in my grip and the resolve in my heart, I would not let the bloodlust consume me. Not today.

The clang of metal and the cries of the fallen were a symphony of chaos, a testament to the desperation on both sides. As I parried and thrust, it became increasingly clear that our side—my Genesi rebels—were outmatched. Cain's forces were relentless, genetically enhanced soldiers who knew nothing but obedience and violence. They weren't just stronger; they were inexhaustible, tireless. My own breaths came in ragged gasps, and my muscles burned with exertion. Each time we took one of them down, two more seemed to take their place.

"Stand fast," I shouted, trying to rally the rebels, but the doubt was a growing pit in my stomach. We had thinned their numbers, yes, but not enough. The truth gnawed at me: we were losing ground. I could see it in the faltering steps of my comrades, hear it in their strained grunts. Even as I fought, part of me began to wonder if this battle was a lost cause.

That's when I saw her—Liz. She was dodging and weaving through the fray with agility that belied her human limitations. Yet, she was unmistakably vulnerable among the superhuman combatants. A Genesi soldier towered over her, his sneer visible even from my position. "You're nothing but a weak human," he growled, raising his weapon.

Something primal within me roared to life. "Not today," I hissed under my breath, launching myself toward them. Liz ducked, a hair's breadth from the descending blade. I intercepted the attacker, my arm snaking out to catch his wrist, and with a swift, calculated motion, I twisted and brought him down.

"Thanks," Liz panted, her eyes wide but fierce. "You've got a handle on that bloodlust thing, huh?"

"Better than most," I replied shortly, pushing down the fear that threatened to overwhelm me. Her acknowledgment was a small victory, and right now, I'd take every one I could get.

"Let's stick together," I said, nodding to her. "We're stronger as one."

"Always," she agreed, and we turned back to face the onslaught, side by side.

With Liz at my side, I waded deeper into the tumultuous tide of battle. The metallic tang of blood filled the air, and the cacophony of war cries fused into a single, monstrous roar.

My twin sai were extensions of my own will, cleaving through the chaos with lethal precision. One, two, three Genesi fell before me, their lifeless forms collapsing in heaps of defeat. I'd dwell on the lives taken after we survive this battle.

"Keep pushing!" I yelled, locking eyes with each rebel I passed, igniting the spark of resolve within them.

As I turned to engage another foe, I froze. A ghost from battles past materialized before me—General Thorn, whom I'd killed with my own hands. His piercing dark eyes locked onto mine, a sinister smile curling his lips as if he'd been expecting me. The air seemed to grow colder, the sounds of battle fading into the background as we stared each other down.

My heart hammered against my ribs, shock rooting me to the spot. Another attacker lunged, nearly catching me off guard. Instinct took over; I ducked and rolled, just narrowly escaping a fatal blow. Regaining my footing, I faced Thorn, my mind racing. *How could he stand there, so alive, when I had killed him?*

"Surprised, Luka?" Thorn's voice cut through the din, smooth and unfazed. "You look like you've seen a ghost."

"Impossible," I managed to spit out, gripping my sai until my knuckles whitened.

"Many things are impossible until they're not," he replied cryptically, his dark gaze never leaving mine.

The battlefield around us blurred into irrelevance. It was him and me once again, a dance of death renewed. Only this time, the stakes felt impossibly higher.

"Your efforts were commendable," Thorn taunted, circling me like a hawk eyeing its prey. "But slitting my throat was merely… an inconvenience." His smile widened, revealing a row of perfect teeth. "Thanks to you, Luka, my transformation is now complete. Cain's genesi code runs through my veins."

My grip on the sai tightened, the weight of his revelation sinking in. I'd been used as a pawn in their sick game of evolution. I lunged forward, aiming for his heart, but he deflected with a grace that was all too familiar. We clashed and parried, our weapons singing a deadly tune.

The sound of metal scraping against metal filled the air as Thorn and I engaged in a furious battle. He was faster and more skilled than before, his movements fluid and precise as he wielded a sword with expert proficiency. But I was determined to end this once and for all.

Our blades clashed, sparks flying in every direction. I could feel the force of each blow reverberating through my arms, but I pushed through the pain, fueled by my anger at being used as a tool.

Thorn taunted me as we fought, mocking my efforts and belittling my skills. But I refused to let his words get to me; instead, they only fueled my determination to defeat him.

We circled each other like predators, searching for an opening in the other's defense. And then it came – a split-second hesitation on Thorn's part – and I seized the opportunity.

I lunged forward, aiming for his heart, but he deflected with a grace that was all too familiar. We clashed and parried, our weapons singing a deadly tune. Sweat dripped from my brow as we continued to fight, neither willing to give an inch.

In the ebb and flow of our combat, a subtle change prickled at the edge of my senses. My hearing, always acute, picked up the faint whine of engines against the cacophony of war cries and clashing steel. Hovercrafts. Approaching fast.

"Expecting company?" I gritted out, dodging a vicious strike from Thorn.

"Wouldn't you like to know?" He chuckled darkly, his eyes glinting with a dangerous light. The sound grew louder, impossible to ignore. It was coming from above – the enemy's reinforcements, no doubt.

"Perhaps this will end sooner than we thought," Thorn sneered, his gaze flicking skyward. "Or maybe you can save them in time, Luka. The choice is yours."

A knot formed in my stomach. Those hovercrafts could decimate us in minutes, and here I was, locked in battle with a man who should've been dead. My friends, my family, the future of our rebellion—all hanging by a thread while death rained from above.

The engines' roar crescendoed, a harbinger of doom that threaded through the clanging of metal and screams of the dying. My heart thundered in my chest, each beat a drum of war that was quickly overshadowing the rhythm of my duel with Thorn.

"Your move, Luka," Thorn taunted, circling me like a hawk eyeing its prey. "End me or save them?"

His words sliced through the fog of battle, sharp and clear, laying bare the brutal choice before me. The weight of leadership bore down on my shoulders, the lives of countless innocents teetering on the edge of my next decision.

I feinted left and spun right, narrowly dodging Thorn's blade as it whistled past my ear. I could end him here, now, ensure he'd never rise again to threaten us. But the ominous drone above grew louder, more insistent, a death knell for my people if I failed to act.

"Damn you, Thorn," I spat, the taste of bile rising in my throat.

A flicker of satisfaction crossed his face before I turned on my heel and sprinted toward the mouth of the mountain. My lungs burned, each breath a searing gasp as I dodged combatants locked in their own dances of death.

"LUKA!" a voice called out—a warning lost in the chaos.

My legs pumped harder, hair coming lose from my braid and streaming behind me like a banner of defiance. I had to reach them, had to warn them. The mouth of the mountain loomed ahead, so close yet impossibly far as the first shadow of a hovercraft blotted out the sun.

"TAKE COVER!" I screamed, but my words were drowned by the deafening shriek of hovercraft engines unleashing their payload.

A brilliant flash of light eclipsed my vision, followed by an earth-shattering blast that rocked the very ground beneath my feet. Heat seared my skin, and a force like the wrath of the gods lifted me from the ground. Time slowed, the world turning silent as I flew backward, the sky and earth a blur of indistinguishable greys.

Then, darkness enveloped me, and I surrendered to its cold embrace.

Chapter 27

Luka

I blinked open my eyes to darkness, the cool dampness of an underground cavern pressing against my senses. For a moment, I just lay there, letting the gentle drip of water somewhere in the distance anchor me back to reality. My mind was groggy, fragmented memories from before I blacked out trying to piece together. Someone must've dragged me down here; it was the only explanation for why I wasn't lying dead on some battlefield.

My hand instinctively reached for my waist, but found nothing—my twin sai, gone. A sweep over my chest confirmed that my knives had vanished too. Panic fluttered in my chest, but I pushed it down. Weapons or not, I was alive. That was all that mattered—for now.

The uneven sound of footsteps echoed through the emptiness, and then Sam filled the entryway, his tall frame silhouetted against the faint light behind him. He looked like hell, dark bruises marring his skin and blood crusted over a split lip. But it was his eyes that caught me, the blue depths hollow, shadows of the battle we'd both survived.

"Sam," I croaked, my voice sounding foreign in the silence.

He approached, concern etching his brow deeper. "Luka, you're awake."

"Hardly by choice," I quipped, pushing myself up despite the room swaying around me. "The bombing?"

"Minimal losses," he said, though his voice was far from relieved. "Entrance to the mountains caved in, though."

"Is that supposed to be good news?" I tried to keep the edge from my words, but worry gnawed at me.

If the entrance was blocked...

"Could've been worse," he muttered, leaning against the cavern wall as if his own body could betray him any minute.

"Sam, the losses," I demanded, my fingers digging into the makeshift mattress beneath me. "Tell me."

He exhaled sharply, a shadow of pain flickering over his face. "Many on our side," he admitted, his gaze drifting away from mine. "Cain's troops... they pulled back too quickly to count."

I closed my eyes, the weight of guilt settling heavily on my chest. If only I had been there with them, maybe we could've prevented this tragedy. But instead, I'd been knocked unconscious and dragged to safety.

"It wasn't your fault," Sam whispered, as if he could read my thoughts.

I scoffed, pushing myself up into a sitting position. "How do you know?"

"Because I was there," he said gravely, meeting my gaze with unflinching honesty.

"Two days," he added, more softly now as if the words themselves were reluctant to leave him. "You've been out for two days, Luka. You were..." His voice trailed off, but the unspoken 'close to death' hung in the air like a specter.

A chill ran down my spine, not from the dampness of the cavern, but from what had almost come to pass. Two days lost to darkness while my people suffered and mourned without me.

"General Thorn," I began, my voice steadier than I felt. "He was there during the battle, he's... changed. He's Genesi." The word tasted bitter, a betrayal to everything we'd fought for. "I could have ended him, Sam. But I needed to warn everyone about the bombs."

"Thorn's alive?" Sam's response was hollow, his eyes clouding over. He shifted uncomfortably, his hands clenching then unclenching at his sides. There was something there, in that split second of hesitation—a secret lurking beneath the surface of his bruised skin.

"Sam," I pressed, narrowing my eyes as I tried to read the unreadable. "What aren't you telling me?"

His lips parted, but no sound came out. Instead, he offered a shake of his head, a silent promise or a plea. "Nothing, Luka. There's nothing." But those blue eyes, usually so clear and resolute, darted away from mine, betraying him.

"Alright then," I murmured, though it rang false between us—another casualty in a war already brimming with deceit and loss.

The cold stone beneath me offered no comfort as I shifted, the ache in my bones a testament to the days I'd lain here, unconscious and vulnerable. "Sam," I croaked, my throat parched and voice barely above a whisper, "after the entrance collapsed, what happened?"

He paced a short distance away, his silhouette a dark smudge against the flickering torchlight. "We dug out an exit," Sam said, turning towards me, his face shadowed by more than just the lack of light. "Helped the wounded, sorted the dead." He paused, a muscle twitching in his jaw. "There was a ceremony for those we lost. I'm sorry you weren't able to be there."

A pang of regret twisted in my gut, and guilt washed over me. They had looked to me for leadership, for hope, and I hadn't been there to mourn with them, to honor the fallen. "I should have been there," I murmured, sorrow heavy on my tongue.

"None of us chooses when we fall, Luka," he replied, his voice soft but firm. But his eyes wouldn't meet mine, and I couldn't shake the feeling that there was something he wasn't saying.

"Sam," I pressed, forcing strength into my limbs as I leaned forward, urgency sharpening my tone. "Why did Cain's forces retreat? It doesn't add up. The bombing—it feels like a diversion."

His blue eyes finally met mine, and there was a storm brewing in their depths. "Maybe they didn't want to risk getting trapped," he suggested, too quickly, too easily. My instincts screamed at me that it was more than that.

"Sam," I said, my voice steady despite the tumult inside me. "You're not telling me everything. What are you hiding?"

For an instant, his facade cracked, guilt flashing across his features so vividly that it might as well have been written in blazing letters across the cavern walls. "I'm not—" His protest died on his lips, and he turned his head away, shoulders tense. "I swear, Luka. There's nothing."

But the atmosphere between us had shifted, charged now with unspoken truths and concealed fears. I knew Sam—knew the weight of secrecy he carried—and this one was heavy, pressing down on him, pushing him away from me. Whatever it was, it threatened to fracture the fragile trust that held our alliance together.

"Okay, Sam," I said, letting the word stretch out, laden with skepticism. And as I watched him wrestle with his conscience, I knew I had to brace myself for the next wave of betrayal that was sure to come crashing down upon us all.

Sam eventually relented, his shoulders sagging with the weight of his confession. "They have a new weapon," he said, his voice barely above a whisper.

My heart dropped into my stomach, dread pooling in its wake. "What kind of weapon?" I asked, my tone flat and emotionless.

"A virus, different to the one we created...one our vaccine is useless against," Sam answered, his eyes now pleading for understanding. "It's biological warfare. The bomb that destroyed the entrance was just the beginning."

I couldn't believe what I was hearing but as I looked into Sam's tormented expression, I knew he wasn't lying.

"They released it in our camp," Sam continued, his voice trembling with anger and grief. "Most of our people are infected."

I felt sick to my stomach at the thought of so many innocent lives being lost to this heinous act. "What about us?" I asked, already fearing the answer.

"We were lucky," Sam replied grimly. "We were outside when they dropped the bomb. But I also suspect that Cain developed this bio weapon to ensure that you and I would be spared."

"He has a purpose for us," I said.

"Yeah," was his simple response.

I nodded, my mind reeling with shock and fear. We had to warn the other camps about this new threat before it was too late. But first, we needed to make sure everyone in our camp was safe.

"Sam," I interjected, the urgency clear in my hoarse voice, "Liz—is she alright?"

He paused his pacing by the cavern's entrance, the dim light casting shadows across his bruised face. "She's safe, Luka," he reassured me, a tired smile creasing his features. "I'll send for her. She'll want to be here with you now that you're finally awake."

A sigh of relief escaped my lips, and I sank back into the makeshift bed. The rough blanket scratched against my skin, but it was a comforting reminder that I was still alive, still fighting.

As the hours stretched into another day, Sam's promise was kept. Liz arrived, her presence like a balm to the raw edges of my spirit. We sat together in the hushed space of the underground hideaway, our conversation ebbing and flowing with the tide of memories.

"Too many gone," she whispered at one point, her eyes glistening with unshed tears.

"I know," I agreed, feeling the weight of their absence. Our shared grief was a silent pact, an acknowledgment of the price we had paid for this fragile hope of freedom.

In the quiet moments, my mind wandered to Harvey and those who had ventured out towards Camille's encampment. Had they made it? Were they safe? I clutched at the thin blanket, willing my thoughts to reach them across the distance.

"Harvey will be okay," Liz said softly, as if reading my fears.

"He always is."

Her words were meant to comfort, but they felt hollow without confirmation. The uncertainty gnawed at me, an insidious whisper that threatened to unravel the threads of resolve I clung to so desperately.

"Let's just focus on getting you better," Liz insisted gently, squeezing my hand. "We need you, Luka. Now more than ever."

***

The sound of footsteps pounding against the earth jolted me from my shallow slumber. My eyes snapped open to the dim light of the cavern, heart hammering in my chest. I pushed myself upright, ignoring the sharp protest of my muscles and the spinning room. "What's happening?" I gasped out.

"Easy, Luka," Liz cautioned, her hands firm on my shoulders as she tried to ease me back onto the makeshift bed.

But Sam was there, at the mouth of the cavern, his face a mask of panic. He looked like he had run through hell and back, breaths ragged, clothes clinging to sweat-slicked skin. Something about his expression set off alarms in my head, a surge of adrenaline that numbed the pain.

"Sam!" I called, my voice cracking with urgency. I swung my legs over the side, every fiber of my being screaming to stand, to fight, to do something. But as I put weight on my feet, the world tilted dangerously, and pain lanced through me, threatening to pull me under once more.

"Whoa there, warrior," Liz murmured, catching me before

I could crumple. Her arms were steady, but I could feel the tremble beneath her calm exterior.

"Tell me," I demanded, breathless, as Liz guided me back to a seated position. "What's wrong?"

Sam dragged a hand down his face, looking momentarily lost before his training seemed to kick in. "It's the convoy," he said, and his voice was a low rumble of contained distress. "We just got word—they didn't all make it to Camille's encampment."

My blood ran cold. The convoy was supposed to be at Camille's encampment by now. We sent them there to keep the non-fighters safe from the battle. "My friends? Are they safe?" My words came out in a rush, the protective instincts that drove me clashing with the stark fear for their welfare.

"Everyone's accounted for…" Sam's hesitation was a tangible thing, hanging heavy in the silence that followed.

"Except for Harvey." His next words landed like a blow, knocking the breath from my lungs.

"Harvey?" My voice broke on his name, my mind reeling. Harvey, with his wry smile, now in Cain's clutches. A thousand scenarios played out in rapid succession, each more horrifying than the last.

"Captured," Sam confirmed, his eyes dark with sorrow. "I'm so sorry, Luka."

"Captured," I repeated numbly, my thoughts spiraling into chaos. I needed to be out there, searching, fighting—anything but this helpless waiting.

"Listen to me," Liz said sharply, her grip tightening as if she could hold me together through sheer will. "You're no good to him or anyone else like this. We'll get him back, but right now, you need to heal."

Her words were a lifeline in the tumultuous sea of my emotions. I nodded, forcing myself to meet Sam's gaze, finding an echo of my own guilt there. I'd sent Harvey away to keep him safe and instead I'd practically handed him over to Cain.

"We'll get him back, Luka," Sam murmured, "I promise."

Chapter 28

Sam

"Tell me everything, Nate. Now." My voice was sharper than a shard of broken glass, and it cut through the tension hanging between us. I leaned across the makeshift table in the dimly lit room that served as our command center, my eyes locking onto his with a desperate urgency.

Nate shifted uncomfortably, the light from the single flickering torch casting deep shadows across his bald head. "Sam, it's not that simple—"

"Start at the beginning," I interrupted, my tone brooking no argument.

I had sent him to lead the convoy, to keep them safe. The weight of their safety pressed down on me like a physical force, a responsibility that I couldn't shake off. When Nate had stumbled back into camp two days after the battle, panic had clawed up my throat. His return signaled one thing: disaster.

As he opened his mouth to recount what had happened, my mind churned with thoughts of Luka. She'd been pacing like a caged animal ever since we'd received the news of Harvey's capture, her guilt an almost tangible entity that filled every corner of the room. It gnawed at me too, the knowledge that my reassurance had pushed her to send Harvey away, straight into Cain's waiting hands. Her face, usually so composed, was now etched with self-reproach, as if she could carve out her mistakes with enough regret.

"Sam, we were ambushed," Nate finally began, dragging me from my thoughts. "We thought we were taking every precaution, but..." His voice trailed off, and the haunted look in his eyes spoke volumes about the horrors they must have faced.

"Listen," Nate's voice cut through the fog of my conflicted thoughts. "The journey was going smooth until we hit the halfway mark. That's when Lewis' encrypted comm system just crashed—dead silence."

I leaned forward, bracing my elbows on my knees, trying to focus on his words rather than the sinking feeling in my gut.

Nate ran a hand over his head, frustration etched across his features. "We knew something was up. So we stopped, tried to figure out what happened. It was like walking into a void where sound used to be."

"Then Ian," he continued, shaking his head with a mixture of anger and disbelief, "decided it'd be smart to investigate outside. I could see it in his eyes, that reckless curiosity. Took me two seconds to realize—it was a trap."

"Did you follow him?" I asked, knowing full well Ian's impulsiveness often led to trouble.

"Of course, I did," Nate admitted. "Couldn't let him walk into it alone. But by the time I stepped out..."

He paused, the memory clearly paining him. His expressive eyes darkened as they met mine, conveying the gravity before his words did.

"Those bloody hovercrafts, Sam. They swarmed us outta nowhere." His hands clenched into fists. "Our other vehicles… gone. It's like they vanished into thin air, and there we were, sitting ducks in the middle of nowhere."

I felt the chill of fear, imagining the scene—a convoy torn apart, friends separated and vulnerable.

"And then?" My voice was barely a whisper, anticipating the worst.

"Then," Nate's voice hardened, "Cain's voice came on, not even in person—the coward. A damn recording demanding Harvey, saying if we didn't deliver, the others would be taken out."

My heart pounded against my ribcage; Cain's manipulations knew no bounds. The power play, the sheer audacity of it…

"Harvey…" The name stuck in my throat. "You handed him over? Why the hell would you give them Harvey?" I snarled, barely containing the rage that was boiling inside me. My fists clenched at my sides as I stared down Nate, waiting for an answer that could somehow make sense of this madness.

"Sam, we didn't just hand him over," Nate shot back, his voice steady, his eyes unwavering in their defense. "We were ready to fight, to go down with everything we had. But Harvey… he chose differently." Nate's tone softened, a somber respect threading through his words. "He stepped up, man—decided to play the hero."

A hero. The word echoed mockingly in my skull. I turned away from Nate, unable to look at him, feeling the weight of guilt pressing down on me. It was a stupid move—I knew it even as I gave the order. Camille's encampment was supposed to be a haven, but I should've seen this coming. I should have predicted that Cain, my own father, would be two steps ahead, waiting for the perfect moment to strike.

As I paced the room, my mind spun with the repercussions of my choices. Luka trusted my judgment, believed in my plans, and now Harvey, her Harvey, was in Cain's clutches. A pawn in a game where the stakes were life and death. And all because I convinced her to send him to safety—which turned out to be anything but.

I gritted my teeth, forcing back the bitter taste of regret. Cain always played dirty, used people's emotions against them like weapons. And in sending Harvey, I'd handed him a loaded gun. If there was one thing I knew about my father, it was that he thrived on control, on wielding power over others. Using Harvey against Luka would be just the kind of twisted move he'd revel in.

I paused, staring at the ground. Every muscle in my body tensed, every scar a reminder of past battles, of losses and hard-won victories. This war was personal, and I had just escalated it beyond measure.

I stopped pacing, fixing my gaze on Nate. "And what happened after that? After they'd cornered you?" I needed to know how it all fell apart.

Nate ran a hand over his head, the gesture oddly calming despite the chaos swirling around us. "Lewis and I were huddled over the comm system, trying to get a signal back," he said, frustration lacing his tone. "We were so focused on reestablishing contact with the other vehicles—thinking if we could just alert them, create some kind of diversion, we wouldn't have to give up Harvey."

"But?" I prodded, knowing there was more he wasn't saying.

"Harvey didn't wait for us to fix the problem." Nate's eyes, usually dancing with mischief, held a somberness I rarely saw. "He just... walked out there. Told them he was Harvey Montgomery and to let the rest of us go."

A cold knot formed in my stomach. "Nobody tried to stop him?"

"We tried, Sam, we did. But by the time we realized what he was doing, it was too late." Nate's voice was tight with guilt. "He made his choice before we could even think of stopping him."

Before I could respond, a voice cut through the heavy air, sharp as a blade. "And what did you do once they took him?" Troian's haughty tone had me snapping my head towards the door frame she'd just materialized at.

Her presence was like a shockwave through the room— imposing, even with her injuries. She leaned against the door frame, arms crossed, a bandage peeking out from under her sleeve where fabric met skin.

"Troian," I acknowledged, surprised. "You should be resting."

Her laugh was devoid of humor. "Resting is for the dead, or have you forgotten that?"

"Answer the question, Nate," she pressed, eyes boring into him. "What did you do once our leverage was taken right out from under our noses?" Her words stung, venomous yet not entirely undeserving.

I watched Nate's jaw clench, the playful spark in his eyes replaced by the hard glint of determination. "We regrouped," he said simply. "Made sure everyone else was safe, then started planning the next move."

"Which was?" Troian's eyebrow arched with challenge, demanding accountability.

"Coming back here," Nate met her gaze without flinching. "To figure out how to get Harvey back."

"Even though you knew the risks?" I asked, my voice low.

"Especially because we knew the risks." Nate's affirmation was unyielding. "Harvey would've done the same for any of us."

The unspoken truth hung heavy between us—the knowledge that loyalty was both our greatest strength and our most exploitable weakness. It bound us together, but in the hands of someone like Cain, it could tear us apart.

"Once communication was lost, we were blind," Nate's voice cut through the tension like a blade. "We waited for any sign from the other vehicles. Hours later, their static-filled messages finally broke through. I told them to press on to Camille's encampment without us."

This clarified the reason for the Comm I had received from Camille, stating that everyone was accounted for except for Harvey.

The room felt smaller as he spoke, the walls pressing in with the weight of his decision. I pictured the convoy snaking through the ruins, vulnerable and exposed.

"Ren, Ian, Skai, Lewis, and I—we turned back." His tone was matter-of-fact, but his eyes held the gravity of their choice. "Harvey's capture...it changed everything. Luka would need all hands on deck."

"So, you came back here?" I murmured, piecing together their harrowing journey through the treacherous mountain paths, retracing steps soaked in uncertainty and fear.

"Yeah," he confirmed, nodding.

"Idiot!" The sharp snort came from Troian, her disdain slicing through the air. "You ignored Sam's orders. You were supposed to keep them all safe." Her posture was rigid, challenging.

I watched the two of them, the undercurrent of their mutual animosity palpable. They had always been like oil and water, forced to coexist in the tight container of command.

Troian's fierce protectiveness over Skai wasn't a secret—to anyone but Skai herself, perhaps. It added a layer of personal stake to her reproach; her snappish exterior barely concealing the tremor of fear beneath. She must have been out of her mind with worry that Nate made the call to return, and Skai had followed. For a moment, my heart went out to her. But there was no time for sentiment—not now.

"Enough," I said sharply, my voice low but carrying the weight of authority. "This isn't about orders or insubordination. We've got bigger problems than your squabbles." My gaze flicked between them, hoping to quell the brewing storm.

"Harvey is out there, with Cain *and* Thorn," I continued, each word heavy with the dread of what lay ahead. "And we're going to get him back. Together."

I shifted my stance, the sudden urge to pace wrestling with the need to stand my ground. Nate's eyes met mine, a silent plea for understanding shimmering in their depths.

"Sam, I had to bring us back," Nate began, his voice steady despite Troian's piercing glare. "The moment we lost Harvey, the mission changed. Luka needs every hand on deck to mount a rescue. You *know* that."

Troian's lips curled into a sneer, her arms folded across her chest like a shield. "Rules are rules, Sam. If we start breaking them whenever it feels right, what's stopping all hell from breaking loose?"

Her words stung like acid; she was right, in a way. But this was different. This was Harvey—our friend, our ally. And beyond that, it was a move against Cain, my father, a man whose shadow loomed over us all like an ever-present threat.

"Troian," I said, my tone brokering no argument, "punishing Nate won't bring Harvey back. It won't change what's happened."

"Then what will?" she shot back, defiance sparking in her eyes.

"Action," I replied simply. "And for that, I need Nate."

She stiffened at my words, her gaze darting between Nate and me as if searching for a crack in our resolve. "You're going to need more than just him, Sam. You're planning to go after Harvey yourself, aren't you?"

The room grew heavy with the unsaid. Yes, I was going after Harvey. Yes, I might not return. Facing my father was a confrontation I'd spent ten years of my life avoiding and now, there was no running from it.

"Troian," I started again, softer this time, "you know as well as I do that this isn't about disobedience. It's about survival. It's about fighting for our own, for our future."

She held my gaze, the fire in her eyes flickering with uncertainty. "And what about the Genesi? Who leads them if you don't come back?"

"The Genesi will have you," I declared, the weight of the mantle I was passing to her settling between us. "As my second, you've got the strength, the command. They'll follow you, Troian. Make sure they're safe when we return."

"Return?" Her voice cracked slightly, betraying the steel of her exterior.

"Or not," I admitted, facing the grim possibility head-on. "If I die out there, if I face Cain and fall… it will be knowing that

I did it to protect our people. To protect our hope of a future where we're not hiding or living in fear of the next attack."

A silence hung in the air, and I could see the conflict raging within her, the desire to fight beside those she cared for most against the duty I was bestowing upon her.

"Very well," she finally conceded, her voice barely above a whisper. "But you better bring him back, Sam. And yourself."

"Plan on it," I murmured, though the hollowness in my chest echoed with doubts.

Chapter 29

Luka

I huddled in the corner of the dimly lit room, knees drawn up to my chest, the chill of the stone floor seeping through my clothes. My breaths came out in ragged gasps, each one a silent accusation. Harvey's face flashed behind my eyelids, his quiet strength and that rare, reassuring smile he reserved for moments when hope seemed lost. I tried to push away the image, but it clung to me, a constant reminder.

If only I hadn't been so certain about sending him to Camille's encampment.

He was meant to be safe.

Now, because of me, he was in Cain's clutches. I could almost hear Harvey's calm voice in my head, trying to argue against the decision, but I'd been too headstrong, too convinced of my own plan.

"Harvey…" I whispered into the silence, my voice breaking. The words I never said to him haunted me, floating up from a place deep inside where I kept things even I was afraid to acknowledge. Every moment that passed now was a moment

I might never get back, a moment lost to tell him that he meant more to me than just my childhood best friend.

Would he understand why I made the choice to send him away? Would he forgive the unspoken truths between us if we never got the chance to lay them bare?

My heart ached with the weight of what went unsaid, what might remain forever unspoken. I needed to see him again, to look into those insightful grey blue eyes and find the forgiveness or the shared secret understanding that lurked there.

The deliberate scuff of a boot pulled me from my spiraling thoughts. I looked up, quickly wiping away the traitorous wetness from my cheeks. Ren stood in the doorway, his silhouette a dark contrast to the hallway's flickering lights.

"Ren," I murmured, my voice steadier than I felt. "What is it?"

He didn't need to say anything; the grim set of his mouth told me enough. But he moved forward anyway, determination etched into every line of his body. Whatever Ren brought with him into this room, it wasn't going to be news I wanted to hear. Yet, in that moment, his presence was a lifeline, pulling me back from the brink of my own despair.

"Ren," I repeated, my voice steadier than I felt. "What is it? Is it about the bio weapon that Cain released?"

Ren shook his head, "No, we have successfully contained the danger and isolated those who have been infected."

I couldn't understand why he seemed so troubled. What other information did he have that could possibly be worse than the effects caused by Cain's biological weapon?

He closed the distance between us in a few strides, a signal of the gravity he carried in his steady gaze. "Cain sent a message," he said, his voice low and even. "A ransom for Harvey."

My heart stalled, then pounded fiercely against my ribs. "What kind of ransom?" I asked, though I feared the answer that would come from Ren's solemn face.

"Yourself," Ren replied. "Cain wants you, Luka. In exchange for Harvey's safety."

I felt the room tilt as if the ground beneath me had crumbled into nothingness. The idea that I could trade myself for Harvey's life was both a torment and a twisted kind of solace. Harvey was out there because of me, and now Cain was using him as bait to reel me in.

"I...I can't believe this," I stammered, trying to wrap my mind around the situation. "Why would Cain want me?"

Ren's jaw clenched and he looked away for a moment before meeting my gaze again. "I think he sees you as a threat," he said slowly. "You've been rallying people against him, trying to undo all of his careful planning."

I nodded, feeling a surge of anger towards Cain for putting Harvey's life on the line just to get to me. But then another thought dawned on me – if I agreed to go with Cain, would he release Harvey?

"What about Harvey?" I asked, my voice tight with emotion.

Ren's expression darkened even more. "Cain didn't mention anything about him once you were in his custody," he said gravely. "But we can assume that if you hand yourself over, he'll let Harvey go."

I closed my eyes and took a deep breath, trying to steady myself. It was clear that there was no easy way out of this situation.

"Don't worry," Ren's voice cut through my spiraling thoughts, firm and resolute. "We're not playing Cain's game.

We need to come up with our own plan—a way to get Harvey back without giving in to Cain's demands."

"Right," I breathed out, trying to latch onto Ren's conviction like a lifeline. My mind raced, possibilities branching out like the intricate roots of an ancient tree. Could we outsmart Cain? What resources did we have left? Who could we count on?

"Listen to me, Luka," Ren implored, his piercing eyes locking onto mine. "You can't just hand yourself over. There has to be another way, and we'll find it. Together."

"Alright," I murmured, but in my head, I was already sifting through potential sacrifices. I couldn't let Harvey pay for my mistakes, not when I could still do something about it. Ren was right; we needed a plan, a clever, calculated risk that could tilt the scales back in our favor.

"Let's gather everyone," Ren suggested, and I nodded. It was time to put our heads together, to pull every idea into the light until we crafted a solution that didn't involve handing me over on a silver platter.

"Thank you, Ren," I said as we stepped into the dim corridor. His presence was grounding, reminding me that despite the fear clawing at my insides, I wasn't alone in this fight.

"Thank me when we save our friend," he replied, his tone leaving no room for doubt. And I realized, that I would walk straight into the lion's den if it meant bringing Harvey home.

Ren's boots echoed off the corridor walls as I strode beside him, each step a drumbeat to my racing heart. "We need Lewis and Liz," I said, more to myself than Ren. The hum of the encampment's generators thrummed in the background, a constant reminder of the fragile bubble of safety we'd managed to create.

"Agreed, Lewis' tech skills will be invaluable." Ren's voice was steady, but his eyes were stormy, mirroring the turmoil in my chest.

As we turned the corner into a secluded aclove, we came face to face with the very people we sought. Liz stopped with an apple half way to her mouth and Lewis looked up as his fingers continued to dance across the holoscreen before him.

"We need to talk," I announced.

"About Harvey?" Liz asked, her voice a soft tremor of concern.

"Yeah," I replied. "We're planning a rescue."

Their nods were quick, filled with the unspoken understanding that our circle of trust was tightening around one of our own.

Before we could dive into details, footsteps approached, and Ian emerged from the shadows with Skai trailing behind him. His sudden presence made me stiffen.

How is it he always knows just where to find me?

"We heard about the ransom for Harvey," Ian said, his tone lacking its usual edge. "We want in."

"Since when do you play the hero?" I couldn't keep the skepticism out of my voice.

"Since it became my family at stake," he shot back, and something in his gaze struck me, a sincerity I hadn't seen before. Maybe desperation truly did make strange bedfellows.

"Alright. We work together," I conceded, and Skai nodded, a silent promise etched in her determined expression.

With our makeshift team assembled, we moved swiftly towards Sam's location. The hastily assembled control room was awash with low, urgent voices and the glow of monitors casting shadows on determined faces. My pulse quickened as we entered.

Nate's head popped up from behind a console, a half-grin on his face. "You're just in time for the brainstorming session."

"Looks like you've started without us," I observed, noting the holographic maps and scribbled notes already cluttering the workspace.

"Sam's got a plan," Nate said, nodding towards where Sam stood, blue eyes fierce beneath furrowed brows.

I moved closer, catching snippets of their conversation—routes, timings, distractions. They were building something complex, a web of strategies that could either save Harvey or entangle us all further.

"Sam, why the hell didn't I know about the ransom?" My voice, sharp as a blade, sliced through the hushed strategizing. I was not aware of my anger towards Sam until I stood in front of him

Sam's head snapped up, his eyes meeting mine in a steely lock. "I sent Ren to find you," he shot back, the defensive edge in his voice mirroring the tension in his posture.

"Ren?" I spat the name like it was poison. The room seemed to close in on us, the air thick with accusation and betrayal. "You should have come yourself!"

"Enough!" Sam barked, slamming a hand down on the console, making Nate flinch. "We don't have time for this."

"Time seems to be all we had until now!" I shot back, my anger boiling over. It was hard enough grappling with guilt without being left out of the loop.

"Look, I'm sorry, okay?" Sam's voice softened marginally. "I thought—"

"Thought what? That I wouldn't want to save Harvey?" I could feel the heat of my fury coloring my cheeks, my fingers curled into fists at my sides.

"Of course not. But this is Cain we're dealing with. He wants *you*, Luka. It changes things." His voice was strained, and I knew the weight of command was heavy on his shoulders.

"It changes nothing," I insisted, piercing him with a glare. "We are getting him back. Together."

There was a collective breath, a moment where everyone seemed to lean in, waiting for the final word.

"Alright," Sam conceded. "Together."

"Good." I nodded sharply. "Let's go rescue Harvey."

Chapter 30

Luka

The dim light from the torches cast long shadows over the holographic map spread between us. My fingers traced the jagged outskirts of the military base, where it was assumed Cain would be holding Harvey.

"Going in alone as bait is not an option, Luka," Sam's voice was firm, his blue eyes meeting mine with a resolve that matched my own.

"Harvey would do it for any of us," I countered, the words tasting bitter with guilt. He was out there because of me, because of a plan that I had orchestrated and executed poorly. The ache in my chest tightened, a silent confession of how much he meant to me, a truth my lips had never spoken.

"Which is exactly why we can't risk you too," Liz chimed in, her gaze sympathetic yet unwavering.

Ren's silence spoke volumes, but his furrowed brow showed his thoughts were in line with the rest. He knew I blamed myself, and he understood the unspoken language of my heart better than anyone.

"Let's focus on strategy, not sacrifice," Ren finally said, his voice cutting through the tension.

"We need to find a way to disable the alarms and security systems without being detected," Liz said, her fingers flying across the keyboard as she accessed schematics of the military facility.

"I can take care of that," Lewis chimed in confidently. "Hacking is my forte."

The room fell silent as all eyes turned towards Ian. He shifted uncomfortably under their scrutiny before finally speaking up.

"I can create a diversion," he said, his voice lacking its usual bravado. "While you guys focus on getting Harvey out, I'll cause chaos outside to draw attention away from the compound."

There was a collective nod of agreement before we delved back into planning.

"We'll need someone on the outside waiting with transport," Nate suggested, looking around at each of us. "Someone who can blend in and not draw attention."

"Me," Ren and I spoke simultaneously.

"I'll handle it," Ren said firmly. "I know my way around that base better than anyone and…"

"I'll handle the transportation," Skai asserted, cutting Ren off. "As much as I hate to admit it, Ren, you're a better fighter."

"Agreed," Sam muttered. "Skai will take care of transport, let's move on."

We huddled closer, piecing together our collective knowledge when Lewis leaned forward, his disheveled curls falling into his intense eyes. "What if we don't have to go in blind?" he proposed, pulling a small device from his pocket. "This cornea slip—it's not perfect, but…"

"Cornea slip?" I raised an eyebrow, Ian and Skai leaning in curiously beside me.

"It's a tech Lars and I have been working on," Lewis explained. "It records everything you see, syncs our locations, and allows communication. If we each wear one..."

"Then we'd have eyes on the inside," Nate finished.

"More than that," I added, a sly grin tugging at my lips despite the gravity of our situation. "We could show the world what Cain really is—a tyrant."

A murmur of agreement swept across the group as we began to envision the possibilities.

"Then it's settled," I said. "We use the cornea slips, we stick to the plan... and we bring Harvey home."

There were murmurs of agreement when Lewis edged closer, his eager eyes scanning our faces for a sign of acceptance. "I should be there," he said, determination lacing his voice. "Harvey would do the same for any of us."

"Absolutely not," Liz snapped, her hands planted firmly on her hips. "It's too dangerous and you're not trained for fieldwork."

"Neither was I before all this," I shot back, more to myself than to them. The guilt coiled tighter inside me, a relentless reminder of my role in Harvey's capture.

"Look, Luka" —Ren's gaze held mine, steady and unyielding— "we can't afford to take unnecessary risks. Lewis is brilliant behind a screen, but out there..." He trailed off, leaving the unsaid fears to linger between us like specters.

We can't lose any more of our family.

"Guys, he's my friend too," Lewis interjected, his jaw set in stubborn defiance. His eyes, so much like Harvey's in their intensity, bored into mine, pleading silently for my support.

246

I swallowed the lump in my throat, torn between my instinct to shield him from harm and the knowledge that refusing him felt like betraying Harvey all over again. I nodded, once, decisively. "Fine. But you stick to the plan, Lewis. No heroics."

He grinned, relief washing over his features. "Wouldn't dream of it," he promised, though we all knew it was a promise made to be broken.

Before we could settle into another round of strategizing, Sam cleared his throat, commanding the room's attention. "There's one more thing we haven't considered," he said, hesitantly. "We need a way to get to the base undetected."

"Go on," I encouraged, watching as he pulled at the edge of the table, his scars stark against his skin—a map of battles fought and won.

"Before I left Delta Force... before I became what I am now," he began, his blue eyes darkening with memories, "my Delta Force team had a hovercraft. It's fast, stealth tech, and still sitting where I left it, near this mountain range."

"Are you suggesting we steal a military-grade aircraft?" Ian asked, eyebrows raised in a mix of amusement and skepticism.

"Already stolen," Sam corrected with a half-smile. "But yes. It's risky, but it's our best shot at getting in and out without drawing attention."

"Until we're ready to draw all the attention," Skai added, the corner of her mouth twitching upward.

"Exactly," I said, feeling the pieces of our desperate plan slotting together with a clarity that left no room for doubt. This would work. It had to. For Harvey, for all of us.

"Then that settles it," Ren declared, his eyes meeting mine in silent solidarity.

Squeezing my eyes shut, I allowed myself one moment—

247

one breath—to hope that somewhere, beyond the walls and watchful eyes of Cain's stronghold, Harvey was doing the same.

"Alright, here's the plan," I said, breaking the charged silence as the group leaned in. "We split into two teams. Sam, you'll take Nate, Ren, Ian, and Skai. You're our stealth wing—use that hovercraft to slip in as backup."

Sam nodded, his jaw set but I could tell he wasn't thrilled with the idea of separating.

"Liz, Lewis, and I will storm the front gates." My voice was steady, my resolve unflinching. "I'll let myself get captured. That's our distraction."

"Are you insane?" Liz's voice cracked, her eyes wide with alarm.

"Trust me, it's the only way. Once I'm inside, I can find Harvey and Sam's team will be waiting to break us out and provide a getaway." My heart clenched at the thought of what condition Harvey might be in when we rescue him, but I pushed on. "Lewis, we need your cornea slips ready."

Lewis brushed his curls back, a flicker of pride in his eyes despite the worry. "They'll record everything we see and hear. Plus, we'll have real-time tracking and mapping capabilities."

"Perfect," I said, feeling a surge of confidence. This technology could change everything—not just for us, but for all those oppressed by Cain's regime.

"Let's get ready and meet back here at dawn," I concluded, the strategy cemented in my mind.

As murmurs of assent rippled through the group, we began to disperse, each to our own quarters to gather what little we owned for the mission ahead. My legs felt heavy as I turned to leave, my thoughts swirling with images of the military base, guards, and the friend I had to save.

Harvey, I'm coming for you.

"Luka," Ren's voice stopped me. His tone was gentle yet insistent, a counterpoint to the chaos raging within me.

"Can it wait, Ren?" I asked, not turning to face him. I didn't want him to see the turmoil in my eyes, the guilt gnawing at my chest.

"Just... walk with me? Please." His words were soft, laced with an emotion I couldn't place.

I hesitated before nodding, and we started down the hallway, our footsteps echoing off the cold stone walls of the mountain that had become both sanctuary and prison.

Ren walked beside me, quiet for several paces. I knew he wanted to talk, to reach out across the gulf of unsaid words between us, but my mind was a whirlwind with only one thought at its center: Harvey.

Harvey, with his chestnut hair that fell in his eyes when he laughed. Harvey, who'd stood by my side since the day we'd met, unwavering and brave. The image of him, possibly bound and beaten behind enemy lines, kept the words lodged firmly in my throat.

"Ren, I... I can't think about anything else right now," I whispered, finally breaking the silence. "I just need to focus on getting Harvey back."

"I know," he replied, his voice soft but resolute. "And we will. We're going to bring him home, Luka."

"Thanks, Ren," I managed, grateful for his support yet unable to shake the dread curling around my heart.

I glanced at Ren's shadowed profile and saw the same fears reflected in his eyes.

The cool stone of the corridor pressed against my back as

I leaned away from Ren's penetrating gaze. His eyes, usually so sharp and unreadable, were clouded with an emotion I couldn't quite name.

"We'll get him back, Luka," Ren said firmly, his voice echoing slightly in the emptiness of the passageway. "I promise you that."

"Ren, this isn't on you—" I started, but he held up a hand to stop me.

"I should've seen it coming, the attack. It was straight out of my father's playbook. I let my guard down, and Harvey paid the price." Ren's words were clipped, tinged with a guilt I knew all too well.

"Hey, we both didn't see this coming," I said, trying to shoulder some of the blame. But deep down, I wondered if my own mistakes had led us here.

"Maybe," Ren conceded, but there was a finality in his tone that told me he wasn't fully swayed by my attempt at solidarity.

We stood there for a moment, caught in the gravity of what lay ahead.

"Tomorrow, we go in there, and we bring him out. No matter what it takes," Ren said. He looked at me then, really looked at me, his gaze unwavering. "Even if it means..." He didn't finish the sentence, but he didn't need to. I heard the unspoken vow in his voice, saw it etched into the hard set of his jaw.

"Ren, don't talk like that. We're all getting out of this, together," I insisted, though a part of me feared the cost of such a promise.

"Harvey means a lot to you," he continued, shifting the subject away from the dark turns of our conversation. "I know that. And I would die to bring him back because... because I know how much he means to you."

My heart clenched at his words, and suddenly the walls of the passageway felt too close, the air too thin. I swallowed hard, trying to push past the lump forming in my throat.

"Ren, I..." The confession bubbled up before I could stop it. "I love him. I love Harvey."

Ren nodded, a sad sort of acceptance in his eyes. "I know, Luka. I've always known."

In the dim light, I could see the ghost of a smile on his lips—a bittersweet curve that spoke of understanding and resignation. It was a look that said he knew his place in my heart, just as I knew mine in his.

"Go get some rest," Ren said, breaking the charged silence. "We have a long day ahead of us."

"Ren..."

"Save it for when we bring him back," he cut in gently, turning to walk down the hallway.

"Goodnight, Ren," I called softly after him.

"Goodnight, Luka," he replied without looking back.

Chapter 31

Luka

I tossed in my makeshift bed, the scratchy fabric of the cot barely registering against my skin. Sleep had eluded me, all I could think about was Harvey. Dawn couldn't come soon enough.

As the muffled sounds of others stirring began to sound, I pushed myself up, muscles coiled tight with anticipation. We met in silence, each of us wearing the same grim determination like a second skin. Our breaths mingled in the cool morning air as we slipped into the hidden underground rail tunnels, the darkness swallowing us whole. It was a path we'd traveled in secret many times before, but today it felt like a descent into the unknown.

"Watch your step," Sam's voice cut through the shadows, his figure a solid presence ahead of me. The rail tunnels wound beneath the earth, remnants of a world that once thrived on order and predictability. Now they were just arteries leading to the heart of our rebellion.

We emerged into an open cavernous space, the hovercraft looming before us like a slumbering beast. Its sleek lines betrayed no hint of its age; it was a relic from Sam's past life in delta force, reborn under his meticulous care. The air was musty and damp, hinting at the dank underground tunnels we had just left.

"Ten years," Sam murmured, more to himself than to us, as we approached the vessel. "And still untraceable." His hand glided over the metallic surface, pride evident in the slight lift of his chin.

"Unbelievable," Lewis breathed out, his usual reserve forgotten as he circled the hovercraft with wide eyes. The tech gleamed under the sparse lighting, its contours sharp and deliberate. "It's like it's not even there."

"Exactly," Sam said, casting a sly grin in Lewis's direction. "That's the point. I've had her cloaking tech upgraded over the years—she'll be nearly invisible to the naked eye when we're airborne."

Lewis let out a low whistle, his fingers itching to explore every inch of the craft. "You're a bloody genius, Sam."

"I bet he had Fox, Stef and Lars perform those upgrades," I teased, the corner of my mouth quirking upward despite the gravity of our situation. "Let's get her in the air."

We boarded the hovercraft, the familiarity of the interior a stark contrast to the alien technology that now powered it. Sam took the pilot's seat, his movements precise and assured. I settled in the seat closest to him, strapping in as the engines hummed to life, a vibration that promised action. Today, we were taking the fight to them. Today, we were saving Harvey.

"Ready?" Sam asked, his blue eyes turning back to meet mine in the dim light.

"Yeah," I replied, my voice steady even as my heart raced.

The thrum of the hovercraft's engines grew to a roar, and

beneath me, the floor vibrated with the promise of ascent. My fingers curled around the armrests, but out of anticipation.

Sam expertly piloted the hovercraft out of the cavern, navigating through tight turns that made my stomach churn

"Feeling it?" Ren asked, his voice barely audible over the din. He was strapped in across from me, his eyes wide with a mixture of excitement and apprehension.

"In every cell," I replied, my gaze fixed on the metal ground. Every sense was heightened; the rush of wind against the hull, the faint scent of ionized air, the weightless sensation that danced in my stomach. My ears cracked and popped as we gained altitude.

As we soared towards the military base, the flight became a blur—a streak of motion through skies that were mercifully clear of enemy craft. The last time we'd fled Delta Force, the journey had been a harrowing six-hour evasion before we'd reached the outskirts of the ghost town and several days of walking before we reached the genesi encampment. But now, the hovercraft cut through the atmosphere with such speed that time itself seemed to contract around us.

The others began chatting amongst themselves, their voices a muted background noise to my thoughts. With each passing second, we grew closer to the military base where Harvey was being held captive. I knew that every part of this plan had been meticulously thought out, but there was still an insidious voice in the back of my mind whispering doubts and fears. I pushed those thoughts aside and focused on the task at hand. We needed to rescue Harvey and bring him back safely. And to do that, we needed to be prepared for anything.

As we approached the base, Sam expertly maneuvered the hovercraft through layers of security systems and patrolling enemy craft. We were nearly invisible thanks to the craft's upgrades, but I couldn't help but hold my breath as we passed within meters of Delta Force crafts without being detected.

"Approaching the landing point," Sam's voice crackled over the intercom. Reality snapped back into focus. I unstrapped myself, stepping close to the viewport. The military base was a dark smudge on the horizon, growing larger with every passing second.

"Remember, this first part is just recon," I reminded the team, though my words felt like they were for me too. "In and out, no heroics."

"Got it, boss," Lewis responded, though his attempt at nonchalance didn't quite reach his eyes. I knew he was thinking about the plan—to use ourselves as bait—and it gnawed at him. It gnawed at all of us.

The hovercraft descended, landing with a grace that belied its size. We disembarked quickly, efficiently, slipping into the roles we'd rehearsed the night before.

"Remember to check your gear," I said, scanning each face. Determination met me in their expressions, but it was Lewis who paused, adjusting the strap of his backpack with more force than necessary.

"Hey," I caught his eye, offering a nod that I hoped conveyed confidence. "We've got this."

He nodded back, the corners of his lips twitching into a fleeting smile. "Yeah, of course, Luka. Lead the way."

And so, we set off, moving through the terrain with practiced stealth. Our mission was simple: scout the military base, finalize our plans.

We made camp in the shadow of the hovercraft, its sleek frame a silent guardian against the afternoon sun. The hum of the cloaking device was barely perceptible, a reassuring whisper that we were still hidden from prying eyes.

"Alright, everyone," Sam's voice cut through the hush of our camp. "Let's get some food in us and catch a few hours of shuteye before their shift changes. We'll need our strength when we split up for the plan."

Forks clinked against metal containers as we ate and around me, muffled conversations peppered the air, each word laced with an undercurrent of tension. Even as we fortified ourselves, we were acutely aware of the looming confrontation.

As the others settled into their makeshift beds, Ren approached me, his shadow blocking out the sun around us. "Luka," he said, his voice low and steady, "promise me you won't pull any heroics behind our backs."

I met Ren's gaze, the intensity of his eyes piercing. "I won't," I assured him, my words firm. "I just need a moment to myself, that's all."

He searched my face, looking for any hint of deceit, but eventually, he nodded, accepting my answer. "Alright. Don't wander too far."

"Trust me, I won't," I replied, a half-truth slipping through my lips.

Ren hesitated for a moment longer before turning away, leaving me to my solitude. I watched him go, a knot forming in my gut, knowing full well the promise I'd just made was one I couldn't keep. Not when Harvey's life hung in the balance.

Silently, I drifted towards the hovercraft, the cool metal soothing under my fingertips as I leaned against it. I closed my eyes, breathing in the scent of earth and engine oil, letting the stillness wash over me. This moment of calm was fleeting, but necessary—a brief respite before the storm broke.

Minutes ticked by as I stood there, lost in my thoughts. But eventually, the sun began its slow descent, casting a golden hue across the landscape. It was time to act.

I made my way back to camp, but stopped short when I heard footsteps approaching. It was Lewis, his eyes scanning the area before settling on me.

"Hey," he said, his voice low. "Going for a walk?"

"I just needed some fresh air," I replied with a shrug.

He nodded and walked over to join me at the edge of camp. We stood there for a moment in silence before he spoke again.

"You know, you can talk to me if something's bothering you," he said gently.

I turned to face him, surprised by his concern. "It's nothing," I insisted with a small smile.

Lewis looked like he wanted to say something further, but instead he just clapped me on the shoulder and said with determination, "We'll get him back Luka."

I observed Lewis as he walked away, keeping an eye on the camp and waiting for the right time to leave without being seen.

Now.

With each step away from the hovercraft, my heart pounded a frantic rhythm that matched the speed of my retreat as I doubled back through the dense undergrowth. I couldn't shake the image of Harvey, his stoic face hiding a well of pain only I knew. There was no choice for me; his life was worth more than any promise I could make.

My genesi speed was a gift and a curse, propelling me forward with reckless velocity toward my singular goal: the military base. Branches snagged at my clothes, leaving thin tears in the fabric, but I barely felt them. Each stride brought me closer to Harvey, to the exchange that would either save him or seal my own fate.

I slowed to a walk as the base came into view, the forcefield shimmered like a mirage around it, an iridescent barrier that hummed with dormant power. Guard towers dotted the perimeter, cold eyes watching for any sign of attack.

Looks like Cain's tech's managed to renew his forcefields then.

The forcefield's glow cast an otherworldly light over the scene, throwing shadows across the barren landscape that stretched before the gates. Here, where the air crackled with energy, I prepared to surrender myself to Cain.

For Harvey, I reminded myself, for a chance to tip the scales back in our favor. My resolve hardened; I was ready to face whatever lay beyond that glowing barrier.

I halted a stone's throw from the gates, my chest heaving as I fumbled with the tiny device in my pocket. The cornea slip was no bigger than a grain of rice, but it held the power to reveal truths that could shatter the world's complacency. With practiced ease, I popped it into place; it adhered to my eye with a faint tingle, syncing instantly. My vision overlaid with a soft, almost imperceptible grid—I could see everything just as before, but now it was being recorded.

Please let this work. Please capture it all for the world to see.

If this went south, if I couldn't pull Harvey from Cain's clutches, then maybe this footage would be enough to turn the tide. And deep down, beneath layers of resolve and desperation, I harbored a flicker of hope that Sam and the others would come for us. They had to.

Taking a final steadying breath, I approached the gate. Shadows loomed over me, cast by the ominous structures behind the forcefield.

"Chancellor Cain!" My voice rang out, clear and firm, echoing off the barrier that separated us. "I am Luka Foster. I've come to surrender myself in exchange for Harvey Montgomery's release."

Silence greeted me first, a poised stillness that bore down hard. Then, the hum of the forcefield seemed to grow louder, as if charged by my declaration. I stood my ground, my hair whipping around my face in the breeze.

This was it, the moment where the countless scenarios I'd run in my head collided with reality. A sudden hiss sliced through the air, a sound out of place amidst the tense quiet. Instinctively, my eyes darted to the source—a shadow detaching itself from the wall of the gatehouse. I had barely a moment to register the dark silhouette leveling an object at me before pain erupted in my neck. My hand flew up to the site, fingers grazing a tiny dart embedded in my skin.

"Damn it," I whispered, the realization crashing over me like a wave.

The world began to tilt, each breath struggling to draw in enough air. With every ounce of willpower left, I tried to keep my eyes open, to remember every detail for the cornea slip. But my vision blurred, smearing the harsh lines of the military base.

Harvey, hold on a little longer.

My knees buckled, and I crumpled to the ground, the cold seeping through my clothes. Powerless, I watched the boots of the guards approach, heard their voices as if through a tunnel. "Got 'er," one said, a note of satisfaction lacing his words.

"Chancellor's going to be pleased," another replied, the sound distant and hollow to my ears.

I fought against the encroaching darkness, trying to cling to consciousness. But the chemicals coursing through me were relentless, dragging me down into oblivion.

As my body surrendered, my mind wrestled with the fear of what lay ahead. With a final effort, I tried to speak, to send a silent plea to my friends, but my voice was lost in the void. They would come. They had to.

Darkness claimed me wholly, and I knew no more.

Chapter 32

Sam

I jolted awake to Ren's hand on my shoulder, the sharp scent of urgency in his breath as he leaned close. "Sam," he hissed, his voice slicing through the haze of sleep that still clung to my brain. "It's Luka. She took off."

My heart slammed against my ribs, a surge of anger heating my veins like molten metal. "What do you mean, 'took off'?"

"Handing herself over to Cain," Ren said, his tone steady but his eyes ablaze with silent fury. "A trade for Harvey."

"Damn it, Luka!" I scrambled up from my makeshift bedroll on the hard ground. My muscles tensed, ready to spring into action. "Wake everyone up. Now."

Ren gave a curt nod and disappeared into our makeshift camp.

I shoved my feet into boots that had seen better days and scrambled to pull on my jacket. My fingers curled into fists. Luka's stunt could ruin everything we'd worked for, could get her killed. And knowing her, she hadn't thought twice about the danger—to herself or to us.

The camp was stirring now, murmurs growing into a cacophony of questions and curses. I strode towards the others gathered, my gaze sweeping over the tired, anxious faces of our group.

"Alright, listen up!" My voice cut through the noise, commanding attention with an authority that felt more like my father's every day. The thought twisted in my gut.

I announced, "Luka's taken off and probably already been captured by Cain." I could hear curses and grumblings from all around me.

"Any idea when she left?" I asked, locking eyes with Nate, who shook his head, his expression grim.

"Last I saw her she was headed into the hovercraft, I assumed for some privacy," he said, rubbing the back of his neck. "Got to be at least an hour ago."

"Great." I rubbed a hand over my face, feeling the roughness of stubble. "We need a new plan."

"We can't just let her walk into Cain's hands," Liz muttered, crossing her arms.

"Damn straight," I agreed. "We go in after her. We stick to the original rescue plan as much as we can, but now it's a two-for-one deal."

We gathered around the holographic map, our voices low and urgent as we discussed our options. Every minute that passed was another minute closer to Luka being caught by Cain's forces.

"Rescuing Harvey was going to be hard enough," Ian pointed out, his words sharp as knives. "Now we've got Luka playing the martyr and Harvey somewhere in that hellhole."

"We'll make adjustments," I said, pacing back and forth, each step imprinting a path in the dirt. "We think on our feet, adapt.

That's how we've survived this long, isn't it?"

"Sam's right," Nate chimed in, "We improvise."

"Let's map out what we know about the base," I suggested. "Entrances, exits, guard rotations—everything. Ian, Liz and Lewis, you'll create the distractions. Draw their attention while Ren, Nate, Skai and I slip in."

"Distractions" was a mild term for the chaos we needed them to cause.

"I have something that can create a diversion," Ren spoke up, his voice soft but determined.

I turned to look at him, surprised. "How?"

Ren reached into his bag and pulled out a small box. "With these." He held up a handful of flashing devices.

"Flash bombs?" I asked, recognizing them from my time as a soldier.

"Yeah," Ren confirmed with a nod. "I've been working on them since we left Delta Force. They temporarily blind and disorient anyone within their range."

A smile tugged at my lips as I studied him. Ren had always been quiet and reserved, but he had skills that could definitely come in handy.

"That could work," Liz said with a grin. "We can use the confusion caused by the flash bombs to slip past unnoticed."

"Alright then," Nate said, clapping his hands together. "Lets move the flash bombs into Ian's gear."

"Whatever happens…" I paused, swallowing the lump in my throat. "…we get them out. Both of them."

"Guys," Lewis' voice cut through the murmurs of the group, "there's something on Luka's feed."

We all crowded around the flickering holographic display that sprouted from his wrist console.

My heart raced against my chest as I watched Luka's video, showing her arrival at the gates of the military base. It appeared that Cain had restored the forcefields.

"Damn it, Luka," I muttered under my breath. She called to the guards, her voice screamed challenge. A guard raised his weapon and fired. The dart hit her neck, and she crumpled, the feed spiraling into darkness as she fell.

"Great," I spat out, clenching my fists so tight my nails bit into my palms. "They've got her, and now we're blind."

Lewis' fingers danced over the console, trying to re-establish the connection, but it was no use. I could see it in the set of his mouth, the way his disheveled curls seemed to droop even more.

"New plan," I said, turning to face him. The group's eyes were on me, looking for the next move. "Lewis, you stay here in the hovercraft. Your job is to keep tabs on our cornea slips. If anyone gets a visual on Luka or Harvey, you direct us to them."

"Got it, Sam," he replied, already adjusting dials and typing commands into his holoscreen.

"Skai," I shifted my gaze to her, "you're on Lewis duty. Nothing gets to him, understood?"

"Understood," she responded, her posture rigid with the responsibility.

"Everyone else, gear up. We're going in blind, but we're not coming out empty-handed." My voice was steady, but inside, my gut churned. Luka's capture had thrown us off balance, and anything could happen once we breached those walls.

Ren was already thinking three moves ahead, his predatory gaze fixed on Lewis. "We need more than a rescue," he said in that intense tone of his, the one that made you listen whether you wanted to or not. "We need everyone to see Cain for what he is. Compile Luka's footage; let's broadcast it nationwide."

"Way ahead of you," Lewis replied, his fingers flying over the console with practiced ease. His disheveled curls bobbed as he nodded, eyes alight with the thrill of challenge. "I've got a backdoor into the mainframe of the public feeds. It'll take some finesse, but consider it done."

I clenched my fists, feeling the weight of the task at hand. "Alright, we're on a tight clock, people. Here's what we know about the base…" My voice trailed off as I tried to conjure a clear image of the compound in my mind — its towering walls, labyrinthine corridors, and hidden cells.

"Security's tightest along the western perimeter," Ren added, pulling up the schematics on a handheld device. The light from the screen threw stark shadows across his angular features. "But there are maintenance tunnels that run underneath. They're our best shot at getting in undetected."

"Right." Liz chimed in, her voice steady despite the gravity of our plan. "Ian and I can handle distractions. We've got enough explosives to make a ruckus—they won't know what hit 'em."

"Good." I looked at each of them, their faces set with determination. "Nate, Ren, and I will go in through the tunnels. Once inside, we split up—search for Luka and Harvey. Remember, don't engage unless absolutely necessary. We're here to get them out, not start another war or get ourselves captured."

"Got it, boss," Nate confirmed, a fire kindling in his eyes.

"Let's gear up then," I said, the urgency propelling us forward. "Time's not on our side."

I snapped the last strap of my armor into place, the cold

leather a stark reminder of the battle ahead. Ren was doing the same beside me, his movements efficient and precise. The silence between us was heavy, each lost in thoughts of what awaited us beyond the camp's deceptive safety.

"Going up against your father… it's not going to be easy," I said finally, breaking the quiet. My voice sounded rough, like gravel being crushed underfoot. "General Thorn, he's… well, he's ruthless."

Ren met my gaze, his eyes hard as flint. "I know," he replied, his tone even but laced with an edge that spoke volumes. "But this is more than personal vendettas, Sam. It's about exposing the truth, showing everyone the monster behind the mask."

"My father isn't any less formidable," I admitted, flexing my fingers around the grip of my weapon. The thought of facing my father twisted my gut.

"Your genesi abilities have changed things," Ren pointed out, adjusting his own gear with a practiced hand. "He won't have the upper hand this time."

"Maybe." I allowed myself a small nod, accepting the truth in his words. "Just… watch your back, okay?"

"Always do." Ren smirked, but the levity didn't reach his eyes. In them, I saw the same steely resolve that mirrored my own.

"Alright, let's round everyone up," I declared, shifting into the role of leader once more. "We've got friends to save."

We gathered the team, their faces grim yet tinged with an unspoken camaraderie. I looked at each one of them, knowing the risks they were willing to take for Luka and Harvey.

"Remember, stay sharp and stick to the plan," I instructed, my voice steady despite the adrenaline coursing through my veins. "Lewis, you're our eyes. Keep the communication lines open."

"Got it. And the footage will be ready for broadcast," Lewis assured, his fingers already dancing over the console at his wrist.

"Skai, make sure the craft's ready for a quick getaway and guard him with your life," I continued, meeting her determined gaze.

"Wouldn't dream of anything else," she replied, a fierce protector to the core.

"Liz and Ian, make the biggest distraction that you can," I said, turning my gaze to their direction.

"Let's blow some shit up," Ian hollered while Liz merely gave a singular nod.

"Ren and Nate, you're with me. We find Luka and Harvey," I said, offering a brief nod.

Our shared history, our future confrontation with our fathers, all of it hung unsaid between Ren and I. Now wasn't the time for hesitation or second-guessing. We had a mission to complete, lives to save, and the weight of our pasts couldn't hold us back.

"Let's do this," Ren responded, his voice cutting through any lingering doubt.

"Move out," I commanded, and together, we moved out.

We're coming Luka.

Chapter 33

Luka

Darkness peeled away from my senses sluggishly as I fought to regain what was left of my consciousness. A dull ache throbbed at the base of my skull, a cruel reminder of the tranquilizer dart's sting that had silenced me at the military base's unforgiving gates.

My eyelids fluttered open, revealing a clinical blur of white and metallic surfaces that soon sharpened into a sterile room—possibly a lab. Harsh light spilled from overhead, casting stark shadows over the rigid lines of cabinets and equipment. The distinct scent of antiseptic hung in the air like a silent threat.

I tried to lift my head, but found it immovable; an invisible weight seemed to press it down. Panic fluttered in my chest as I realized I was strapped down, my arms pinned against the cold, hard surface of a surgical table. My heart hammered against my ribcage, each beat a drumroll of dread for what was to come.

Then, slicing through the sterile silence, came a soft male chuckle—a sound so familiar and unnerving that it echoed in the hollows of my fear. I couldn't see him, but there was no mistaking who it belonged to. Chancellor Cain. His laughter crept along my spine, raising goosebumps on my flesh even as the rest of me lay numb from the tranquilizer's lingering poison.

"Awake at last, Luka?" The voice was smooth and mocking— the auditory signature of my captor, my enemy. Despite my confinement, my resolve steeled within me, and I braced for whatever twisted game Cain had in store.

Chancellor Cain strode into view, General Thorn a silent shadow at his side. I strained against my restraints, my voice echoing against the sterile walls. "Where is Harvey?"

"Ah, Luka," Cain began, his tone as smooth as the surface of the table pinning me down, "a deal is a deal. You'll be reunited with your friend very soon."

My heart sank. 'Very soon' had an ominous ring to it. Cain's words were never without multiple layers of deceit. The truth hit me like a punch in the gut—he was never going to let Harvey go.

"Was it you?" I spat out, the question burning behind my lips. "Did you order my father's murder?"

Cain's expression didn't falter as he looked down at me, the slight curve of his mouth revealing a sliver of satisfaction. "Christopher Foster became a liability. He discovered things that were not meant for him." He paused, letting the weight of his words sink in. "General Thorn carried out what needed to be done."

The room seemed to spin, and it wasn't from the drugs anymore. Thorn, the man who had taken everything from me, stood there, his face impassive.

"Killing me... that wasn't planned, was it?" The accusation

269

hung between us, a tangible thing.

"No," Cain admitted, his gaze locking onto mine, unblinking and remorseless. "We couldn't have any witnesses. But we were... surprised to hear of your survival." His eyes narrowed slightly. "It made us wonder if Christopher had hidden something within you—perhaps the genesi coding... maybe even a cure."

My voice came out stronger than I felt, the words cutting through the sterile air of the lab. "What do you want with me, Cain? Why was it so important to have me back?"

He circled the table like a shark, his gaze cold and calculating. "You've been quite the elusive prey, Luka," he began, a sardonic lilt in his voice. "But then, you played right into our hands. We knew allowing you to escape Delta Force would eventually lead us to the genesi encampments. They've been a thorn in our side for far too long."

"Is that all then?" I spat, struggling against the restraints. "I was just bait?"

His chuckle was devoid of humor. "Hardly. Your father's work on your DNA makes you an invaluable asset. You see, we need your superior genes to develop new strands of the genesi coding, evolve our arsenal." The pride swelled in his voice. "And let's not forget about the possible cure hidden within you. My geneticists have been working tirelessly, but alas, some puzzles require a... key."

I took a slow breath, letting my fear simmer into something more useful—anger, determination. The cornea slip embedded in my left eye itched slightly, a reminder it was recording everything. "So you're just going to pick me apart, is that it?" I asked, feigning ignorance.

"Something like that," Cain said, his thin smile revealing

nothing of his thoughts. "But oh, the plans we have for your genes. With them, we'll cleanse this nation."

"Cleanse?" The word hung heavy between us.

"Indeed. The genesi rebels will be eradicated. And as for the surplus population—" Cain spread his arms wide as if embracing the room, "—a necessary culling for a brighter future."

"Genocide," I whispered, the reality of his plan settling like lead in my stomach.

Sam had been right.

"Survival," he corrected smoothly. "The strong will prevail, as they always have. And once the genesi army has served its purpose, we'll heal them, erase their memories. I'll be hailed as the savior, uniting humanity under one cause, one leader."

"Yourself," I concluded.

"Of course." His eyes gleamed with the reflection of his ambition. "A world reborn under my guidance, cleansed of rebellion and disorder."

"Sounds like a nightmare," I retorted, buying time as my mind raced for any possibility of escape.

"Only for those who stand against progress," Chancellor Cain replied, his gaze locking onto mine, unyielding and filled with the promise of power. "As for you, Luka Foster, your part in this new world order is just beginning."

I swallowed hard, my heart pounding against my ribs. But beneath the fear, a flicker of hope ignited. He didn't know it, but every word he uttered was being documented, a testament to his tyranny—if only I could find a way to use it.

"But now that you're aware of my plans, I can't allow you to leave." Cain said, his voice slicing through the sterile silence of the lab.

A chill ran down my spine as I processed his words, my heart thudding in my chest. This was it—the end of the line. I'd always known that standing up to Cain might mean paying the ultimate price, but facing the reality was another matter entirely. Yet, as I lay there, strapped to the cold metal table, acceptance washed over me. If my death meant that the truth about Cain's atrocities could be exposed, then so be it.

"But let it not be said that your Chacellor isn't a man of his word," he continued, a cruel smirk tugging at the corners of his mouth. "You made a deal for Harvey's release, and I intend to honor it."

Confusion clouded my thoughts. His words were laced with a poison that I couldn't quite identify.

How could he possibly let Harvey go after everything that had been revealed?

The door hissed open, and a figure stepped into the room, standing just out of my line of sight. My breath caught in my throat as I strained against my restraints, desperate to see who it was.

"Harvey?" I called out tentatively, hope and dread warring within me.

The figure shifted, and then Harvey came into view—but he was not the Harvey I knew. His eyes, once warm and vibrant, were now dull and lifeless. A pale, sickly sheen covered his skin, and his movements were mechanical, devoid of the gentle easiness that had defined him.

"Wh-what have you done to him?" I stammered, horror clawing at my insides.

"An improvement," Cain replied nonchalantly. "Harvey is now part of my genesi army—enhanced, obedient, and most importantly, under my control."

I stared at the shell of the person who had been my anchor, fighting back tears. "You turned him into a weapon?"

"An effective one," Cain confirmed. "And he will fulfill his first assignment by dealing with you."

"Harvey, please," I pleaded, desperate for any sign of recognition in his eyes. There was none. He was gone, lost to Cain's twisted experiment.

Cain stepped back, a satisfied glint in his eye as he watched the scene unfold. "Goodbye, Luka Foster. It's time for you to say farewell to your friend."

Harvey's approach was quiet, deliberate. Each step he took was measured and precise, the muscles in his jaw clenched in a way that wasn't his own. My heart raced, adrenaline surging through my veins even as I lay immobilized on the cold, unforgiving surface of the surgical table.

Focus Luka, concentrate and use all of your strength to break the through the restraints.

"Harvey," I whispered, a last-ditch effort to reach whatever fragment of him might still exist within the mind-controlled shell he'd become. "This isn't you."

But my words were like whispers in a storm. He stood over me, his face devoid of the compassion I had come to rely on. His hands, once so capable of comfort and care, now bore the intent to harm. The dark grey blue eyes that had often met mine with shared secrets and silent understandings were now empty—voids where a soul used to reside.

"Harvey!" I called out again, more forcefully, hoping to ignite a spark of recognition. But it seemed Cain's programming had taken root too deeply; the Harvey I knew was buried under layers of genetic commands.

His hand reached out, and the coldness of his touch sent

shivers down my spine. It wasn't just his skin that was ice—it was the very essence of him, chilled by the manipulation he'd undergone. Harvey's fingers wrapped around my throat, squeezing with a strength that betrayed his athletic build, a strength that was no longer governed by human conscience.

"Fight it, Harvey. Please," I gasped, but my voice was barely audible under the pressure of his grip.

I could see the struggle in his eyes for a moment—a flicker of the old Harvey—before it was extinguished by the overriding compulsion instilled by Cain. His grasp tightened, and I struggled for air, my body writhing against the restraints.

"Remember who you are!" I choked out, the edges of my vision starting to blur. "You're not a killer!"

Yet, as darkness crept into my sight, I knew that the Harvey I was speaking to might be gone forever. This was how I would die—not at the hands of an enemy, but by the hands of someone I loved, twisted into a weapon by the very monster we had vowed to fight against.

My lungs screamed for air, my thoughts scattering like leaves in the wind. And as I faced the end, it wasn't fear that consumed me—it was sorrow for Harvey, for the life he wouldn't live and the choices he was no longer free to make.

"Forgive me," I managed to whisper, unsure if the plea was for Harvey or myself. Then, everything went still.

Chapter 34

Sam

The chill of the metal shaft pressed against my palms as we inched our way through the narrow vent. Nate's quiet grunts echoed behind me, a reminder that we were all here, together, trying not to alert the patrols that roamed just beyond the thin walls of the military base.

"Remember," I whispered back to Nate and Ren without turning my head, "Ian and Liz are out there setting up the distractions. If all goes well, they'll buy us the time we need."

Nate let out a low chuckle, his voice barely a breath. "Yeah, if Ian doesn't blow something up prematurely."

Ren tried to lighten the tense atmosphere in the room by teasing, "Leave it to Ian to mess up a flash bomb."

I smiled despite the tension knotting my stomach. Trusting part of the plan to others left me feeling exposed, vulnerable, but it was necessary. Ian and Liz had their roles, just as we had ours.

We reached the end of the shaft, and I peered through the slits of the vent cover into the corridor below. The coast was clear. With a nod to Ren, whose eyes sharpened with focus,

I carefully pushed the cover open, muscles tensed for any sudden alarms.

Dropping silently to the ground, I signaled for them to follow. Once we were all out, I took the lead, scanning the hallway for any signs of traps or hidden sensors. My genesi abilities heightened my senses, allowing me to pick up on the subtlest vibrations, the faintest shifts in air currents that signaled danger.

"Sam, wait." Nate's hand on my shoulder stopped me mid-stride. His gaze locked onto mine, intense and probing. "You sure about this? About going in blind?"

"Harvey and Luka are down there," I replied, my voice laced with conviction. "We don't leave family behind."

Nate nodded once, sharply, and we proceeded, each step measured and deliberate. The underground laboratories weren't far now; I could almost sense the desperation seeping through the walls, a silent cry from Harvey and Luka, urging us forward.

"Keep your eyes peeled," I cautioned, leading the way through the dimly lit corridor. "There's bound to be more security the closer we get."

"Got it," Nate murmured, his vigilant gaze missing nothing as he followed on my heels.

We moved as one entity, shadows flickering among the stark white walls, a shiver ran down my spine, and I froze. The dull echo of boots on concrete snapped our synchronized stealth into a moment of chaos. "Patrol," I hissed, the word slicing through the silence like a knife. I motioned with a swift, flat hand — down, stay quiet. Nate and Ren melted into the shadows as if born from darkness itself.

My back pressed against the cold wall, heartbeat pounding

in my ears, I peeked around the corner. Two guards, oblivious to their imminent downfall, chatted about something trivial—their voices a grating contrast to the gravity of our mission.

"Three… two…" I counted under my breath, synchronizing our assault without a sound. On one, we struck—three specters emerging to claim victory over life and death.

I lunged, my genesi strength an asset I never underestimated. My hand found the first guard's mouth, stifling any cry for backup, while my other arm locked in a chokehold. Beside me, Ren and Nate were equally efficient, their targets dropping silently to the ground before they even understood what happened.

"Patrol neutralized," I whispered into the comms, barely catching my breath. We couldn't afford to linger; every second mattered when Harvey and Luka's lives were on the line.

"Excellent work." Lewis' voice crackled through the earpiece, a thread of relief woven into his usually composed tone. "I've managed to bypass the base's security protocols. You should be able to move through most doors now."

"Copy that," I replied, scanning the corridor ahead. The way was clear—for now.

"Stay sharp," I cautioned, signaling the team to advance. "Lewis, keep an eye out for anything you can manipulate from your end. It could make all the difference."

"Understood, Sam. I'll monitor the systems and alert you to any changes."

With that assurance, we continued our descent into the belly of the beast, ready to face whatever lay ahead.

The first locked door loomed ahead, a silent sentinel mocking our progress. I approached, pressing my palm against the cold metal, feeling the hum of security mechanisms just beyond.

"Stand by," Lewis' voice buzzed in my ear. "Accessing mainframe… got it. The code is coming through now."

Digits flickered in my vision as I typed them into the keypad. With a satisfying click, the door slid open, revealing another dim corridor lined with more doors, each one promising to be a new riddle.

"Keep sending those codes, Lewis. We don't have time for delays," I said, my words clipped as we moved forward. Ren gave me an approving nod, his eyes reflecting the same urgency I felt pulsing through my veins.

"Already on it, Sam. You'll have an open path straight to the labs," he assured me, his voice crackling with static but steady as ever.

We were halfway down the corridor when Liz's breathless voice in my ear cut through the commotion of our hasty advance.

"Sam—we've hit trouble," she gasped, and the unmistakable sounds of a scuffle filtered through the line. The hairs on the back of my neck stood on end. "It's going south fast—"

Her transmission ended abruptly, replaced by the sound of my own pounding heart in my ears. My grip on my weapon tightened as I fought the instinct to turn back and help.

"Damn it, Lewis, what's happening with Liz and Ian?" I demanded, my voice betraying a rare edge of panic.

"Working on it, Sam," Lewis replied, the usually calm cadence of his speech fractured by concern. "I'm rerouting power to create a diversion. It should give them a chance to…"

His voice trailed off, leaving us suspended in uncertainty. I didn't need to see Nate's face to know he was thinking the same thing: every second we hesitated, our friends were fighting for their lives.

"Keep moving," I ordered, shoving aside the fear that clawed at my chest. "We have to trust they can handle it. Our job is to get Harvey and Luka out."

Ren nodded, and Nate grunted in agreement. We pressed on, the silence of the corridor punctuated only by the soft beep of door codes and the distant echoes of chaos we were powerless to stop.

We huddled in the shadow of a towering storage rack, the dim light from the overhead panels casting long shadows across our faces. Nate's breathing was steady, a counterpoint to Ren's soft, nervous shifts beside me. I kept my gaze fixed on the muted glow of my comm unit, willing it to crackle to life with Lewis' voice.

"Any word?" Ren whispered, his voice barely audible above the hum of machinery.

"Nothing yet," I murmured, scanning the area for any sign of approaching danger. We needed that distraction, and every fiber of my being screamed to jump into the fray with Liz and Ian. But Harvey and Luka were depending on us.

Time stretched thin, a taut wire ready to snap. Then, without warning, the base shuddered violently beneath our feet. A deep, thunderous roar filled the air, shaking the walls and sending debris cascading from above. Instinctively, we ducked, covering our heads as dust and small fragments rained down.

"Was that—?" Ren's question was cut short by another violent tremor.

"The distraction," I said, the words tasting like ash in my mouth. There was no time to wonder if Liz and Ian had made it out. No time for anything but action.

"Move!" With a surge of adrenaline, we sprang to our feet, racing through the corridors. Alarms wailed, a cacophony of sound that seemed to scream along with the base itself. Through the haze of smoke and confusion, I caught glimpses of enemy soldiers scrambling, their silhouettes blurred and chaotic.

"Left here!" I shouted over the noise, taking the lead. The floor seemed to undulate beneath us, threatening to throw off our balance. Another explosion rocked the structure, closer this time, its fiery breath licking at our heels.

"Sam, watch out!" Nate barked. I veiled right, narrowly avoiding a chunk of ceiling as it crashed down where I'd been seconds before. We were trapped in a deadly maze, the base morphing into a beast intent on devouring us whole.

"Almost there!" Ren called out, pointing ahead to the reinforced doors marking the entrance to the laboratories.

With one last burst of effort, we sprinted towards salvation, the heat of the blast scorching our backs. I slammed my palm against the access panel, and miraculously, the doors slid open. We dove through the threshold just as the world behind us erupted into chaos, the doors sealing shut with a hiss.

Chapter 35

Luka

"Finish it, now!" Chancellor Cain's voice sliced through the ringing in my ears.

I wriggled, twisted, and turned, my fingers clawing desperately at the straps binding me to the cold lab table.

Focus Luka.

The leather bit into my wrists, but I refused to give in. With a violent jerk, one strap gave way, then another.

"Montgomery!" General Thorn's voice was like a blade over ice, sharp and chilling. "Stop her!"

His orders didn't matter. My mind clung to the hope that the explosion had been Sam and the others. As I freed my last restraint and leaped off the table, my heart hammered with anticipation of their arrival, of our plan coming to fruition amidst this chaos.

"Troops," Thorn was barking into his comm piece, cool and calculated even now, "locate the source of that blast immediately."

My feet hit the ground, muscles tensed for the next move. If that explosion was our doing, then we had a chance. We just had to survive long enough to take it.

Harvey lunged at me again, his movements mechanical, void of the boy I knew—the one who laughed too loud and dreamed too big. His hands, once a source of comfort, now aimed to kill. Cain and Thorn stood off to the side, their eyes gleaming with a sickening blend of anticipation and control. They needed Harvey to end me, to prove that their mind control was absolute.

I dodged Harvey's attack, my fists clenched and ready for a fight. I couldn't believe this was the same person who had once been my best friend. His eyes were cold and empty, his movements precise and calculated. He was nothing but a weapon now.

"Harvey, snap out of it," I pleaded, hoping to reach some part of him that was still human, still Harvey. But there was no response. He continued to come at me with deadly intent, his mind overtaken by the programming Cain and Thorn had instilled in him.

"Come on, Harvey," I gasped between dodges and parries of his relentless assault. "You're stronger than this." My voice broke, carried on waves of desperation. It wasn't just my life at stake; it was Harvey's soul, trapped in a prison of their making.

I could see the conflict flicker in his darkened eyes, a silent battle raging behind the facade they had forced upon him. But each time that spark ignited, it was smothered by another command from Thorn's twisted lips.

"Kill her!" Thorn's voice echoed, bouncing off the sterile walls of the lab. Harvey seemed to grow stronger with each repetition, his movements more precise, more deadly.

A scuffle of boots and the clang of metal on metal distracted me for a fraction of a second. That was all it took. Harvey's fist connected with my jaw, sending pain splintering through my skull, stars exploding in my vision. I stumbled back, my defenses crumbling.

Concentrate.

The sounds grew louder, closer—reinforcements or rescuers? My hope hung on the latter.

"Harvey, please." My plea was a whisper lost in the commotion, a last-ditch effort to reach whatever part of him remained untouched. "Don't let them win."

As another blow was about to land, certainty of my end flashed before me—but it never came. Instead, Harvey's body jerked away violently, as if yanked by an unseen force. Confusion washed over me until I saw Nate standing there, his muscular frame positioned between Harvey and me.

"Missed me?" Nate's mouth curved into that familiar mischievous grin. Relief and terror mingled within me, knowing our fight was far from over but grateful for the momentary reprieve.

I sucked in a ragged breath, my gaze darted across the chaos-filled lab, taking in the violence with a clarity that belied the terror clawing at my insides. Sam, muscles taut with fury, was a blur of motion against his father, Cain, each exchange a dance of anger and desperation. Ren, wiry and fierce, grappled with Thorn, their struggle punctuated by grunts and the sharp sound of fist meeting flesh.

"Get up, Luka," Nate said tersely, pulling me to my feet. His hand was steady, a lifeline in the maelstrom.

Harvey was rising too, shaking off Nate's blow. His eyes

had the glazed look of one who wasn't fully present, and I knew the mind control still had its hooks sunk deep into him.

"Harvey, fight it!" I called out, but my voice was lost in the cacophony.

Nate and I circled Harvey, wary. "We need to snap him out of it," I muttered.

How do you save someone from their own mind?

Before we could act, a barked command cut through the noise. General Thorn had Ren by the throat, a knife glinting dangerously close to his jugular. "Enough!" Thorn roared. "Surrender, or I end him!"

The room held its breath. Ren's eyes met mine, an apology and a plea all in one. I felt Nate tense beside me, ready to spring.

Then, a gurgling sound—wet and ugly—filled the space. Cain's formidable frame crumpled to the floor, Sam standing over him, face a mask of anguish and resolve. For a heartbeat, our eyes locked, and a silent understanding passed between us: he would take care of Ren; I would deal with Harvey.

"Go!" I hissed to Nate, and together we launched ourselves at Harvey. It was a dance of desperation, two friends trying to reach the man buried beneath the layers of manipulation. "Come back to us, Harvey," I pleaded between blows. "We need you."

Everything hinged on breaking the grip of control. *Everything.*

Nate and I, we moved as one—a fluid force against the storm that was Harvey. Sweat stung my eyes as his fist came dangerously close to connecting with my cheek. It was like sparring with a ghost, one who knew your every move before you made it. "Harvey!" My voice cracked like a whip, trying to reach him through the chaos.

"Remember who you are!" Nate bellowed next to me, dodging a kick meant to incapacitate. We had to be careful; we didn't want to hurt him, but we couldn't pull our punches too much.

"Think, Harvey! You're not their puppet!" I grunted as I blocked another strike. Something flickered behind his eyes then—recognition or confusion, I couldn't tell. But it was enough to fuel my hope.

"Your family! We're your family!" I shouted, locking eyes with him as we clashed again. "And we love you. I love you."

And then, it happened—something in those grey blue depths shattered. Like watching a dam burst, Harvey's features crumpled from steely determination to bewildered horror. He stumbled back, hands flying up to his head as if he could physically pull away the dark veil that Cain had draped over his mind.

"Lu-Luka?" His voice was a hoarse whisper, drenched in fear and relief. I nodded, panting, letting the surge of triumph wash over me.

"Welcome back," I said, my smile strained but genuine.

He stumbled towards me, features contorted with agony. "I'm so sorry," he choked out. "I didn't know what I was doing."

"It's okay Harvey," I murmured. Nate and I exchanged a look, there would be time for emotions later; right now we needed to focus on getting out of here alive.

I turned my attention away from Harvey for the first time since the fight began, surveying the room quickly. The sight that greeted me was a battlefield frozen in time. Cain's lifeless form lay sprawled on the ground, a silent testament to Sam's grim victory. Blood seeped into the concrete, a stark contrast

285

to his pale skin.

Sam was there, towering and formidable, standing guard over Ren like a sentinel. General Thorn, lay unconscious at his feet, a bruised heap of treachery and failed ambition.

"Ren!" The word tore from my throat as I noticed the way he slouched, an unnatural angle to his shoulders. Dread coiled in my stomach as I sprinted towards them. Sam's eyes were dark pools of grief and fury, the blue of them nearly swallowed by dilated pupils.

"Sam, what—"

"Thorn got him. Before I could..." Sam's voice broke, a rare crack in his armor. My gaze fell to Ren, to the blood blossoming across his shirt, and a cold numbness spread through my veins.

"Ren," I whispered, kneeling beside him. His eyes found mine, and the intensity I'd always seen there was dimming, fading like the last light of day. "Hold on. Please."

"Luka," he breathed, and even that small word was laden with pain. "It's okay."

But it wasn't okay. Nothing about this was okay. I pressed my hand against the wound, a futile gesture.

His hand trembled in mine, his grip feeble where it used to be unyielding. "Don't be afraid, Luka," Ren rasped, a shadow of a smirk playing on his lips. "You always were the brave one."

"Shut up, Ren. You're going to make it through this," I said, though the quiver in my voice betrayed me. My hands, slick with his blood, were useless against the tide of red that wouldn't stop.

I looked around desperately, searching for anything that could help us. My eyes landed on General Thorn's body lying nearby, and I scrambled towards him.

"Sam, help me!" I called out to him as I reached for Thorn's jacket pocket. I fished out a small knife and quickly returned to Ren's side.

"What are you doing?" Sam asked, his voice filled with confusion and concern.

"I-I have to do something," I replied shakily, my fingers gripping the knife tightly.

"Digging the bullet out won't save him Luka," Sam said shortly before adding after a pause, "it nicked an artery."

My heart dropped at Sam's words, my fear and panic increasing tenfold. I knew he was right, but I couldn't just sit there and do nothing as Ren bled out in front of me.

"I can't just let him die," I whispered, trying to keep my voice steady.

With shaking hands, I applied pressure to the bullet hole. Ren winced in pain and hissed through clenched teeth as my hand came into contact with his wound. His grip on my hand weakened even further and guilt washed over me for causing him more pain.

"I'm sorry," I whispered softly, tears streaming down my face now.

"Don't be," Ren replied weakly. "I wouldn't want anyone else by my side."

His words only made me cry harder as I continued working on stopping the bleeding. Sam stood nearby, watching us both with concern etched on his face.

"Promise me," Ren coughed, wincing as each breath seemed to cost him more than he had left, "Unity. For all of us. Genesi and humans."

"Unity," I choked out, tears blurring the harsh lines of the lab around us. "I promise."

Ren's eyes locked onto mine, and for a moment, his strength flickered back, fierce and bright. "Promise me. United... .Free..." He squeezed my hand one last time before his gaze softened and the light in his eyes extinguished like a candle snuffed by the wind.

"Ren!" I screamed, but he was gone. His body lay still, the battle having left him, leaving a silence that was deafening.

Chapter 36

Luka

Twelve months. Twelve months since we'd clawed our way out of the shadows, since Cain's fall and Thorn's demise. Twelve long, aching months without Ren, whose laughter had once filled our ranks with hope. His voice was just an echo now, a ghost in the wind that whispered through the crumbling city walls. I could still hear him sometimes, urging me on when the night grew too silent, too heavy with the weight of his absence.

"Keep moving, Luka," he would say, his words as sharp and clear as if he were standing beside me, hand on my shoulder. But when I turned, there was only emptiness, a void where he should have been. We'd won, yes, but victory had never tasted so bitter.

I remember the exact moment Lewis came to us with the footage, his eyes alight with something fierce and unyielding. He'd spliced together truths that had been hidden for far too long. The cornea slip, once a tool for Cain's surveillance, had become the key to unlocking the chains he'd wrapped around the nation's mind. Lewis showed us all—every man, woman, and child—how Cain had confessed to his own twisted plans, his voice cold and detached, speaking of a tyranny dressed as salvation.

But it didn't end there. Lewis made sure the world saw the Genesi not as monsters, but as they truly were: mothers, fathers, children... people. People who laughed and cried, who bled the same color, who yearned for nothing more than peace and a place to call home. It was a message that couldn't be ignored, a call to stand united.

"Are you ready?" Lewis had asked me then, a slight tremble in his voice betraying the gravity of what we were about to do.

"Time to change the world," I'd replied, a sly grin finding its way onto my face, despite the sorrow that lingered like a shadow.

Change came like the first rays of dawn after the longest night. Slowly, steadily, washing away the dark. There was resistance, of course. There always is when old fears are challenged, when the unknown stretches wide and vast before a people used to walls and barriers. But we stood firm, our resolve unshakeable.

"Ren would have been proud," Sam often said, his blue eyes reflecting a sky free of forcefields. He'd taken to the role of ambassador with a gruff dedication that somehow bridged the gap between human and Genesi hearts.

"Ren believed in this more than any of us," I'd reply, clenching my fists to still the tremor of loss that never quite left.

Lewis was right. It was time to be one people, one heartbeat. And as I watched the message play out, broadcast to every screen, every soul within our battered nation, I felt it. The shift. The beginning of something new. Something whole.

"United," I whispered to the memory of Ren, to the flickering images on the screen, to anyone who would listen. "Finally, united. Finally, free."

The sterile scent of the lab brought my thoughts back to the present. Around me, equipment hummed and flickered with life, a symphony of progress. The world outside had begun to reform itself, a mosaic pieced together from shards of what once was and what could be.

"Are you ready?" Harvey's voice was steady, but I caught the subtle strain behind it. He knew, as well as I did, that this step—our transformation back into humans—was more than a simple medical procedure; it was symbolic, a closing of the chapter that had been written in blood and sacrifice.

"Ever since we defeated Cain, I've been ready for a new start," I said, my words more for myself than him.

"A new world order," Harvey muttered, looking around at the lab. "Feels like a new universe."

I nodded in agreement, taking in the pristine white walls and advanced medical equipment that surrounded us. It was a far cry from the war-torn landscape we had grown up in.

"Sam's out there, doing his part," I mused aloud, thinking about our friend who had taken on the role of ambassador and liaison between humans and Genesi. "Liz is commanding Delta Force now, steering them away from conflict and towards protection."

Harvey smiled proudly at their achievements. "And you," he said, turning to me with a glint in his eye. "You're leading this project to turn us back into humans."

I shrugged off his praise, feeling a familiar twinge of guilt in my chest. Ren should have been here with us, taking charge alongside me. But his selfless sacrifice during the final battle against Cain had ensured our victory and paved the way for this new world.

"We wouldn't be here without Ren," I said quietly.

Harvey's expression softened at the mention of our fallen friend. We both knew that he would always hold a special place in our hearts and minds.

"But we have to move forward," Harvey said firmly. "We owe it to him and all those who fought alongside us."

I took a deep breath, trying to push aside my lingering guilt and grief. He was right. We had to keep moving forward.

His soft voice echoed the familiar phrase that had propelled us through the war: "A united front."

"United," I affirmed, feeling the weight of that word. It was a promise, a hope we were all clinging to, especially since the senate had hesitated to replace the Chancellor, choosing instead to explore the possibilities of democracy.

"It's time," I declared, moving toward the apparatus that would administer the cure and laying down on the cold metal table before me. My skin prickled at the sight of the gleaming needle and vials of clear liquid.

"Easy does it," the technician reassured me, her hands deft as she prepared the injection. Harvey squeezed my hand—a silent vow that mirrored my own determination. We were about to shed our Genesi traits, but not the memories, not the lessons learned.

I closed my eyes and took a deep breath as she injected the serum into my arm. I felt a slight pinch, followed by a cool sensation spreading through my body. It was over quickly, and I opened my eyes to see Harvey receiving his injection.

Harvey nodded, his eyes holding mine as the cure flowed through my veins, a tide washing away the last remnants of division.

For a moment, we lay there in silence, waiting for something to happen. Then, without warning, a surge of energy shot through me like an electric shock. My body flailed on the table, and I reached across to Harvey for support.

"Are you okay?" he asked with concern.

"I think so," I said, trying to steady myself. "It just feels... strange."

Strange was an understatement. My body felt like it was on fire one second and then freezing cold the next. My vision blurred as if someone had splashed water in my eyes. Then suddenly everything cleared up and I could see clearly again. Feeling returned to my limbs first—a pins-and-needles sensation that made me wince. Then, as if a heavy veil were lifting from my eyes, the lab came back into focus. I was human again.

"Did it work?" My voice sounded foreign to my own ears—rougher, like I'd lost the melodic lilt of the genesi.

Harvey was beside me, his hand no longer radiating the warmth I had grown accustomed to. "It feels strange," he admitted, rubbing his arms as if to coax back the heat we had forfeited.

"Strange doesn't begin to cover it," I murmured, swinging my legs over the side of the table and rising cautiously. My body obeyed, but it was like learning to walk all over again—everything felt heavier.

We moved to a pair of chairs, and I caught Harvey's gaze. It was searching, as if he were trying to find remnants of our former selves within these unfamiliar human contours. Together, we were stepping into the future—one without walls, one where every person, human or Genesi, could stand under the open sky and simply be.

"Remember how Ren used to say we'd cross any desert, climb any mountain?" I said softly, a sad smile tugging at the corner of my mouth.

"Only to find more mountains," Harvey finished with a sigh. "I miss him. Every step forward feels like we're leaving him further behind."

"Ren gave us a path," I reminded him, feeling the ache of loss anew. "We promised to walk it, no matter the cost."

"Doesn't make it easier, does it? The sacrifices..." His voice trailed off, and I saw the shadow of doubt clouding his eyes— the same shadow that haunted me.

"Nothing worth fighting for is ever easy." I clenched my fists, feeling a surge of human resolve. "Cain's gone, the walls are down, but the real battle starts now. To live up to what we've achieved, what we've lost..."

"Ren would be proud," Harvey said, his voice steadier now. "Of you, especially."

"Of us, Harvey. We did this together." I reached out, feeling the roughness of his skin—so different from before. It was a stark reminder of our choice, our new reality.

"United," he repeated, the word a solemn pledge between us.

"Free," I finished.

We sat in silence for a time, each lost in thought. The lab around us hummed with the quiet activity of technicians and machines, a symphony of progress. But even as we embarked on this next chapter, Ren's memory lingered, a silent companion on the journey we had yet to complete.

As night fell over the city, I stood at the window of the lab, watching the stars twinkle in a sky unmarred by forcefields.

My father's words came to me then, a whisper from the past.

A world united, not divided.

We were a testament to his dream. Humans and genesi, once separated by fear and misunderstanding, now mingled under the open heavens. The road ahead would be fraught with challenges, doubts, and tests of faith.

But as I looked upon the fragile beginnings of a society reborn, I couldn't help but feel a spark of hope ignite within me. This new world was raw, uncharted, terrifying.

And yet, it was ours to shape.

"Here's to a future where we can be who we are, not what we are," I whispered into the twilight.

"Here's to unity."

My heart swelled with a fierce determination. For my father, for Ren, for every soul seeking a place in this world—we would rise, again and again, to meet each dawn with unwavering conviction.

Together.

Epilogue

Luka

I trailed my fingers over the spines of dusty books, all that was left of him in this dim study. The air was thick with the scent of old paper and memories. My heart felt heavy as I stopped in front of his desk, where an old photograph lay. It was creased at the corners from years of being held, studied, and silently cried upon. There we were—my parents and me, a tiny version with pigtailed hair and wide, hopeful eyes.

"Hope you're proud, Dad," I whispered to the smiling man in the photo who never got to see what became of his little girl.

The sound of small, unsteady footsteps interrupted my somber nostalgia. A burst of sunlight seemed to follow the toddler into the room, dispelling shadows and bringing life to the space once more. "Mummy!" he squealed with delight, his cherub face beaming up at me.

"Hey, Ren," I said, scooping him up into my arms. His warmth seeped into my bones, chasing away the chill of the past. He wrapped his little arms around my neck, his head nestling against my shoulder.

"Who dis?" Ren's tiny finger pointed at the photograph still clutched in my hand.

"Someone very important," I answered, my voice soft but filled with a strength I had learned over the years. "That's your grandfather, Ren. He was a great man."

"Like you, Mummy?"

"Something like that, little one." I kissed the top of his head, feeling a resolve settle within me, a fierce protectiveness for the new world we were building—where the ghosts of yesterday would not cloud the sunshine of tomorrow.

The creak of the study door heralded Harvey's arrival, his silhouette framed by the dim hallway light. "There you are," he said, a note of relief coloring his voice as he stepped into the room.

"Lost track of time," I mumbled, still holding Ren close. I could feel Harvey's eyes on us, that gaze which always seemed to understand more than I spoke out loud. In his presence, my walls, carefully built and fiercely guarded, seemed to crumble without permission.

As Ren played with a strand of my hair, my thoughts drifted. Motherhood had never been part of my plan. My entire being had been honed for one singular purpose—to unravel the web of lies and deceit that led to my father's death. Yet here I was, a protector of new life rather than an avenger of the lost. It was a role I never envisioned, a facet of myself I never dared to explore until it unfolded before me, demanding recognition and tenderness I wasn't sure I possessed.

"Everyone's starting to gather," Harvey said, breaking through my reverie. His tone held a weight, signaling the shift from our quiet sanctuary to the reality waiting beyond these walls.

"Already?" I set Ren down, watching as he toddled uncertainly toward Harvey, who caught him with practiced ease.

"Time doesn't stand still, not even for memories," Harvey replied, his words echoing the very lesson the past years had etched upon my soul.

As he returned Ren to the floor, I took a deep breath, steeling myself for the gathering. Once a year, we came together at my mother's house. It was a tradition etched in grief and solidarity, a remembrance of the price our freedom demanded.

My heart clenched at the thought of those absent faces, the ones who remained vibrant in memory but were lost to our reality. But the sting of loss never truly faded; it lingered, a ghostly ache in every reunion.

"Let's not keep them waiting," I said finally, my resolve hardening. Today was about honoring those we carried in our hearts, the living and the departed alike. We owed them our courage, our laughter, and our unyielding spirit.

"Lead the way," Harvey responded, extending a hand.

I placed my palm in his, feeling the familiar roughness of his skin, the unspoken promise that no matter how dark the path, we'd walk it together.

Ren pulled on my pant leg, his small face scrunched up with determination. "Walk!" he demanded, his voice a commanding chirp that seemed to echo the authority I often had to wield.

"Alright, little commander," I chuckled. His tiny feet hitting the cool floor with purpose, and he toddled forward with an unsteady but eager gait.

I exchanged a glance with Harvey, his eyes twinkling with a silent laugh we both shared at our son's burgeoning independence. This was a new battlefield for us, one filled with toy soldiers and storybooks, so far removed from the one we were accustomed to.

"Come on Ren, where you go, we'll follow," Harvey called out to him, his words a tender echo of a promise made long ago in a world that had demanded too much from too many.

Harvey took a step, his hand squeezing mine as we began to follow our son.

As Ren led us through the house, my heart swelled with pride and love for this little boy who had changed our world in ways we never thought possible.

He darted around corners, his tiny feet pattering on the hardwood floors as he giggled with delight. The house was filled with the familiar faces of our friends and comrades, all gathered together for this annual tradition.

I couldn't help but smile at the sight of them all, a mix of old and new faces, each one carrying their own story of survival and resilience.

Ren reached the living room, where a large table was set up with various dishes and drinks. He let out a squeal as he ran towards it, his arms reaching out for a platter of cookies that sat on top.

"Careful there buddy," Harvey said, gently guiding Ren away from the edge of the table. "Let's save those treats for after dinner."

Ren pouted for a moment before finding another toy to play with. I took this opportunity to scan the room once more, taking in the sights and sounds that surrounded me.

My eyes landed on my mother's face, her features etched with both joy and sadness as she welcomed each person who entered. She had been through so much in her life, yet she continued to be a source of strength and support for our community.

Next to her stood Harvey's father, looking proud and content as he conversed with some of our guests. I couldn't help but feel grateful for their presence in our lives, especially now that we had Ren to raise in this ever-changing world.

A tap on my shoulder brought me back to reality. I turned to see Harvey smiling down at me. "Ready?" he asked softly.

I nodded, taking a deep breath before following him towards our family and friends, toward our future.

About the Author

Tristen lives in Newcastle, Australia with her husband and two kids. Tristen wrote her debut novel, The Genesi Code when she was 21 and it was published later in 2017 which is available on Amazon.

She took a brief hiatus from writing to start her family however, she is now back at it and has since published 2 romance novellas which form part of an interconnected series.

Tristen also writes and designs preschool activity workbooks for kids in her spare time.

You can connect with me on:
- https://www.tristenwillis.com
- https://www.tiktok.com/@authortristenwillis
- https://www.instagram.com/authortristenwillis

Subscribe to my newsletter:

✉ https://subscribepage.io/jBvYk5

Also by Tristen Willis

Tristen is a multi genre author who's taste in writing varies much like her taste in reading.

The Happy Hour Hookup

Ruby Daniels had her life turned upside down when a surprise meeting at work informed her that she would be forced to move teams and work under a team leader that she absolutely despised, Aiden.

Being forced to work under Aiden stirred up mixed feelings from when Ruby and Aiden used to be on friendlier terms and Ruby makes a foolhardy decision one Friday night at after work drinks.

Now forced to face her bad decision and her mixed feelings, Ruby must decide if taking a chance and risking it all on someone she knows could be the ruin of her career is worth it.

Love Bytes And Gossip

Hannah Upton's life has been flipped upside down following a devastating breakup. Despite her heartache, she's determined to focus on herself - that is until she meets Jeremy, the new I.T. guy.

Suddenly, Hannah is being forced out of her comfort zone and instead of dealing with her feelings, she dives into the latest workplace scandal. She is known as the Gossip Queen of BHI, after all, and she won't rest until she solves this mystery.

But as she digs deeper, she begins to realize that the stakes are higher than she ever imagined - and she must face her feelings if she hopes to succeed.

Preschool Activity Workbook Ages 3-5: Non-Coloured Edition - 150 activities including letter tracing, numbers and counting, shapes, colours and more: Non-Coloured Edition
Results from reading this book: "Transform your child's learning and give them a head start in school with The Preschool Activity Workbook!"

Benefits: This book will improve your child's readiness for school and make learning fun and engaging.

- Build a strong foundation for your child's academic success
    - Empower your child with essential preschool skills
    - Experience the joy of learning with fun illustrations and activities
    - Boost your child's confidence and self-esteem
    - Develop problem-solving and critical thinking skills for real-life applications

What's in the book:

- Alphabet and letter tracing exercises to improve letter recognition and writing skills
    - Fun coloring pages to reinforce colors and shapes
    - Sequencing activities to develop logical thinking and understanding of order
    - Grouping exercises to enhance cognitive skills and understanding of similarities and differences
    - Number and counting exercises to introduce basic math

concepts

Other features:

- 150 pages of engaging activities
    - Kid-friendly illustrations to make learning enjoyable
    - Durable glossy cover for long-lasting use
    - Suitable for ages 3-5

Don't miss out on this opportunity to give your child the gift of learning!